Shadows from the Past
Sandrine Perrot - Brittany Mystery Series
Book 6

Christophe Villain

Copyright © 2023 by Christophe Villain

All rights reserved.

No part of this book may be reproduced in any form or by any electronic or mechanical means, including information storage and retrieval systems, without written permission from the author, except for the use of brief quotations in a book review.

Christophe Villain
Pettenkoferstr. 2
45470 Muelheim
Germany
author@christophe-villain.com

Coverdesign by Giusy Amé
Translation by Rose Bodenheimer
Copy editing and proofreading by Elizabeth Ward

List of Characters

- Sandrine Perrot: Investigator from Saint-Malo
- Adel Azarou: Assistant to Sandrine Perrot
- Léon Martinau: Club owner in Saint-Malo and Sandrine's romantic partner
- Miriam Mignon: Artist hoping for a career in Paris
- Antoine de Chezac: Prosecutor in Saint-Malo
- Auguste de Saint-Clair: Wealthy entrepreneur and murder suspect from Paris
- Jamila Azarou: Intern and younger sister of Adel
- Rosalie Simonas: Author and best friend of Sandrine Perrot
- Inès Boni: Office manager at the police station
- Luc Poutin: Brigadier under investigation
- Renard Dubois: Brigadier and best friend of Luc Poutin
- Sébastian Hermé: Prosecutor from Rennes
- Charles Jogu: Police Commander (Rennes)
- Marie Baud: Police Major (Rennes)
- Arianne Briand: Editor-in-chief of the local radio station
- Alexandre Mason: Forensic pathologist

Investigators from Rennes

Sandrine parked her Citroën 2CV in the courtyard of the police station in Saint-Malo, closed the car's roll-top roof and tossed the cap she had worn during the drive onto the back seat. There was not a cloud in the sky, and the temperature was already approaching 68 F early in the morning. It promised to be a glorious day, and she toyed with the idea of spending her lunch break at Plage du Sillon. A dip in the cold water would be refreshing. The beach bag with her bikini, sunscreen and towels was within easy reach on the passenger seat. The fact that she didn't have a current case to work on, only a pile of accumulated overtime and paperwork that needed her attention, further solidified her plan. In a good mood, she got out of the car and climbed the stairs to the open-plan office where her workstation was located.

"Hello, Sandrine," Inès Boni greeted her. "The prosecutor from Rennes and his colleagues have already arrived and are with Commissaire Matisse."

"So soon?" She checked the time; it was half-past eight. Sébastian Hermé must have left early. It took about an hour from Rennes to Saint-Malo, and even longer in late July during the peak holiday season. They both drove French classics—she in a red and black Citroën 2CV, Charleston model, powered by a robust 29 horsepower, and he in a bright yellow 1972 Alpine A110, which allowed the prosecutor to navigate the Brittany country roads significantly faster than she could. But in the inevitable traffic, his sports car was of no use.

"That doesn't concern me much for now. I'll stay at the police station today and work on reports and protocols. If Matisse wants to speak to me, he knows where to find me," she said.

She held a certain regard for Sébastian Hermé, but she wasn't particularly looking forward to his stay in Saint-Malo. His role as a Juge d'instruction, a prosecutor, was to examine the allegations against Brigadier Poutin, who had planted drugs on her friend Léon Martinau during a raid at his club. She reminded herself to keep a distance from the investigation. Poutin had wanted to discredit her due to his actions against her friend. So, she would likely be questioned as a witness, even though she could contribute very little. On the night in question, she had been in Le Mont-Saint-Michel, investigating the Barnais murder case. She trusted that Hermé, whom she had found competent and clever, would fully uncover the background.

Sandrine sat down at her desk. Adel Azarou, her assistant, nodded to her.

"They arrived about half an hour ago," he said. "The three of them."

"Who did he bring with him?"

"A Capitaine and a Major de Police, a woman," said Renard Dubois, turning to them. The senior brigadier was sitting two desks away. "Who seems to be quite humourless."

"It was to be expected. He needs a few investigators he can trust," Sandrine replied.

"We can handle our own affairs; we don't need anyone from Rennes for that," Dubois retorted with a bitter tone.

"It's standard procedure. The investigation involves police officers from Saint-Malo, so there can't be the slightest hint of bias," she replied. "Besides, they won't discover anything different from that which we will."

"A pure waste of time and money," grumbled the brigadier.

Sandrine understood him well. Sébastian Hermé and his team were here to lead the investigation against Luc Poutin. The man had worked closely with Renard Dubois for many years. They were close friends, and Dubois was even the godfather of Poutin's daughter. Yet, in the end, Dubois couldn't bring himself to cover up his friend's criminal activities, for which Sandrine highly respected him.

Inès' phone vibrated, and she looked at the display.

"Commissaire Matisse. He says to send you to him as soon as you arrive. They've moved to the conference room," she said. "Have you arrived already, or do you need a coffee to fortify yourself before heading there?"

"Thank you. I'm not sure how Hermé plans to proceed, but I want as little to do with it as possible. Who else do they want to see besides me?"

"For now, they're only expecting you."

Sandrine opened a desk drawer, dropped the car keys inside, and placed her gun next to them.

"If you decide to take a detour to the promenade and want to show off with a convertible, feel free to take my 2CV; it has a roll-top roof," she offered to Adel with a cheerful smile.

"Don't worry, I wouldn't even consider touching that thing. I'd be afraid it would flip over at the first turn, or I'd get seasick from all the wobbling." Her always fashionably dressed and somewhat vain assistant laughed and waved his hands in refusal.

They always used his official car, a new Renault 306 when they were on duty together. She'd never been able to persuade him to ride in the 2CV. Sometimes she suspected he was embarrassed to be seen in it by friends or colleagues. Besides, he loved to drive himself, and she enjoyed being chauffeured.

The door to the conference room was open, but she lightly tapped the doorframe nonetheless. Several heads turned in her direction, and she entered. Her boss, Commissaire Matisse, and the prosecutor, Sébastian Hermé, sat facing each other at the head of the long table. Sandrine didn't know the two uniformed police officers, who scrutinised her attentively. They must be the investigators Hermé had brought from Rennes. To her surprise, Antoine de Chezac, the prosecutor responsible for Saint-Malo, was also present, either out of pure courtesy to his colleagues or to keep an eye on the investigation. The man didn't hide his dislike for her. He hadn't questioned Brigadier Poutin's actions, and had even supported them to some extent. Sometimes she wondered how much his open hostility towards her had facilitated the brigadier's actions. Well, it was now Hermé and his team's job to find out.

"Come in and have a seat." Commissaire Matisse, looking particularly formal in his grey double-breasted suit, gestured to an empty chair. She grasped the backrest and moved it slightly to the side. She wanted to sit as far away from de Chezac as possible.

"Capitaine Perrot, good to see you again," Hermé greeted her cheerfully. Unlike Commissaire Matisse, he appeared rather casual in dark trousers and a white shirt without a tie, accentuated by the golden earring and subtle makeup. They had investigated the death of a book lover together in Bécherel and he had provided helpful information in the de Tréchet murder case. They liked each other and usually addressed each other informally but in the context of this meeting, a more formal tone was appropriate.

"Monsieur Hermé, it's good to see you, even if the circumstances are rather unpleasant," she said.

"Unfortunately, I have to agree with that. But we aim to conduct the investigation swiftly and professionally, without stirring up too much dust," Hermé replied. The last part was directed towards de Chezac, who nodded in agreement.

"We could have easily handled this without assistance from Rennes," he said. The careerist did not take kindly to playing second fiddle in his own jurisdiction, Sandrine surmised. Especially since the investigation was veering beyond the actions of the brigadier and also scrutinising the fact that he had turned a blind eye to Poutin's behaviour.

"There's no doubt about that," Hermé reassured him in a conciliatory tone. "We are only here to comply with regulations."

From the corner of her eye, Sandrine noticed the sceptical face of the major, a woman in her forties, sitting with a straight back in her chair, scrutinising those present with a critical gaze. She wore a uniform that was immaculately pressed and starched. Her black hair was slicked back into a tight bun. Sandrine couldn't discern any makeup. The woman seemed to be trying not to appear too feminine, at least while on duty.

"Do I get access to the investigation?" De Chezac's question came swiftly and forcefully, as if he wanted to catch his colleague off guard and extract a concession.

"Of course. After all, we both work towards the same higher goal: achieving justice." Hermé smiled at him and briefly played with the golden earring in his left earlobe. His nails were perfectly manicured, and his eyes were accentuated by subtle eyeliner. De Chezac probably saw him as someone who valued a harmonious working relationship and thought he could manipulate or, in a worst-case scenario, someone he could intimidate with a harsh tone.

Sandrine forced herself to suppress a grin. Sébastian Hermé wasn't easily intimidated. Besides, he had just lied to de Chezac with the face of an honest man. De Chezac would only have access to documents that Hermé approved or those he wanted his colleague to see if he was interested in his reaction. She believed she could size up the prosecutor quite well. Underestimating him could end dramatically.

The investigation revolved around Brigadier Poutin's fabrication of a crime. However, it wasn't clear how far Hermé's investigations would extend. Was he content with bringing the brigadier to court, or was he interested in the masterminds behind the act? If there were any. So far, she had no evidence or a strong motive to justify such an action.

"We will provide Prosecutor Hermé and his team with an office for the duration of the investigation." Commissaire Matisse, little interested in the bickering between the two lawyers, moved on to organising the investigation, something that fell within his purview; he wanted to get it done quickly.

Sandrine suspected that he would welcome it if the Rennes police officers completed their work swiftly and without drawing attention and soon left his police station.

"That's very generous of you," Hermé thanked him. "I'd like to take this opportunity to introduce my team. As far as I know, Capitaine Perrot hasn't met my colleagues yet. Capitaine Jogu and Major Baud are experienced investigators from the gendarmerie and will support me in the investigation." The man with a receding hairline and a blonde goatee nodded amiably at her, while the woman gazed at her emotionlessly.

"We've heard quite a bit about you," Capitaine Jogu said to her without specifying what exactly they had heard.

"Pleased to meet you." Sandrine offered a cautious smile that shattered against the stone-faced demeanour of the woman. Capitaine Jogu seemed to be the more approachable of the two, but Sandrine reminded herself to wait and see. They weren't here to make friends but to conduct interrogations that could land a colleague in front of a judge. An extremely unpleasant task they probably hadn't eagerly accepted. They likely hadn't expected a warm welcome.

"Be prepared for an interrogation today. It may take a while," Major Baud instructed Sandrine with a harsh tone. Matisse raised his eyebrows, and Hermé shot his colleague an astonished look. Only de Chezac seemed to enjoy the major's attempt to intimidate Sandrine. Suppressing a grin had completely failed, if he had even tried.

"Am I being accused of something?" Sandrine responded, seeking eye contact with the woman.

"We are still at the beginning of the investigation," Baud replied evasively, leaving the possibility hanging.

"Capitaine Perrot has not committed any wrongdoing," Commissaire Matisse interjected.

"We are here to thoroughly clarify incidents, including the role Capitaine Perrot played." Baud rejected the objection. She clearly didn't act any less harshly towards superiors than towards potential suspects.

"Of course, I am at your disposal," Sandrine said. Fanning the flames of conflict between Major Baud and her boss was not in her interest. "However, I have a job to do and won't always be available at the office. But I'm sure we can find a suitable time if we coordinate in advance."

"That settles it then," Capitaine Jogu decided. The man had an unexpectedly deep voice, exuding enough authority to put an end to the discussion.

Someone knocked on the door and opened it without waiting for an invitation. Inès Boni looked in and addressed Sandrine.

"Jean-Claude needs you. A body has been found."

"That will certainly have to wait for at least another fifteen minutes," Major Baud objected.

Inès glanced at the slim watch on her wrist briefly. "The low tide has begun, and the receding water could erase traces. At least, that's what the head of forensics said."

"They need Capitaine Perrot to hold the body in place so it doesn't float away, is that it?"

Inès Boni didn't handle sarcasm particularly well, and she was about to respond, but Sandrine beat her to it.

"They'll manage it just fine," Sandrine said and stood up. She had no intention of letting the woman interfere in her work or watching her condescend the officers at the police station. "But the team knows that I like to examine the scene of a body that's been found as early as possible. That seems more important to me at the moment than continuing our conversation. Either leave your appointment request on my desk or inform Mademoiselle Boni, our office manager, and I'll do my best to accommodate it. Until then, I wish you a pleasant day in Saint-Malo."

She nodded to Matisse and Hermé before turning around and leaving the room with Inès.

"Why was that woman so aggressive?" the office manager asked.

"Just some barking to show who's giving the orders and who has to obey."

"As I can see, you're not willing to jump when she snaps her fingers."

"No way, especially not when a body has been found. That takes priority."

They reached her desk. Adel Azarou already had the car keys in his hand. Sandrine retrieved the holster from her desk and placed her Glock 17 inside. It was unlikely she would need it at a crime scene, but in a murder case, she never knew who she would encounter throughout the day.

"Do you know any more details?" she asked her assistant.

"A sailor found the body of a woman on the rocks in front of Tour Bidouane. It's part of the city wall and located in front of Maison du Québec. Jean-Claude couldn't determine if she died there or was washed up by the tide. He just arrived as well. He'll have more information by the time we get there."

"A crime or an accident?"

"We'll find out. The forensic pathologist has been notified and might already be on the scene."

"Then we better get going and see it for ourselves."

The Dead Woman on the Beach

Adel Azarou drove through the Grand Porte and crossed the old town of Saint-Malo. In front of the Passage de la Poudrière, a police officer blocked the entrance to the narrow alley. Behind him were parked the forensics van, an ambulance, and several patrol cars, making it impossible to pass through.

"It's best if you go back a bit and take the Porte de Champs-Vauverts. There's a path to the foot of the tower where the body was found," the policeman said after they had identified themselves. "You can leave the car here."

Sandrine thanked him and walked back with Adel to the gate in the city wall, which was barely ten to thirteen feet high at this point. Behind the inconspicuous passage was a footpath running parallel. Instead of descending to the beach, they chose a path that branched off towards the tower, which was only slightly higher than the city wall. The horseshoe-shaped tower stood on a projecting cliff several feet above the beach. From here, they could already see Jean-Claude Mazet and the forensic team members who were on the rocks below. The water was still high, and the waves reached the lower edge of the dark rocks jutting steeply out of the sandy beach. It was just past nine-thirty. The tide had peaked about an hour ago, and the water was receding. Saint-Malo was known for its strong tides, with a rise of more than fourteen metres during spring being common, but they were far from that at the moment.

"We need to determine how high the water rose this morning," she said, more to herself than to Adel.

"Jean-Claude will know and note it in the report."

Sandrine nodded. The forensic technician and his team were meticulous, which she was very grateful for. Unfortunately, she'd had a somewhat different experience when she worked for the Paris police department.

The head of the forensics team approached them.

"Bonjour, Capitaine Perrot. Salut, Adel," he greeted them.

"Bonjour, Monsieur Mazet. At least you could cool off a bit," she remarked. The blue disposable overall, with its legs tucked into scratched rubber boots, was wet up to just above the knees and slightly tight around his belly.

"One of the few pleasant aspects in this weather. I'd rather be out on my boat enjoying the breeze than sweating here," he replied.

"I can imagine," said Sandrine, although she had no knowledge of sailing. Léon often talked about a joint tour, but the opportunity had not yet arisen. She assumed he knew how to handle a boat, but that was just a guess. Probably because most Bretons she knew loved the sea. "What do we have here?" she asked the forensic technician.

"A sailor spotted a woman lying lifeless on the rocks below the tower. He couldn't get close enough with his boat to check if she was still alive, so he notified us. The doctor could only confirm her death. She must have died several hours ago; rigor mortis has already set in."

"An accident or a case for us?" she inquired.

"The woman, maybe in her late twenties, was completely naked and has a considerable number of wounds, although most of them are superficial. The most crucial are the strangulation marks on her neck. Without going too far out on a limb, I would assume foul play."

"Is this the crime scene, or just where the body was found?" she asked.

"I can't say for sure yet. If she was killed here on the beach, the tide has washed away most of the evidence thus we found very little usable information. Her clothes are missing, as are any other belongings that might have been hers. We're cordoning off the area extensively and waiting for low tide. Hopefully, we'll get lucky and find some useful evidence heavy enough to have sunk between the rocks or remain on the beach."

"If she died elsewhere, how did the body end up here? Washed ashore, or was it placed here?" she inquired.

"In front of us are Petit Bé and Grand Bé." The forensic technician pointed to the two islands that were only a stone's throw away from them in the water. "They form a natural barrier, just like the footpath that leads to Grand Bé during low tide. I don't believe the woman was driven here by the tide. Her body was too high on the rocks for that. The waves barely touched her, if at all. Only during very high spring tides and with strong winds does the sea reach the foundations of the tower. This morning, the high tide was much lower. No chance she was washed ashore."

"Your hypothesis?" Adel asked.

"Normally, I would have assumed that the crime scene was on the tower, and the assailant threw her down during the attack or after her death. That would explain some of the wounds."

"But?" Sandrine inquired.

"The body was too far from the tower, about five to six metres. Impossible to throw her that far, and it's not steep enough for her to roll or slide to the discovery site. But we'll search the area directly under the tower for clues as soon as the rest of my team arrives. There's still a lot to do."

Sandrine looked at the Tour Bidouane. Strictly speaking, it

was not a tower but rather a protrusion in the masonry of the city fortifications, just slightly higher than the adjacent wall. From there, the defenders of the city had an unobstructed view over the sea and the fortifications on the islands, but also to the south and northeast along the city walls. In the lower part, the gun ports for the cannons were still recognisable.

"So, we can rule it out as the crime scene?" Adel asked.

"Not at all. It's still my top choice. I just need to figure out how the body got from up there to down here. It's going to be tricky, but we'll get there. I can provide more details this afternoon. Until then, you'll have to wait." The man knew how impatient Sandrine could be, but he was cautious not to commit until all the evidence had been collected and analysed.

"Has access to the tower been secured?" she asked.

"Of course. Nobody is getting up there until we've finished our work, and the door to the interior has been locked all night. We'll be done down here soon, and then it's the tower's turn. Until then, police officers are guarding it."

"Good job," said Sandrine. "We'll check it out later."

It was only a short distance until they encountered two paramedics standing next to a stretcher with a body bag. A man she didn't know was talking to them.

"Can we take a look at the body?" she asked the paramedics.

The stranger turned to her. "And who are you?" he replied with raised eyebrows.

"I'm Capitaine Perrot. This is Brigadier Chief de Police Azarou. We're leading the investigation."

"Oh. Nice to meet you. Dr Hervé has told me a lot about you." He turned to Adel. "And about you, of course," he added, extending a hand for a greeting.

"And who are we dealing with?" Sandrine scrutinised the man. The open bag on the ground revealed that he was a doctor.

"I'm Dr Alexandre Mason, standing in for Dr Hervé. I hope to fill his shoes as best I can."

"And where is our doctor?" She had already worked on several cases with him and knew how to get as much information as possible.

"He accepted the offer of early retirement and," he glanced at his watch, "should be on his way for a vacation. The Caribbean, as far as I know. His eldest daughter lives in Martinique."

"Lucky him," muttered Azarou.

"What can you tell us about the deceased?" Sandrine returned to the investigation.

The man knelt beside the body bag and unzipped it. The pale face of a young and remarkably beautiful woman emerged. Her blond hair, with some seaweed entangled in it, clung damply to her bloodless skin, and someone had closed her eyes. The narrow lips were slightly parted, and the tip of her tongue was visible. A red mark coiled around her neck. Sandrine took a step back. Memories of an old case flooded her mind, and the surroundings seemed to spin. She leaned forward, resting her hands on her thighs. Her breath was rapid and shallow, and her heart pounded against her chest. *This can't be.* But the images of the victims flashed before her mind's eye.

"Are you feeling unwell?" she heard the doctor ask.

Adel waved it off, and the man fell silent. The brigadier knew her well enough not to assume that the sight of a corpse would throw her off track; they had seen too many of them already. She breathed slowly until her pulse calmed down. *It's just a coincidence,* she tried to reassure herself, but an unpleasant premonition gripped her painfully and wouldn't be dispelled.

"It's okay," she said, carefully straightening up. "Just the heat, and I'm probably a bit dehydrated. My blood pressure briefly dropped," she lied. It was none of the man's business what troubled her. She ignored the sceptical look Adel gave her.

She would talk to him later. Currently, there was nothing she could tell him without jeopardising his objectivity in the investigation.

"What's the cause of death?" Adel asked, refocusing on the case. "She looks badly beaten." He gestured to the extensive abrasions on her shoulder.

"These are just superficial wounds that wouldn't have killed her. It's different with the bone fractures."

"Was she sexually assaulted?" Sandrine resumed the questioning.

"There are no external signs of that, but I won't know more until after the autopsy." The doctor pulled a shiny chrome telescopic rod from his pocket and opened the zipper of the body bag a bit more. He tapped the tip of the rod on the woman's occiput—the back of the head where the skull meets the neck. The skin was torn, the hair matted, and a piece of bone was exposed.

"This wound would have been lethal under normal circumstances, but it was inflicted post-mortem. That's what killed her." He pointed with the rod at the dark bruise encircling her neck.

"Strangulation," Sandrine stated.

"Of course, this is only preliminary, but I doubt the examination will reveal anything else."

"It looks like the marks from a rope or something similar. Was the murder weapon found?" Sandrine waited anxiously for the doctor's answer, even though she knew what he was going to say; if it had been, the forensic team would have mentioned it.

"There was nothing with the body. The killer may have thrown the rope into the sea. Maybe the forensic team will find something."

"Where are the other wounds from?" Sandrine continued.

"I can't say for sure yet. Perhaps the killer vented their rage on her and beat her, or the waves tossed her back and forth on the rocks. However, I find the latter unlikely; by the time the waves reached her, their force was significantly diminished."

"A fall from a great height?"

The doctor turned towards the tower and nodded thoughtfully. "That's also Monsieur Mazet's assumption. The tower is a little over sixty-five feet high, and some of the rocks below are quite sharp-edged. That would explain the post-mortem injuries. If my initial assessment is correct, the victim died late at night, around one or two in the morning. At that time, it was low tide, and the rocks were definitely exposed. The water wouldn't have slowed her fall, explaining the severe injuries."

Sandrine walked a few steps towards the tower. It had to have happened up there. She no longer doubted that. The question was: how did the body end up so far from the wall? They would figure that out.

"Thank you for your initial assessment. When can we expect the autopsy report?"

"I'll expedite it," he promised.

"I would appreciate that."

"One more thing," the doctor said. "Between the time of death and the body being moved, at least half an hour to an hour must have passed. The discoloration of the skin is well developed and not consistent with a body lying down."

"Instead?" Sandrine pressed.

"The woman must have been in a sitting position at the time of her death or shortly thereafter. After the heart stopped beating, the blood sank into the back of the legs and buttocks, relatively evenly."

"So, she was sitting with her legs extended on the ground. Perhaps leaning against a wall." She pointed at the tower. "The killer murdered her up there and left her behind."

"She would have been found there for sure, and quite early in the morning. Tourists like to climb up there. Besides, the parapet on the tower isn't particularly high, maybe up to an adult's knees. So, she should have been easily visible from here if she had been left sitting there," the doctor speculated.

"I would assume that was the intention of the perpetrator. He wanted her to be found," Sandrine said. She turned to Adel. "I bet it was a staged scene. My gut feeling says she was sitting against the wall, directly opposite the entrance, so that anyone entering the tower would have noticed her." *A message to me.* She shook her head. *Nonsense. He's long forgotten about you.*

"If the killer went through the trouble of luring the woman to the tower, strangling her, and staging the crime scene, why did we find the body on the rocks at the base of the tower? Under different circumstances, the tides could have carried her out to sea, and no one would have found her." The brigadier sounded sceptical, and Sandrine had no argument to dispel his doubts.

"I have no idea," she said hesitantly. "It's just a hypothesis. Maybe I'm wrong. Let's see what the forensic team finds." She hoped she was wrong, but her instinct told her otherwise.

"There's nothing to do here for now. We'll inspect the tower once the forensics team has collected all the evidence. Now, I'd like to speak to the person who found the body," Sandrine decided. "Do you know where we can find him?"

"Inès texted me his name. A Monsieur Sélon. He's waiting for us at the bar on Plage de Bon-Secours," Adel replied.

"Is that the one near the tidal pool and the sailing school?"

"Exactly." Adel checked his phone's display. "They should be open now."

"Then let's go. They might have some coffee. I could use one."

They left the crime scene, walked along the city wall, and descended the steep staircase to the beach. On the left, a broad ramp led to the city, lined with sailboats, catamarans, and some canoes from the sailing club and rental businesses. On the lower level was the Bar l'Embraque. At this early hour, only one of the tables on the terrace was occupied.

"Monsieur Sélon?" Sandrine inquired.

He looked up at her, a tanned, athletic-looking man in his fifties with dark-blue knee-length shorts, a light T-shirt, and white sailing shoes. A lightweight waterproof and windproof jacket hung over a chair.

"You're from the police?" He stood up and extended his hand.

"Capitaine Perrot," she introduced herself. "And Brigadier Chief de Police Azarou from the Saint-Malo police station."

"Please, have a seat." He pulled out a chair for her.

"Thank you."

"Coffee?" he asked.

"Yes, please."

He signalled to the waiter, who stood behind the counter polishing glasses, and held up his cup with three fingers.

"You found the body this morning," Sandrine began.

"Unfortunately, yes. I have a stressful job, and I wanted to enjoy some sea breeze before heading to the office." He looked at his watch. "Where they've been expecting me for more than an hour already."

"We'll make it quick," she assured him.

"Someone died; I certainly won't complain about losing a few work hours. If I can help you, I'd be happy to."

"Thank you. Unfortunately, not everyone shares your perspective."

"In fact, I can't contribute much. I got up early to enjoy the sunrise on the sea. It's wonderfully peaceful out there, just a few seagulls, and no one chattering in your ear."

"I can imagine it's very relaxing."

The man nodded. "Around half past eight, the tide reached its peak, and I returned about half an hour earlier than usual. I saw someone on the rocks, half in the water. The waves were playing with her arm, and at first, it looked like she was waving to me." He blew air through his lips. "Creepy. I still get goosebumps thinking about it. That image won't leave my mind any time soon."

"Such things tend to stay with you," she agreed.

"I don't envy you for your job. You must see corpses more often."

"It's unfortunately part of the job." Sandrine glanced at the tidal pool, its platform already protruding well above the sea, while the parapet walls remained submerged. It had only been a few months since she had pulled a murder suspect's body out of there. She would probably never swim in the tidal pool again without thinking about it.

"I drove as close as I could, but the rocks are treacherous. It wasn't possible to moor without damaging the boat," the man said, pulling her back from her memories.

"How far was the body in the water?" Azarou asked.

"The waves were reaching her outstretched arms, but it was obvious she wouldn't drift away. I took out my phone and called the police. After that, I went to the beach." He turned his head and pointed at a small sailboat. The sail was furled, the mast tilted, and it was already on a trailer, ready to be taken off the beach.

"Did you see anyone else nearby?"

"There were a few people on the beach, some walkers, and a few daring swimmers who ventured into the cold water. They're usually up here near the tidal pool, even when it's completely submerged, like now."

"And near the tower?"

"I didn't see anyone. There were a few people on the wall, joggers, it seemed, but I didn't notice anyone on the tower."

Sandrine took out her phone and showed him the picture she had taken of the deceased.

"Does she look familiar to you? Perhaps a female sailor who also liked to admire the sunrise?"

He took the phone and examined the picture for a moment, then handed it back and shook his head. "A beautiful woman. I would have noticed and remembered her if I had met her. I'm sorry."

"It would have been a big coincidence, but I had to ask."

"Is she from around here? A Malouine?"

"We can't say for certain yet."

The waiter brought the coffee, nodded to the man, whom he apparently knew, and placed the cups on the table.

"If you don't have any further questions, I'd like to be on my way," Monsieur Sélon requested.

"Not at the moment. If anything else comes up, we'll give you a call."

The man quickly drank his coffee, stood up, and bade farewell.

"There's something small I'd like to talk to you about," the brigadier began. "It's somewhat personal."

"Sure, as long as you're not looking for relationship advice. I'm not very good at that."

"Between me and Geneviève, things are going excellently," he defended. "But it's about family."

"Tell me."

"You know my little sister."

"Jamila? Of course. A nice young woman."

"She applied for an internship with us, but you already know that. I didn't object, because..."

"Because you didn't expect her to be accepted." Sandrine got straight to the point.

"Well, she's not the kind of girl you'd assume would dream of a career as a policewoman."

"Don't be fooled. I think she knows exactly what she wants."

"In any case, she was accepted and starts with us today."

"What a surprise." In reality, it wasn't. She had advised the girl to apply and had directed her to Inès, who had helped her fill out the paperwork. Commissaire Matisse hadn't hesitated to use a bit of influence, partly because he owed Sandrine more than one favour, and partly because he held Adel in high regard and assumed the brigadier would support his sister's application, even if that was only partially true.

"However one might see it, I do wonder where she would be best placed. I'd prefer her to be in the administration, far away from all kinds of danger and bad influences."

Sandrine knew exactly what arguments he would present to give Jamila the safest but also the dullest job possible, one that would quell any interest in police work.

"I think you're right; our department really isn't suitable for an intern. When I consider who we deal with every day, murderers and criminals, I believe she'd be much better off with Inès or in the forensics department."

"Thank you for seeing it the same way. Jamila is still very young, and some of her decisions are rather spontaneous and not well thought out."

Adel wanted to protect his little sister from the unpleasant aspects of working in the force. Unfortunately, it seemed that was precisely the aspect of police work that Jamila wanted to experience. It would help the relationship between the siblings if it was Sandrine who placed her in the office and not him. At least for a while, until Adel got used to her presence at the police station. Sandrine didn't believe in coddling people, and the girl didn't seem interested in being sheltered.

"Inès will take this matter into her own hands," she assured him.

Certainly, he must have been thinking of an internship in the archives, where she would scan or file old case records. She would be bored to death there and forget any thoughts of a career in the police force. In Sandrine's opinion, she was much better off in forensics. The work was diverse and interesting, but she wouldn't come into contact with any hardcore criminals. Inès had already spoken to Jean-Claude Mazet and set everything in motion. Sandrine didn't particularly like ambushing Adel, but when it came to his sister, he often seemed overly protective. The young woman was tougher than he gave her credit for.

"Maybe I'll meet her during her lunch break," Sandrine said.

"She'd be delighted; she sees you as a role model."

"Only because she doesn't know me well," she shrugged. That was probably another reason why Adel was sceptical about her internship. While he liked Sandrine, and they made a good team, it didn't mean he welcomed or approved of his little sister emulating her.

Sandrine and Adel remained seated, enjoying the view and the morning calm. The sea was receding, and the diving platform was now almost completely above water, while the outlines of the boundary walls were clearly visible below the surface. Some teenagers swam out and climbed onto the platform. Sandrine shivered at the thought of jumping into the cold water. It was vacation time, and the beach was now speckled with colourful towels and a few umbrellas. A motorboat towed a row of small sailboats out into the bay. It reminded her of a mother duck leading her ducklings. She felt at home in Saint-Malo now, and there was nothing pulling her back to the bustling streets of Paris.

Soon, the beach would become crowded. By then, Jean-Claude Mazet should have finished examining the crime scene. Sandrine tore open the paper sachet and poured the sugar into her coffee. She stirred thoughtfully. So far, they didn't have much to go on in their pursuit of the killer.

"Where do we stand?" Adel asked, tapping his cookie against the rim of his cup. She knew him well enough to recognise that he was concerned about her behaviour at the crime scene, even if he didn't voice it and was waiting for an explanation.

"The ligature mark around the victim's neck reminded me of my last investigation in Paris. Three young women were strangled with a necktie. Those victims resembled the young woman who was killed last night. Some cases just don't let you go, and then pop up like a jack-in-the-box when you least expect it."

"Did you catch him?" Adel asked.

"No. He's still at large," she replied.

Adel fell silent, his gaze following a sailboat slowly passing behind the islands. A light breeze had picked up, carrying children's laughter to them. None of the beach-goers seemed to have any inkling of what had occurred just 600 feet away. Sandrine hoped it would stay that way for a while, until the news inevitably spread.

"Do you think this guy might be lurking in Saint-Malo now?" He finally broke his silence.

"No," she replied firmly. "Why would he? His territory is Paris, he knows his way around there. Here, he'd be a stranger and therefore conspicuous."

"You said the victims resembled each other, and the cause of death is identical. We should definitely keep it in mind."

"The press called him the Necktie Killer because he strangled his victims with a silk tie. Unlike our perpetrator, he always left it around the neck of the women. He would never forego the chance to show the police who committed the crime. The man is a massive narcissist, essentially signing his own work. So, no, he hasn't followed me to Brittany. Why would he? I'm insignificant to him." She tried to sound determined, even though she wasn't entirely convinced. It wasn't just the ligature mark that had hit her like a blow, but also the victim's appearance: blonde, blue-eyed, petite, and extremely attractive, she matched the women from the Parisian murder spree exactly. *Coincidence, nothing more.* Sandrine brushed the thought aside. These fantasies would only distract from the investigation. *I want to catch the real killer, not chase a ghost.*

"I'm inclined to believe it's a male perpetrator," Adel said. "To strangle someone who's desperately fighting for their life takes a lot of strength."

"I would also assume that. They should definitely check for date rape drugs in her bloodstream. With that stuff, she wouldn't have been able to resist."

"True," Adel agreed, jotting a note in his phone's planner.

"Furthermore, the two of them probably knew each other," Sandrine continued. "Who goes for a midnight stroll on the walls with a stranger? There's no one else around at that hour. Especially not on the tower."

"There are no clues to the victim's identity. Her clothes are nowhere to be found, nor a bag with an ID, driver's license, or credit card. Nothing. It's too early for a missing person's report, and we can't exactly walk around the city with the photo of the deceased."

"If we can't make progress with the identification, I'll ask Matisse for permission to release the image of the victim. Until we know who the victim is, we won't make much progress."

"Good idea," Azel replied.

"The two of them knew each other and went for a night walk on the wall. It was warm, the temperature hardly dropped below 68 F and the sky was clear. What are you thinking?"

"It practically screams romantic getaway," Adel remarked.

"They probably knew each other very well, maybe even a couple," she said.

"But the evening didn't go as planned. They argued, and the

altercation got out of hand. In the end, she was dead. A crime of passion?"

"I don't think so. He completely undressed her, placed her on the ground, and leaned her against the tower's wall. That sounds more like staging than a crime of passion. And he stayed with his victim, maybe even his lover, for at least half an hour, only to throw her over the wall afterward? He then collected her clothes and took them with him. It doesn't add up."

"He realized the gravity of what he'd done and panicked. He needed that half-hour to calm down and figure out how to handle the situation and save his own skin."

"Why didn't he leave straight away then?" she asked.

"If they were a couple, he'd immediately become the focus of the investigation. There were probably witnesses who knew they were planning to spend the evening together. So, he had to get rid of the body. He took everything that could help identify her and threw her over the wall."

"He must have known she'd be found at the base of the tower the next morning. Not a particularly clever plan."

"Don't forget, it was dark," Adel said. "The guy heard the waves but probably couldn't see how high the sea actually was. He miscalculated; the tide didn't come up high enough to wash the body away."

"So, not a local. A Malouin would be familiar with the tides and know that Tour Bidouane is rarely inundated."

"Which won't make it easier to track him down." Adel sighed in frustration. "The city is swarming with tourists right now."

Sandrine took a sip of her coffee. "That doesn't mean she's not from Saint-Malo. Maybe she had a fling with a tourist. Or a business arrangement."

"Do you want me to check escort services?"

"Yes. We have so little to go on right now that I'll be grateful for any lead."

"Exactly the people I was looking for," they heard someone call. Sandrine turned her head. A woman in her mid-twenties was approaching them briskly, weaving her way through the tables like a football player dribbling towards the goal. It was Arianne Briand, the editor-in-chief of the local radio station. Her jeans were torn in a few places, a black T-shirt with the local radio's logo hung loosely over her hips, and the strap of a backpack was slung over her shoulder. In her left hand, she held a dictation device, which she seemed to be turning on.

"So, you've tracked us down. Congratulations," Sandrine said and extended a hand in greeting. The woman had helped her with information several times before and defended her when she came under fire. Sandrine wouldn't go so far as to call her a friend, but they respected and liked each other.

"Do you have a dead body?" The journalist immediately got to the point and placed the dictation device on the table between herself and the two investigators.

"Who told you that?" Sandrine asked.

"Do we really have to go through this charade?" she asked, rolling her eyes, while Sandrine just shrugged. "Alright. It's obvious. The police have cordoned off Tour Bidouane and part of the beach. The guys from forensics are running around in their blue overalls like a bunch of Smurfs, and the new forensic pathologist just drove off in his Renault. An ambulance is parked behind the wall."

"Maybe a celebrity's dog was kidnapped or..." Adel tried to make a joke.

"Nonsense," she cut him off. "Do you really want to waste my time? I need to prepare the news and require credible information."

Sandrine reached for the Dictaphone and turned it off. "Who spilled the beans?"

"I won't reveal my sources."

"I bet it was the paramedics. They were probably bored," Adel guessed. "Maybe a coffee or the prospect of a free concert ticket, which your radio station often gives away, made them too willing to inform the press."

"No comment." The hint of a grin on the journalist's lean face told Sandrine that her colleague had hit the mark. "But Deborah Binet from *Ouest France* beat me to the coffee."

"Nice hairstyle, by the way. Wasn't your hair bright red not too long ago?" Arianne Briand ran her hand over her millimetre-short hair, dyed as blue as the sea.

"Variety is the spice of life," she said, looking around, probably afraid that her competitors might also locate Sandrine and Adel. "To the point, what happened?"

"A police matter."

"The public has a right to know what's going on in their city."

"Absolutely," Sandrine agreed. "That's why there will be a press release from the police station." More like a press appearance by Antoine de Chezac.

"But I'm going to find out what happened anyway. It's better for the local radio to report authentic news than wild theories spreading on social media."

Sandrine couldn't disagree with her on that point.

"Plus, I need to prepare for the press conference. You surely want me to ask your boss the right questions, don't you?"

Sandrine sighed, and Adel chuckled quietly. Arianne Briand had brought up an excellent point. They knew the prosecutor well enough to know that he didn't always stick to the facts when they made him look bad.

"All right. The whole town probably knows by now anyway. We found a female body at the base of the tower and are investigating what happened."

"Accident or murder?" The woman leaned forward and scrutinised Sandrine intensely. She would recognise a lie.

"We're ruling out natural death. Everything else is still open, and I don't want to speculate."

"An accident or a violent crime?"

"The investigation isn't complete yet. We're waiting for the final report from the forensic pathologist and the forensics team, then we'll inform the press." Sandrine evaded the question, even though there were hardly any doubts about the cause of death.

Arianne Briand nodded thoughtfully. She understood what Sandrine was hinting at but didn't want to say officially.

"Who is she?"

"We're still in the process of identifying the deceased." Which wouldn't be easy. So far, they had no leads, and all her personal belongings had disappeared.

"Maybe I can help. I know a bunch of people in Saint-Malo, that's part of my job," she offered, not entirely selflessly, but she had a point. The journalist got around and knew many residents of Saint-Malo and the surrounding area. Sandrine glanced at Adel, who nodded almost imperceptibly.

"All right." She took out her phone and uploaded the picture of the victim.

"May I?" The journalist took the phone and looked at the photo for a while. "Hard to say, but she looks vaguely familiar, probably a Malouine. Let me think about it." Arianne handed the phone back.

"Before you ask, we can't present a suspect or witnesses. This happened last night."

"It would have been too good to be true." She put the Dictaphone in her pocket and leaned back in her chair.

"I hear that a team from Rennes has arrived in Saint-Malo. Is that true?" Her question sounded casual, as if she wasn't exactly sure what was happening in the city. Her local radio station had extensively covered the drug bust at Équinoxe, Sandrine's boyfriend's club.

"When a police officer is accused of misconduct, as in this case, the investigation is handed over to another department to avoid conflicts of interest. Pure routine. Accordingly, the case was assigned to a prosecutor from Rennes. I can't say more about it since I don't have any further information. We," she gestured to herself and Adel, "will participate in these investigations at most as witnesses. If you need information, you'll have to contact the police station or the new prosecutor directly."

"Sébastian Hermé, isn't it?"

"As I can see, you're well-informed."

"Will there be a press conference for these investigations as well? After all, the case here has caused quite a stir. Léon Martinau and Équinoxe have fallen into disrepute."

"Is that so?" Sandrine brushed a strand of hair from her face, trying to appear calm. The accusations against her boyfriend had weighed heavily on her at the time. It could easily have led to him losing the license to operate his club, perhaps even facing a trial. Fortunately, it hadn't come to that, mainly thanks to Adel's investigations. In fact, Léon claimed that Équinoxe was doing better than ever. Bad publicity is still publicity. Something must be true about that saying.

"Didn't this police officer confess to planting drugs on him during a raid?"

"I can't comment on that. As I mentioned, I'm not involved in the investigations, but I believe it will be clarified." Both statements were true. She trusted Sébastian Hermé to get to the bottom of the incident and take the necessary steps.

"Do you think he acted on his own or was he used by someone further up in the hierarchy? There's a rumour going around."

Sandrine waved it off. "That's wishful thinking on the part of some journalists who want to inflate the accusations against a police officer to make sensational headlines, maybe even on a national scale. There's no concrete evidence to prove that the man acted on someone else's orders. Why would there be a police conspiracy against a harmless club in Saint-Malo? Forget this nonsense."

"Perhaps it wasn't about Léon Martinau or the club, but someone in his immediate circle," speculated Arianne Briand, echoing Sandrine's own but unspoken suspicion.

"We're in Saint-Malo, Brittany, not in an American conspiracy thriller." Sandrine brushed off the journalist's notions. She couldn't afford a report on the local radio if she wanted to track down the person behind Brigadier Poutin's criminal activities. It would only alarm him unnecessarily and make him more cautious.

"Well, I'll keep an eye on the developments."

"Please do. We need to head out now."

"To the crime scene?"

"To Tour Bidouane."

"Then I'll see you there. Thanks for the information."

"If you happen to remember where you've seen the woman before, give me a call. It would be helpful."

"I will," promised the journalist before they parted ways.

***

Sandrine and Adel walked back along the city wall towards Tour Bidouane. Two bright red wooden doors leading into the interior of the tower were locked, with the entrance to the upper platform open, guarded by a police officer who was turning away tourists. They displayed their ID badges, and he let them through. The distance from the entrance on the city wall to the tower was hardly ten to twelve feet. Sandrine led the way up the narrow spiral staircase and stepped aside as she emerged into the open to make way for Adel. The tower was roughly three times as long as it was wide, with a surrounding wall barely more than knee-high. To prevent accidents, a sturdy iron railing had been installed. Her gaze immediately turned to the opposite side, where she suspected the victim had been placed by her murderer. Except for some small markers set up by the forensics team, there was nothing unusual to see. On an ordinary day, she wouldn't have paid much attention to the spot on the wall but would have admired the view of the bay.

Jean-Claude Mazet stood at the far end of the tower, looking down at the rocks.

"May we?" Sandrine called out.

The forensics expert turned around and nodded at her. One of his colleagues handed them two pairs of disposable overshoes, which they put on before approaching him. They always carried gloves in their pockets.

"We're done up here. Just a few more photos, and the tower can be reopened," said the forensic expert.

"Did you find anything?" Sandrine asked.

"I believe so." He pointed downwards. "My team found skin, blood, and hair at a spot directly below us. Someone pushed the body under the railing and rolled it over the wall."

Sandrine crouched down. There was enough space between the railing and the wall to climb through. The top of the wide masonry slanted outward. It wouldn't have been too difficult to roll or push a body over the edge. She estimated it to be about sixty-five feet to the rocks at the base of the tower.

"Hair, blood, and skin traces? The body must have been dragged over the masonry, and not very gently. Probably the killer was in a hurry to get rid of it before being seen up here," Adel concluded.

"We've taken samples. As soon as the results come back from the lab, I'll send them to you. I expect a positive result in the DNA analysis, although there wasn't a significant amount of blood. This suggests that she was strangled here, and the injuries occurred when she hit the rocks below. After that, the perpetrator moved her again and dragged her towards the water. Some of the abrasions likely resulted from this. But I unlikely we'll find any traces on the rocks."

"The new forensic pathologist had the same suspicion," Sandrine commented.

"What we didn't find were her clothes, ID, bag, or anything else she might have had with her. Also, there's no sign of the object used for strangulation," added Adel.

"The perpetrator likely took everything with him. Either he wanted to make it harder for us to identify the victim, or her belongings could potentially lead us to his trail. Probably both," Sandrine surmised.

"What do you think he used to strangle the woman?" Adel inquired.

"I won't commit to that just yet. Based on the imprint, it's most likely a belt, scarf, or rope," the forensic expert responded.

"A rope would suggest a premeditated act. Who carries something like that around at night?"

Mazet agreed with the brigadier's assessment. "There are always a few fibres left behind. Tomorrow, I will be able to provide more details."

Sandrine leaned on the metal railing, which was already so worn only remnants of paint remained.

"Isn't that the big boss down there?" Mazet asked sarcastically.

Sandrine glanced down. He was right. On the path leading to the tower, de Chezac was talking to a dozen people, who were holding out cameras and microphones towards him. Arianne Briand's bright blue hair stood out from the crowd. Deborah Binet, the reporter from *Ouest France*, stood a few steps away. She was dressed conservatively as always, but she had swapped her usual high-heeled shoes for something more practical in order to navigate the rocky path. Most likely, her high heels were in her handbag, which she always carried.

"If he's good at anything, it's putting on a show." Disapproval resonated in Mazet's voice. The head of forensics was an advocate of competent, calm work before results were published. Surely he was wondering which unproven facts the prosecutor was currently putting out into the world before his eyes. In that regard, Sandrine felt similarly.

"He certainly knows how to hog the spotlight," she agreed. The prosecutor had chosen a place where he not only had the location of the body behind him but also the sea and Fort National, one of the city's landmarks. A gentle breeze played in his hair. The tan from the sun and the rolled-up sleeves of his shirt would surely look good in the pictures. The man practically lived for his public appearances, where he portrayed himself as a vigorous advocate of law and order.

"He only met with us briefly; I can't say if he's already spoken with the new medical examiner. If so, it was likely just over the phone," Mazet replied.

"We'll find out from the newspaper tomorrow." Adel stepped up beside her, also leaning against the railing.

"It'll happen faster than that. Look down there, Deborah Binet is standing there. Knowing the journalist, she'll ambush us and drill us for details that de Chezac couldn't give her," replied Sandrine, who had dealt with the woman frequently before.

On the city wall, a crowd of onlookers had gathered, observing the scene at the beach. A police operation provided an interesting diversion from their vacations or city tours, which few wanted to miss. Sandrine scanned the crowd, but she didn't spot any familiar faces.

"Do you think he's here, watching us?" Adel asked, coming closer to her. A hint of his aftershave wafted her way. Sometimes it felt like he could read her thoughts.

"I don't know, but it wouldn't be unusual. Some revel in their criminal deeds to feel important, while others live in fear of being discovered and watch the police, as if they could draw conclusions from our investigations," Sandrine responded.

"How do we proceed?" Adel inquired.

"Our top priority is to identify the woman, then find witnesses," Sandrine confirmed.

"How do you plan to do that? It isn't exactly bustling here in the middle of the night. The bar at Plage de Bon-Secours closes at 10 p.m., and the restaurants along the wall not much later."

"It was Sunday night. Perhaps someone on their way home from one of the bars chose the path over the city wall, or a resident might have seen something during the night. We'll have to send officers door to door to interview the residents. Maybe we'll get lucky and find a surveillance camera that recorded something," Sandrine said, outlining the plan.

"A lot of work, but we don't have much choice," Adel acknowledged.

"We'll wait for the results from forensics and the forensic pathologist." Sandrine checked her watch. "Let's head back to the police station before de Chezac starts breathing down our necks."

"Good idea," Adel agreed.

Shadows from the Past

"Go on ahead, I need to talk to Inès," Sandrine said as they entered the police station.

"Sure thing. Since we need it more urgently than they do, hopefully our guests have vacated the briefing room," Adel replied.

"They definitely have. Matisse has assigned them their own office," Sandrine assured him. It was something Matisse hadn't offered her yet. But she felt more comfortable in the open workspace. It gave her a sense of being part of the team that she wouldn't have in a closed room.

"Come in," the office manager, Inès, responded, quickly typing something into a spreadsheet before turning her chair to face Sandrine. "I hear there's a case for us."

"The body on the beach? Definitely a homicide. But the perpetrator didn't make it easy for us to identify her. I hope a missing person's report comes in soon."

"Unfortunately not today. I've already checked. I'm sorry."

"I didn't expect it to be that quick," Sandrine replied.

"In any case, I've reserved the briefing room for your investigation. The team from Rennes has taken up a free space on the ground floor, far from our office."

"Have they indicated how long they'll be staying?" Sandrine inquired.

"The woman has requested all the files and evidence Poutin worked on in the past year, as well as any documents related to Équinoxe."

"That last one will likely be a thin file," Sandrine remarked. Léon had assured her that no raid on his club had ever yielded anything beyond a few grams of marijuana. She believed him; why would he lie to her?

"I've taken a look at the file myself, considering I visit there quite often," Inès said. "Multiple noise complaints and a guest once blocked a fire lane. Nothing dramatic."

"It's all part of your job. You're just getting an overview. I'd do the same," Sandrine replied. "I should be glad they're doing it thoroughly, but I don't like how aggressively Major Baud is acting." She took a visitor's chair and sat down next to Inès. "Could you do me a favour, one that nobody should know about for now, at least not yet?"

"Something illegal?" Inès grinned mischievously, as if such a task would be particularly enjoyable for her.

"No, but not entirely following the rules either."

"Sure thing. Shoot!"

Sandrine picked up a pen from the desk, tore a piece of paper from a pad, and quickly wrote a name on it before sliding it over to the office manager.

"Can you find out if this man is staying in Saint-Malo or the surrounding area?"

"Hotels won't be a problem, but with private rentals, it's usually off the books," Inès cautioned.

"The man is most likely staying in a hotel. The more upscale, the better. Try nothing below five stars. But it's probably a false alarm."

"Understood. I'll be discreet."

"Thank you," Sandrine said. She got up, pushed the chair

back into place, and followed Adel into the briefing room. Along the way, she called Martin Alary, an old friend and colleague from Paris.

Adel had used the time to prepare the room. Cork boards lined one long wall, tables were set up, and on the monitor at the head of the room, he was uploading photos of the victim. Renard Dubois had joined them and was attaching images of the crime scene and a map of Saint-Malo's old town to one of the cork boards. All that was left to do was to bring in some thermos flasks filled with coffee and a tin of Breton butter cookies, which Inès kept locked in her office. Over the next few days, more leads would come in, and the evidence would slowly fill the boards, connecting the dots until they made sense. For now, they had next to nothing in their hands, as evidenced by the empty spaces on the cork boards.

"What should I do?" Dubois asked.

"I need you to coordinate the search for witnesses. Organise interviews with the residents in the vicinity. Someone might have noticed something," Sandrine instructed.

"I'm on it. Surveillance cameras?"

"Mazet said he'd take care of that. Tomorrow, the newspapers will report on the case, and I need someone to sift through the tips from the public, weed out the nonsense, and find the needle in the haystack," she explained.

"I'm your man for that," Dubois assured her.

"I have no doubt."

"First, I have to meet with our colleagues from Rennes. They want to interrogate me," he grimaced, as if he'd rather go to the dentist than be questioned by Major Baud. Hence, he'd used the term "interrogate" instead of "interview." He was a cop and understood the difference.

"You haven't done anything wrong, so there's no reason to worry," Sandrine reassured him.

"What do you think will happen to Luc?" Renard seemed more concerned about his old friend Luc Poutin than himself.

"His time in the police force is over, that much seems clear. He was never an exemplary cop, but his record is clean, so I think he'll get off with a light punishment at most. If he's willing to testify about what led him to plant drugs on someone, that might help him," Sandrine speculated.

"To be honest, he never liked you," Dubois admitted.

"That was obvious, but did it push him to commit a crime like this?" Sandrine doubted it.

"I wonder about that, too," Dubois replied quietly. He also seemed to doubt that the idea of framing her boyfriend for a crime had originated with him.

"You better get going; Major Baud doesn't seem like someone who enjoys waiting," Sandrine advised.

"Not at all. She gives the impression that she could become very bossy if I don't show up on time," he said, taking a deep breath and heading off.

"When do you have to report in?" Adel asked.

"No idea. It seems they're saving me for last," Sandrine replied. Major Baud had likely collected clues or contradictions that she could use to make Sandrine's life difficult. She wondered what she had done to earn the woman's animosity.

The door swung open, and de Chezac walked in.

"There are my detectives," he said, emphasising the word 'my' as if the era of serfdom had never ended. "We need to issue a press release. What do we have?" He took a chair and sat down.

"So far, not much," Sandrine replied. "The woman was strangled on Tour Bidouane, then thrown down by someone and discovered by a sailor this morning. We can't say much more about the sequence of events yet."

"When you use the word 'someone,' you must be talking about the perpetrator. If another person had found the body, they would have informed the police instead of tampering with the corpse and tossing it from the tower. Don't unnecessarily complicate the case."

"It's likely that's what happened, but it's by no means certain. We have to keep all possibilities open. Between the woman's death and her fall onto the rocks, at least half an hour passed, as evidenced by the post-mortem discoloration of the skin. She died in a sitting position, not lying on the rocks."

"So the perpetrator sat there for a while, observing his victim. It's truly strange what goes on in the minds of these monsters."

"Then he would have taken a big risk of being discovered while sitting there next to the corpse. The tower is easily visible from the wall and adjacent houses. If I were in his place, I would have quickly disposed of the body and vanished."

"Who else would have any interest in throwing the body down? Drunk guys passing by who thought it would be funny?" An arrogant smile crept across his lips. "You should forget that theory quickly. We'd make fools of ourselves with that one. I see it more as a crime of passion, not premeditated but impulsive. The perpetrator panicked once he realised what he had done. Understandable that he needed some time to calm down and come up with a plan to dispose of the body."

"That's certainly possible," she admitted.

"Not just possible, but likely. I'd say it's almost certain," he insisted. "A crime of passion. They probably had an argument, and it ended with her death."

"She was strangled," Sandrine observed. "That doesn't happen quickly; it takes some time. Enough time for one to regain their composure. Furthermore, he must have had a tool with him."

"Almost everyone has one." De Chezac tapped his belt that held his trousers.

"Or a necktie," Adel added, nodding towards the examining magistrate's tie.

The smile on Antoine de Chezac's face froze, and his gaze met Sandrine's, who forced herself to suppress her emotions. She and de Chezac shared a history. Before he came to Saint-Malo, he had been in charge of the investigation into the Necktie Killer in Paris. Their cooperation had been far from harmonious, and Sandrine had made a mistake that had almost ended her career in the police.

"Don't get yourself caught up in this again," he warned her. "Last time, it almost cost you your job."

"So far, our investigation doesn't point in that direction," she replied calmly. "There's no indication that this crime is connected to those series of murders in Paris."

"Don't forget that," he said emphatically. He stood up abruptly. "Make sure you catch the guy who did this." Without saying goodbye, he turned around and marched out.

"What was that?" Adel asked in surprise, looking at her with a questioning gaze.

"A warning not to delve into a theory I can't prove and one that goes against his beliefs." *Above all, he would have to admit that he was wrong, which he would never do.*

"Can you explain what's bothering him so much?"

"A long story that doesn't paint me in a good light. And it's not relevant to our case."

"The story about that Necktie Killer?"

"Yes, my last case in Paris and the reason I moved to Brittany. But it has nothing to do with our investigation." *At least I can't prove it does, and I don't want to rely solely on my gut feeling.*

"Fair enough." He didn't sound convinced but wouldn't

press further. Adel knew that she would talk to him about it when she was ready, if it had any relevance to their case.

There was a knock on the door. Inès entered, followed by a young woman in faded jeans, trainers, and a dark blue T-shirt with the word "POLICE" printed on it, holding a stack of files in her hands.

"Welcome, Jamila," Sandrine greeted Adel's younger sister. "As I can see, Inès has already given you some work."

"Oh, yes." She managed to nod and roll her eyes at the same time. "Sorting files. Must be a great way to start getting into police work."

"I think it is. At least it's a realistic one," Sandrine replied. "Generally, I spend more time sitting at a desk typing reports than chasing criminals."

"I'll make sure she doesn't get bored," Inès reassured. "And not get involved in anything too dangerous," she added, winking at Adel.

"Maybe I can go out with Sandrine sometime," Jamila suggested.

"With Capitaine Perrot," her brother immediately corrected her with emphasis.

"Of course. Sorry, I guess I still need to get used to the ranks," she said to Sandrine. "Or to Brigadier Chief de Police Azarou," she continued in her brother's direction.

"I'll see what can be arranged," Sandrine promised without committing herself.

"I did some asking around and maybe found a witness," Inès said.

"Who? They witnessed the crime?" Sandrine inquired.

"I'm not exactly sure yet. An old school friend, Jules, works at a youth centre, and a few schoolgirls mentioned that they were on the beach last night around the time of the incident. Near the tower."

"We need to talk to them," Sandrine decided. "Do you have the address?"

"That might be tricky. They don't particularly like cops. He was sceptical about whether they'd talk to you at all."

"I could help," Jamila surprisingly offered.

"How so?" Adel asked.

"The youth centre Mademoiselle Boni mentioned is near my school, and I know a lot of the kids who go there."

Inès suppressed a grin when Jamila referred to her as 'Mademoiselle Boni'.

"You do?" Adel asked instantly, furrowing his brow. Clearly, he didn't think highly of the boys from the youth centre.

"Sure. Don't look at me like it's something bad. Everyone goes there. I do some tutoring or help with homework. They don't have anyone else, nor the money to pay for someone."

Sandrine leaned back in her chair. It was Jamila's first day of her internship, and she left it to Adel to decide whether she could go out or stay with the files.

"Come on, I know them; they're more likely to talk to me than if you give them your disapproving looks," Jamila urged.

Adel looked at Sandrine, who shrugged. It was his decision.

"Alright, but after that, you go back to work with Inès, understood?"

"Definitely," she agreed wholeheartedly.

"I mean it."

"Jules is with the group at Plage de Bon-Secours," Inès informed them. "With this weather, it sounds like a great outing."

"Then Jamila and I will head out. We'll take a patrol car that will bring us back afterward," Sandrine decided.

"I'm working in forensics to help review the surveillance cameras. I promised Marie," Adel said. He sounded like he'd rather retract his promise and accompany them instead.

"I'll take good care of her. What could happen at the beach, besides getting a little sunburn?"

The young woman smiled gently, with a hint of barely concealed triumph. She had achieved her goal: trading the boring files for a beach visit on her first day and working on a current case with Sandrine. She seemed very pleased with herself.

* * *

The patrol car drove through the narrow Porte Saint-Pierre and parked at the top of the ramp leading down to the beach, mostly used by sailors who brought their boats in on light trailers. The tide had receded further, and the beach was much busier than in the morning. It was lunchtime, and there were no empty tables at the beach bar, the same place they'd met the sailor earlier. A gentle breeze blew, and the row of boats and catamarans from rental shops had significantly thinned out. Business was good, which was not surprising for a day in late July.

"I see them over there." Jamila pointed towards the tidal pool. "I know the girls on the diving platform from school."

"Let's go then." Sandrine pulled at her T-shirt to fully conceal her weapon and holster. Jamila was as fashion-conscious as her brother, but on her first day at the police, she had opted for something practical. The girl rolled up her trousers and took off her shoes, holding them in her hand. Walking barefoot on the soft sand was easier. Sandrine left her shoes on, as she might have to go back to the rocks in front of Tour Bidouane. Besides, she hated sand in her socks.

"I'm Capitaine Perrot from the Saint-Malo Police Department," she introduced herself to the man Jamila had pointed out. "Inès Boni said you might have some information for me."

"Jules," he said, extending his hand out for a friendly handshake. "Hello, Jamila, I didn't know you were working for the police."

"Internship. My first day."

"Have fun with that," the social worker from the youth centre replied, with a look that suggested he had doubts about how much fun an internship with the police could be.

"Thank you. I have, so far." She was probably thinking about the stack of files waiting for her at the police station.

"The others are in the water. Could you get Céline and Ninette?" he asked Jamila.

"Sure," she said, placing her shoes on the sand and heading towards the tidal pool.

"They can't tell you much, but I thought every little helps. Usually, we limit our contacts with the police. Many of the kids haven't had good experiences with your colleagues."

"I'm glad you're still willing to talk to us."

"Inès can be very persuasive when she wants something."

Jamila returned with two girls with whom she conversed animatedly. Sandrine hoped they would remain talkative and not clam up as soon as they had to deal with the police.

"This is Capitaine Perrot," Jamila introduced her. "You can tell her what you saw."

One of the girls looked at Sandrine, and Jamila nodded encouragingly. "Go ahead, Ninette."

"Alright. Our club closed, and we weren't tired yet," she began, then hesitated.

"Her boyfriend owns the Équinoxe?" her friend asked. "Supposed to be a cool place."

"Which club were you at?" Sandrine avoided the question.

"One over there," the girl named Céline replied vaguely. "In any case, we stayed here on the beach for a while."

"Did you notice anything unusual?"

"Somebody got killed, they say," Ninette chimed in.

"Someone has died," Sandrine replied. "We don't know the details yet."

"Damn, that could have been one of us," Ninette said, looking towards Tour Bidouane.

"That's rather unlikely," Sandrine tried to reassure her. "Did you observe anything unusual?"

"Nothing unusual. There are always people hanging around here at all hours, and some of them are really creepy," Céline said. "We were just sitting here chatting, when I heard something from the direction of the tower. At first, I didn't think much of it, but then we decided to go check it out."

"That was brave but not very smart," Jamila commented.

"Oh, come on," Ninette brushed it off. "I thought it might be some Peeping Tom hoping to spy on couples. They usually run away if they get caught in the act."

"And? Was it one of those?" Sandrine asked.

"I don't think so. Someone was hanging around the tower and climbing over the rocks. A really dumb idea in the middle of the night. It was pitch dark, and you could easily break a leg."

"Could you see the person?"

"Like I said, it was dark, and I didn't have a flashlight with me since we hadn't planned on coming here."

"Man or woman?"

"Looked more like a man. He was wearing dark clothes, even though that doesn't help much," Ninette said.

"I called out, and he stared at us for a while, then he vanished." Céline pointed to the stairs leading from the beach to the city wall. "Up there."

From that path, he could only have turned to the right and disappeared through the city gate.

"After that, we went back to the others. There's nothing more to say," Céline said, raising her hands apologetically. "It must have been around 2 a.m. It's the holidays, so it's not a big deal."

"Thank you, that already helps." At least she now knew when the victim had been thrown from the tower and dragged towards the water. And who had interrupted the process. It had been nearly low tide around two in the morning. To get the body into the sea, someone would have had to drag or carry it quite a distance, not an easy task, especially in the dark. Someone must have been very desperate.

"Do you think..." Ninette began, but Jamila lightly elbowed her in the side.

"Let's get back in the water." Ninette and Céline said their goodbyes and ran back to the pool.

"They won't get in trouble, will they?" Jules asked.

"Not from me. But tomorrow, those two will have to come to the police station and give their statements."

"Do you think they saw the young woman's murderer?" Jules sounded concerned.

"I don't think they were in danger," she reassured him. "But at night, you don't necessarily encounter nice people here."

"I keep telling them that," he said, looking at Sandrine and grinning. "They're 16 or 17. Did you listen to your parents or teachers at that age?"

"Not really."

The man said his goodbyes and rejoined his group.

"What do you think—was that all they had to say, or did they leave something out?"

"On the way here, she told me the same story. There wasn't more. Fortunately, or it could have ended badly. Who knows how a murderer will react when caught off guard."

"I don't think it was the killer. At 2 a.m., the woman was already dead, had been for at least an hour or two."

"Then who else could it have been?"

"Good question. That's exactly what we need to find out."

"You can do it," Jamila said with conviction.

"Thank you, but especially for being here. They might not have told me anything."

"I don't think they would have. They were afraid of getting into trouble."

"Why? It's the holidays, and sitting on the beach at night is not illegal."

"The club they came from doesn't check IDs very closely. They had fake copies with them."

"I see."

"That's why they thought it was cool to talk to the girlfriend of the owner of Équinoxe."

"The girlfriend?" Sandrine whistled softly in astonishment. "You told them that?"

"Sure. It's the coolest club in Saint-Malo, and they'd like to go there, but they only let you in if you're 18, and the guys at the door are clever and don't fall for fake IDs."

"You didn't make any promises to them, did you?"

"No," she protested indignantly. "At least not directly. Just that I'd inquire if there might be an exception for witnesses of crimes."

"I see. Then you'll have to ask Léon. He owns the club, not me."

"I only know him by sight," she protested. "Although..."

"Although what?"

"You have really good taste," she said, grinning.

"Thank you." She smiled. "I'll tell him."

"Don't. Otherwise, he might think I have a crush on him." She waved it off.

"Oh, where would he get that idea? After all, he's quite ancient compared to you."

"That's true," Jamila said thoughtfully.

"Take the patrol car. The officer will drop you off at the police station."

"And you?"

"I'll walk. It's not too far, and I could use a nice stroll to help me think."

"I could think along with you," she offered.

"Very kind of you, but I'm sure Inès is already waiting for you with the case files."

Jamila sighed deeply in disappointment before making her way to the patrol car waiting at the top of the ramp.

Sandrine watched the girl until she got in, and the patrol car slowly drove through the narrow gate. Adel would be relieved when she returned safely. He worried too much. It was her first day; it would likely ease over the course of her internship.

Sandrine turned around and marched towards the tower. That's where the woman had been killed and thrown down soon after. The more she thought about it, the less believable it seemed that the murderer had spent an extended period of time with the body. Her gaze shifted from the rocks up to the platform. She suddenly froze. Leaning by the railing was a man tall enough to stand out from the crowd. His blond hair gently fluttered in the summer breeze, and he was wearing a red jacket.

This can't be happening.

Instinctively, she took a step back as their gazes met. He must have been waiting for her up there, for there was no other way to explain the eerie resemblance to the man from her last case in Paris. Ariste de Saint-Clair. He had looked down on her as she came from the location of a body, from a bridge over the Canal Saint-Martin. Her hands clenched into fists until it hurt, nails digging into her flesh. She couldn't say how long they had stared at each other—maybe a few seconds, maybe minutes— when he turned away. Shortly after, he disappeared as if he had never existed. Chasing after him would be pointless. The man would have vanished before she even made it to the old town. Her heart continued to beat heavily against her chest, and her breath was shallow and fast for the second time that day. Why was he here? *Is he trying to send me a message? Of course, that's it. To let me know that he's safe from me, no matter what crimes he commits.*

She stood motionless on the beach for a while, her gaze scanning the city wall. Death had followed her from Paris.

From Tour Bidouane to the police station was just over a half an hour walk. Time she needed to sort out her thoughts. Instead of taking the direct route to the police station, she walked a few more steps along the pedestrian promenade on the Digue de Rochebonne and sat on a bench in front of one of the small hotels lining the beach. Cyclists, families with young children carrying plastic shovels and pails, couples, and some inline skaters populated the promenade, but she paid them little attention. Her thoughts revolved around the dead woman and the unexpected appearance of the man from her past—her only suspect in the Necktie Killer case. There was just one conclusion: that he was behind everything that had happened in the past few months. But what was his goal? To finally get her out of the police force? He had come close to achieving that in Paris, as she had made some serious mistakes. But not in Saint-Malo. *I've learned my lesson.*

A shadow fell across her face, and she looked up. A man stood in front of her. She squinted against the sun. It was Brigadier Poutin. He gazed down at her, scrutinising her with hostility, then stepped aside and sat down beside her.

"Did I say the seat was free?"

"This is a public bench. Anyone can sit here if they want," he replied in a curt tone.

"What do you want?" she asked irritably. She needed peace to think about de Saint-Clair, and she didn't want to deal with the brigadier any more than necessary. He was just a minor player in this game. In fact, he'd already been taken out of it and was watching from the sidelines.

"You never respected me," he said, to her surprise. Sandrine looked at him. The man had never cared much about his appearance, but now he seemed even more unkempt. His shirt hung out of his trousers and sweaty stains showed under the armpits. His trousers were creased as if he had been sleeping in them, and his shoes desperately needed a brush.

"You mostly avoided work and used Dubois to cover for your laziness," she replied. "And by the way, the feeling's mutual."

"Parisians like you, coming here acting all high and mighty, think everyone in the provinces is dumb and should dance to your tune," he spat out, barely comprehensible.

"I didn't choose this. I had already written my resignation and closed the chapter on my career as a police officer when Commissaire Matisse basically forced me into that murder case."

"In Paris, you were dismissed," he said, his voice dripping with sarcasm.

"One could say that," Sandrine replied. He wasn't entirely wrong.

"Nothing will happen to me," the brigadier suddenly asserted, confidently. "My record is spotless, and all in all, I've committed fewer offences than you."

"What are you talking about?" Sandrine asked.

"An entry in my service record, early retirement, perhaps a demotion. That's the worst that will come out of this drama. The guys from Rennes bark a lot but can't really bite. I have friends in the police department," he added with a grin. It was the second time that day someone seemed to consider themselves untouchable. First Ariste de Saint-Clair, and now the brigadier. However, the two were of completely different calibre. Poutin was a simple brigadier with few friends, while de Saint-Clair was a wealthy and influential aristocrat from Paris.

"Has Hermé interrogated you yet?" Sandrine inquired.

"He and the whole gang. There was nothing I wanted to tell them. A pure waste of time," he replied.

"A confession could help you," she suggested.

"I don't need help," he said confidently. He seemed to genuinely believe that he wouldn't face harsh consequences or a conviction.

"Framing Léon by planting drugs in order to harm me wasn't your idea. Someone is pulling the strings and making you dance like a puppet," Sandrine remarked.

"Believe whatever you want. But nobody orders me around," he retorted.

"Consider whether you're still useful to your puppeteers. They'll drop you like a hot potato. Do you really think these people respect someone like you? You better watch out before you end up in jail or something happens to you," she warned, attempting to puncture his arrogance or at least sow some seed of doubt. But it seemed to be in vain.

The man chuckled bitterly. "If you still think I'm a simpleton, you're sorely mistaken." Brigadier Poutin leaned on the bench with both hands and stood up clumsily. Without another word, he walked away, disappearing among the tourists on the path.

* * *

Sandrine observed Inès sitting in her glass-enclosed office and approached her.

"Hello, Sandrine. Did the interrogation yield anything?"

"Yes. Jules and the girls were very helpful. Having Jamila there made a difference; she knew the girls from school." And it helped that they were hoping for free entry to Équinoxe.

"She was quite excited to be on a real assignment on her first day. I suppose office work will seem doubly boring to her now."

"Who wouldn't enjoy going to the beach during working

hours?" Sandrine thought of the swimsuit in her car. But her enthusiasm for a beach outing had waned.

"Regarding the other matter..." Inès closed the door to the office. "I couldn't trace this man to any of the exclusive hotels. There's no property registered under his name where he could be residing. I'm sorry, but I'm afraid he's not in Saint-Malo."

"Thank you for your help. You can stop the search." This morning, it was just a hunch, but now she knew he was in Saint-Malo and not afraid to be seen by her. She still needed to figure out how to deal with it. It was time to talk to Adel. He had to know what had happened in Paris, at least most of it.

Sandrine approached the brigadier, who was reading a report from the forensics department.

"I need to talk to you."

Adel looked up at her in surprise.

"But not here."

He looked around as if searching for unwanted eavesdroppers.

"Alright," he said softly, and stood up. Sandrine led the way into the conference room and closed the door behind them.

"The forensic experts found traces on the victim's neck," Adel confirmed.

"Silk, right?" assumed Sandrine.

"Exactly. But also traces of synthetic fibres. I just received the report from the forensics department. Have you already met with Jean-Claude?"

"No, it was just a guess."

Adel took a seat at the table. "Go on, I'm curious."

"This morning, I told you about Paris."

"That Necktie Murderer?"

"It was my last case," she began and hesitated. It was difficult for her to talk about it. She still felt anger towards the perpetrator, her superiors, but most of all towards herself when she recalled it. "Over the course of a year, three young women were strangled in Paris and left at historically significant locations. The last one was in a tunnel of the Canal Saint-Martin, another one in the basement of the Opéra Garnier."

"Where the Phantom of the Opera is said to have lived? I read about the murders in the newspaper, but I didn't know you worked on that case."

"I was just one of many in the team. Commandant Henry led the homicide division, and Antoine de Chezac was the prosecutor."

"Our de Chezac? I wouldn't have thought they'd assign him to such high-profile cases. Did you catch the guy?"

"No. After I left Paris, the murders stopped. They never managed to identify the perpetrator."

"Not a great record for de Chezac. Was he transferred to us because of that?"

"That was one of my assumptions, but I was wrong. In fact, he initiated the transfer himself. I can't say for sure why. Maybe he believes that gaining experience in the provinces will help him on his way to the Ministry of the Interior. Besides, he's a fan of fresh oysters, so he's in the right place here."

"And you believe the Parisian murders are connected to our case?" Wrinkles appeared on his forehead. The possibility of a serial killer being in Saint-Malo disturbed him.

"The victims were all in their early to mid-twenties, exceptionally good-looking, petite, blonde and blue-eyed," Sandrine described. "All of the women had a connection to the art school. They either studied there, worked as models for artists, or exhibited their work in galleries."

"They were strangled?"

"Without exception. They were drugged beforehand and, when they were defenceless, strangled with a silk tie," Sandrine explained.

"Like our victim. The description matches. Let's wait and see if the forensic team finds traces of a sedative," Adel added, nodding. Her theory seemed to make sense to him. "The crime scene at Tour Bidouane is also historically significant. We might be dealing with the same perpetrator."

"There are differences that confuse me," Sandrine said. "In Paris, a silk tie with an embroidered rose was always left behind. It hung around the neck of the victims like a personal seal. The police should have known who was responsible for the crime."

"Silk traces were found on the victim's neck here."

"But also synthetic fibres, which is puzzling. Moreover, no tie was left behind, and someone attempted to dispose of the body in the sea. If he had succeeded, she might never have been found. That contradicts the actions of our man from Paris."

"It almost looks like someone committed the crime, and another person tried to eliminate the evidence," the brigadier speculated.

"That's also my impression."

"Why do we need to hide away here then? We're just discussing our case."

"I had a suspect back then: Ariste de Saint-Clair, a filthy rich aristocrat with a family tree dating back to the early Middle Ages. I could establish a connection to at least two of the women."

"And?"

"Commandant Henry and de Chezac questioned him, but I was kept out of it. The man could provide an alibi for each of the crimes. So, he was removed from the list of suspects, and I was ordered not to approach him again. At least not without the express permission of my superiors."

"Well, if he had alibis, that's not unusual."

"Alibis from people who were economically dependent on him. One of them was transferred to South America shortly thereafter." Sandrine shook her head. "Those alibis didn't mean much."

"What else besides the connections to the women?"

"He always appeared at the crime scenes, usually before the press, as if he knew what was happening. He was last seen on a pedestrian bridge over the Canal Saint-Martin, watching as the body was being transported away. The man was convinced that I could never prove anything against him. He sought contact with me, as if he wanted to taunt me."

"I understand."

"Not entirely. Today, I saw him. He was on Tour Bidouane, looking down at me as I re-examined the crime scene. For a moment, we locked eyes, as he did at a crime scene in Paris, then he disappeared. He must be somewhere in Saint-Malo."

"If he's here, we'll find him."

Sandrine wasn't so sure about that. Inès' search had yielded nothing. Perhaps he was staying with friends or a business partner. He had no shortage of connections.

"I hope so," she said hesitantly. "An unknown person gained access to his Paris apartment."

"An unknown person?" Adel repeated, studying her closely, as if he had more than just a suspicion about who that person might have been.

"He suspected it was me."

Adel nodded. She hadn't admitted it, but between them, it was clear that it had indeed been her.

"How did he figure that out?"

"His security system was more sophisticated than this unknown person had assumed. In any case, she was recorded in his living room by a surveillance camera. The next day, he filed a report with the police and had de Chezac hound me. He claimed it was me. I was taken off the case and put on leave. The house in Brittany seemed like the perfect place to distance myself from police work. So, I packed my things and came here. Matisse assigned me to our first case, and that's how I ended up here."

"They couldn't prove anything against you, otherwise they

wouldn't have put you on leave; they would have fired and prosecuted you," he stated.

"How could they? I wasn't even in the apartment," she claimed. If Adel were ever forced to make a statement, she didn't want him to have to lie.

"Of course not. It wouldn't fit your profile at all," he remarked ironically. He knew full well how skilful she was with a lock-pick and that she occasionally operated in the grey areas of police work. Did he suspect her of breaking and entering? Most likely.

"The unknown person couldn't be identified in the footage. An average-sized person wearing a ski mask and black clothing. There are thousands of people like that in Paris, and nowadays, every other burglar looks the same."

"Did this unknown person find anything incriminating in the apartment?" he asked.

Sandrine leaned back in her chair and looked at Adel for a moment. She had told him what needed to be said, but she didn't want to drag him further into her problems. Investigating de Saint-Clair at all could harm his career.

"No idea," she said. "The intruder didn't report to the police, and de Saint-Clair refrained from stating whether anything had been stolen."

"The man is intelligent. By accusing you, he cast doubt on any evidence that might be found in his apartment, and as a bonus, he got rid of the best detective on the force. Very clever."

"Oh yes, he's undoubtedly that. But also a huge narcissist who believes he's immune to police investigations. That's what he wanted to rub in my face when he appeared on the tower."

"How do we proceed?" Adel asked.

"Same as always. We gather evidence and draw our conclusions from there until we find the perpetrator."

"Do you want to go after this de Saint-Clair?"

Adel hit a sensitive spot with that question. Directly

accusing him was impossible. He would scream and cry police harassment. She chuckled bitterly at the thought of how well that would go down with prosecutor de Chezac.

"De Chezac knows him and our history in Paris. He'll block any investigation that points in his direction. They're both from the same elitist clique."

"You think he's protecting him?"

"Intentionally?" She shook her head thoughtfully. "I wouldn't go that far, but don't birds of a feather flock together?"

"Then I don't see what we can do," he said with resignation.

"My theory stands. Someone," she refrained from mentioning the name, "killed the woman. We might not be able to approach this person directly. We need to employ a different tactic."

"We won't take any illegal shortcuts," Adel interjected.

"Definitely not." She had learned that de Saint-Clair expected it and was well-prepared. She wouldn't fall into one of his traps again. "I won't even mention his name to de Chezac until we have concrete evidence on the table."

"Really?" He scrutinised her sceptically.

"It wouldn't help, only cause more trouble. The less our prosecutor knows about our actions, the better," she replied, especially since she couldn't guarantee that he didn't already know de Saint-Clair was in town. Maybe they had already had a superb dinner together.

"So we won't mention him and leave him alone. How do you plan to gather evidence against the man? Call me confused, and you'll have hit the bull's eye."

"We'll follow any leads that point in his direction, but his name won't go on there," she pointed at the bulletin boards at the head of the room, "or into any files."

Sandrine got up and went to one of the bulletin boards. She took an empty index card from the table and pinned it to the wall. She wrote the number 2 on it.

"And who is this?" Adel asked.

"The woman was murdered between one and one-thirty. Let's assume the killer left her there to be found the next morning."

"I'm with you so far."

"My theory: about half an hour later, a second person appeared." She tapped the index card with the number.

"Maybe he came back," Adel suggested.

"No," she firmly rejected. "The motive is entirely different. The one who showed up later wanted to clean up the crime scene and eliminate all evidence. First, he removed the tie from the victim's neck and took it with him. If we had found the body with the tie around her neck, the connection to the murders in Paris would have been too obvious. Even de Chezac couldn't have dismissed it."

"All right."

"After that, the body had to disappear. Carrying it over the city wall wouldn't work. The risk of being noticed was far too great."

"So he threw her from the tower."

"The postmortem injuries indicate that. It was low tide around two in the morning. To make the body disappear into the sea, he had to carry it quite a distance. Difficult, but doable. But his plan went awry right at that spot. He ran into a group of teenagers who were winding down the night on the beach. When the teens approached, our man panicked, fled the beach before they could recognise him, and left the body where our sailor found it this morning."

"As a working hypothesis, not bad. That would at least explain Jean-Claude's problem of why the body was found so far from the tower."

"We need to find this man. That's what we're focusing on."

"And we're leaving the murderer out of it?"

"If we have Person Number Two, we can close the case. The

two of them must know each other, I'd bet my life on it. He must have found out about the murder for some reason, otherwise why would he have shown up there?"

"Of course. He wanted to clean up the crime scene and eliminate as much evidence as possible to protect the killer," Adel said. "Or himself, because he's involved in the whole story."

"The question isn't just who he is, but also how he found out about the murder. Nobody walks over the city walls on a mere suspicion and searches for a body. Our killer detailed everything he did."

Adel leaned back and interlocked his hands behind his neck. He stared thoughtfully at the ceiling for a while.

"Why? If I were to kill someone, I would keep my mouth shut. Any accomplice is one too many."

"It must be someone the killer is absolutely sure will never betray him. Ariste de Saint-Clair is a power-hungry narcissist who loves to humiliate others and demonstrate how helpless they are."

"Why did he come here? He must know that you would immediately recognise the type of murder and suspect him. The man would have you on his back until you convicted him."

"De Saint-Clair feels infinitely superior. After all, he's already bested me once, and the rest of us are provincial cops he doesn't take seriously. I hope that arrogance will help us bring him down."

"Do you think this guy is behind the drugs that Poutin framed your friend with?"

"It's possible. De Saint-Clair had already tried to get me fired from the police in Paris. Unfortunately, he didn't have enough evidence to pin anything serious on me. Maybe he tried it again here and found a willing accomplice in Poutin."

Now the brigadier's big talk began to make sense. He relied on de Saint-Clair's influence to get him out of trouble, and he would compensate the man with a bundle of money for the inevitable consequences. She hoped he wasn't wrong; if his word went up against de Saint-Clair's, nobody would believe him. The man probably had more than one accomplice. *The question was, who was it?*

"At least you disappeared from Paris, that was a success for him. And they couldn't pin anything on him," Adel said, bringing her back from her thoughts.

"But I'm still with the police," she replied. And she possessed two pieces of evidence that she had stolen from his apartment: a tie similar to the ones used in the murders and a file with an encryption she couldn't crack. Unfortunately, neither could be used in any case against the man since they had been obtained unlawfully.

"Then Poutin could be our Suspect Number Two," Adel speculated.

"Doubtful. Planting drugs on someone, he went along with, but getting involved in a murder may have become too hot for him. He has too many scruples for that."

"Or someone from the Rennes team. They show up, and a murder happens."

"I'm convinced Hermé wanted the case," Sandrine said. "But I can't imagine him as an accomplice. I can't yet assess Commandant Jogu and Major Baud."

"With the right sum of money, anyone can be tempted. Maybe they're supposed to make sure that Poutin's case gets swept under the rug."

Sandrine leaned back in her chair. So far, she had had a hard time explaining Major Baud's aggressive behaviour, but she seemed determined to involve her in the investigation, not just as a witness.

"I talked to Poutin today," she said.

"Why? The investigation is ongoing; anything you mention to him can be brought up."

"I was sitting on a bench on the promenade during my lunch break, and he sat down next to me without asking."

"What did he say?"

"Not much, other than calling me a lousy and arrogant cop. But he was convinced he would get away relatively unscathed."

"So he really believes someone is protecting him, which goes against the Rennes team. It can't be anyone from here, as our police department is kept out of the loop."

"Then let's take a closer look at who they've sent us." She knew it was a sensitive matter to investigate fellow police officers, especially those who were working on a case in which she was a victim. Based on a gut feeling, she knew she wouldn't get access to a colleague's personnel files, phone records, or bank statements. Hermé would definitely resist.

"Let's call it a day for now," she suggested. "Tomorrow, we should receive more information from forensics and the coroner. The top priority is to determine the identity of the victim."

"Good idea. The next few days will surely bring a lot of overtime."

On her way to her desk, she stopped next to Renard Dubois and took a seat across from him.

"Poutin came to see me," she said without any preamble. "I didn't get the impression that he's doing well. To be honest, he looked dishevelled."

"That's an understatement." Brigadier Dubois leaned forward, resting his arms on his desk. "The kids have been out of the house for a while. He sent Anne, his wife, to her sister's place in Normandy until the investigation against him is over. She's taking it pretty hard. None of us could believe he got involved in criminal activities. I visit him regularly and bring some food, which he mostly leaves untouched. I'm afraid he's drinking more than he should."

"The investigators from Rennes have questioned him already?"

"Yes. But he's keeping silent. I advised him to spill the beans and put everything on the table, but he refuses. The scatterbrain believes he can ride it out."

"Perhaps he hopes someone will come to his rescue," Sandrine probed, curious to see what Dubois thought of her theory.

"Come to his rescue?" he repeated slowly. "He was never one to seek approval from others and didn't make a secret of it. Besides me, there's no one here he was close to. No, there's no backup he could rely on."

"Then I don't know what's motivating him to stay quiet."

"Pure stubbornness. He's as stubborn as an ox. Once he's convinced of something, you can't make him think or change his mind."

"Too bad. I must admit some guilt as well. I never praised or promoted him much. It's not surprising he didn't like me."

"There are plenty of people I don't like, but I don't manufacture evidence to put them in jail. He clearly went too far, and there's no excuse for that."

"Yet you still bring him food?"

"Of course. He's my friend after all. But that doesn't mean he shouldn't face the consequences of his actions."

"It's good that he has someone like you as a friend."

"I do what I can, even though it's not much," Dubois said. "Even though he got himself into this mess."

"How far along are you with interviewing the neighbours?" She redirected the conversation to the current investigation.

"So far, we haven't found any witnesses who could contribute anything. At that hour, everyone was in their beds asleep. Strangulation is quieter than a gunshot that would have startled the neighbours out of their beds."

"Then let's hope for a security camera that captured something. The forensics experts are still working on it."

"I wouldn't expect too much from that. Most cameras in the

area belong to businesses or ATMs and are installed at street level to capture burglars or graffiti vandals, not high enough to see the crime scene."

"I feared as much. Nevertheless, we have to give it a try."

Sandrine went to her desk and sat down. She ignored the pile of files; her thoughts were with Brigadier Poutin. Why did he act as if there was someone protecting him when talking to her, but made no such insinuations to his best friend? Was he lying to conceal his fears, or was there more to it? She wouldn't find out today. She retrieved the key to her Citroën from the desk drawer. The gun was already in her hand, ready to be put away, but she decided to take it with her, which she rarely did when driving home from the precinct.

Brigadier Poutin

Sandrine was jogging along her favourite route: from the garden down the stairs, and along the coast to Pointe du Grouin. Today, on her way back, she took a short break at Port Mer Beach to watch the sunset. She enjoyed the peaceful atmosphere as the edge of the sun touched the horizon and slowly dipped below. It was these tranquil moments she remembered when she went about her job and was confronted with the violence that people inflicted on each other.

In the twilight, she climbed the concrete stairs that led from the hiking trail to her garden. The scent of charcoal smoke hung in the air. Léon was standing in front of a grill on the lawn next to the old sheepfold, which her aunt had converted into a guesthouse where Sandrine now lived.

"There you are," he called out and waved to her. "Right on time for dinner."

"How did you know when I would come home?" she asked.

"I'm tracking your phone. When you were passing through Port Mer, I fired up the grill."

"You're doing what?"

"Just kidding," Léon laughed. "Rosalie told me when you

left. I know the route, and I know how fast you are, so it wasn't too difficult to estimate when dinner should be ready."

"Stop teasing me," she said, lightly punching his shoulder.

"Ouch."

"Drama queen," she joked. In martial arts training, she hit him much harder, and he took it in his stride. "You'd better tell me what I can look forward to."

"How do you know you'll like it?"

"Because you're at the grill," she replied. There wasn't much more to say. Léon was a talented cook who usually hit her taste buds perfectly. One of the ways they complemented each other. He loved to cook, and she loved to be pampered by him. *If this continues, I'll have to extend my jogging route, or soon my trousers won't fit.*

Léon lifted a metal tray on which a dozen opened oysters were resting.

"Oysters à la Léon," he said, smiling at her.

"And what would that be?"

"Oysters, brushed with a herb butter containing tarragon, dill, spring onions, a hint of garlic, and the usual suspects: salt, pepper, and a generous dash of Tabasco. On top are crumbled croutons."

"Your invention?"

"The name? Yes. But the recipe is stolen. Nevertheless, it's good." He lifted the lid of the charcoal grill and placed the metal tray on the rack. "350 degrees," he muttered, glanced at the thermostat, and closed the grill again.

"How much time do I have?"

"Ten minutes."

"Then I better hurry," she said, tugging at her damp T-shirt. A shower was urgently needed. She ran to the terrace door and was surprised to find it locked. She had given him a key to her house, but he never entered when she wasn't home. Another reason why she loved him. Her privacy was important to her.

"Are you bringing wine?" Léon called after her as she unlocked the door and went inside.

Sandrine set the last oyster shell aside, tore off some bread, and dabbed at the remaining crumbs on her plate.

"It was delicious."

"Better than your cafeteria?" he inquired, fishing for more compliments.

"Just about," she teased him and reached for her wine glass. In the kitchen, she had found a Sancerre Rosé, which she knew Léon liked. It had maintained its temperature in the wine cooler, and condensation covered the glass.

"We need to talk," she said.

"About what?"

"The investigation against Poutin has begun. Sébastian Hermé arrived with a team from Rennes."

"The prosecutor we met in Bécherel? The one with the cute earring?"

"That's him."

"He seems like a nice person. Not exactly your typical prosecutor, as far as I know. I don't know many who wear makeup. When I think of that de Chezac..." he shook his head disapprovingly. Antoine de Chezac had pressured him hard about the drug bust. As far as they knew, an apology was still pending.

"They will question you."

"No problem, everyone in Saint-Malo knows where to find me."

"But there's more." She hesitated, but he needed to know. In one way or another, it would also affect him, so she told him about her encounter with the brigadier and her suspicion that he relied on protection within the police department.

"That sounds mysterious. And not in a good way." He studied her and waited.

"Furthermore, we found a body on the beach this morning."

"I already heard about it. It was on the local radio."

"If only that were it."

He took her hand gently in his. "If something is bothering you, you'd better get it off your chest."

She sighed softly. It was time for confessions she didn't want to postpone any longer, and she told him about the events in Paris, just as she told him about the encounter with de Saint-Clair at the beach.

He listened without interrupting, and after she finished the story, he remained silent for a while.

"A lot is coming our way," he finally said. "Now everything makes more sense."

"Do you think so?"

"You can deny it, but of course you were in his apartment. I know you well enough for that. What did you take with you?"

"What makes you think I took something?"

Léon was a realist who didn't chase after fantasies, and Sandrine was curious if he was thinking in the same direction as she was. If so, it would help alleviate some of her self-doubts.

"It makes sense. The guy set a trap for you because you were hot on his heels while he had your colleagues wrapped around his finger. You were emotionally involved, otherwise you wouldn't have fallen for it. At least you were smart enough to keep your balaclava on. That saved you from going to jail."

"I will absolutely not admit that I was in the apartment and took something from there."

"Of course not. How could I claim not to know anything during a possible interrogation?"

She nodded in agreement. One of her top priorities was to keep him out of the mess she had created.

"This de Saint-Clair tried to destroy your career and get you kicked out of the police force. Why would he do that? He had ironclad alibis and your bosses in his pocket." Léon took his wine glass and sipped from it as he contemplated the situation. "The only possibility is that you discovered something and took it with you so you could incriminate him. As a civilian, you're only half as dangerous to him as you would be as a Capitaine de Police."

"Could he be behind Poutin's actions?"

"There's no doubt about it. He wanted to attack you and chose the detour through me. As the girlfriend of a convicted drug dealer, your credibility would be ruined. They probably would have pushed you onto a back burner if you hadn't quit on your own."

She nodded. His thoughts led to the same conclusion as her own. De Saint-Clair must be the man from whom Brigadier Poutin expected salvation. But did he really pull enough weight to influence Sébastian Hermé's investigations? Probably not. There must be someone else from whom he sought help.

"What about de Chezac?" Léon asked. "Do you have support from his side?"

"Unlikely. He shielded the man in Paris before me and would have to admit to making a mistake back then, which the narcissistic guy will never do. He would rather let a murderer go free or have me walk the plank."

"So, what did this unknown person take with them?" He returned to his suspicion.

"The women were all strangled with silk ties that were at least 50 years old, probably older. There was a small rose embroidered on the back on all of them. This detail was never made public. It was only known to the team working on the case," she explained.

"If someone was seeking publicity and confessed to the murders, they would lack the necessary knowledge of the crime. Clever," he commented.

"Hypothetically, the intruder could have found an identical

tie in the man's dressing room, maybe even several in different styles," she speculated.

"But without a search warrant, that wouldn't have any legal relevance. That's why this guy won't lose sleep over it. Those ties were probably sold quite frequently in their time. He could easily explain them away. If it were me, I would have destroyed the remaining ties a long time ago."

"De Saint-Clair paid me a farewell visit in Paris. He mentioned a USB stick in a hidden compartment of his desk. The intruder found it and copied the file to an old cell phone. It's visible on the surveillance video that was running."

"What was on it?" he inquired.

"I have no idea," she replied truthfully. "He assured me that the file is extremely well-encrypted and impossible for anyone to crack. I have no reason to doubt him."

"I suspect he's not a liar," Léon commented.

"Most likely not, aside from denying the murders," she added. She had asked her uncle, who was well-connected in the Paris underworld, to use his contacts; thus far no one had been able to crack the encryption.

"But he believes you can somehow figure it out. The content could likely be his downfall. That's why he's after you. And he won't rest until he achieves his goal."

"The question is, what does he want to achieve?" she pondered.

"That you leave the police force, what else?" Léon responded.

"Or that I disappear altogether," she muttered.

"That won't happen." His voice was resolute; he sought her gaze. "You have friends here who would look out for you."

Tears welled up in her eyes at his words, and her heart raced. Her phone's vibration interrupted her response.

"Perrot," she answered and listened briefly. "I'm on my way," she said and pocketed her phone.

"Work?" Léon asked.
"*Merde*," she cursed.
"What happened?"
"We have another body."
"Another young woman?"
"No, this time an older man." She stood up, leaned down, and kissed him. "I have to go. Don't wait up for me; it's going to be late." Fortunately, she had only drunk half a glass, and the Sancerre was very light.
"I'll be here when you come back," he assured her.

            * * *

Sandrine parked her motorcycle on the side of the road behind a police car and approached the inconspicuous cottage at the end of the cul-de-sac. A white Renault pulled up next to her, and Adel got out.
"What happened?" he asked.
"No idea, I haven't been inside yet," she replied.
She led the way. The police officer standing in front of the house nodded to her and pointed to the garage attached to the side. "Not a pretty sight," he muttered as they passed by.
The gate was half-open. She entered and froze.
"*Merde.*"
"Quite an understatement," Adel muttered.
Brigadier Poutin's body lay on a gurney, still in the same stained clothes he had worn when she had seen him that afternoon. Even his shirt was still hanging out of his trousers. There was a half-empty bottle of Cognac on the concrete floor. He had probably mustered up some liquid courage before taking his own life. Someone had closed his eyes, making him look almost as if he were sleeping. But the red mark around his neck captured her gaze. Adel cleared his throat; Sandrine tore her eyes away from the sight.

The forensic team had cut the rope above the knot. The loose end hung from a crossbeam. In the corner lay a chair from which he must have jumped. She hoped his neck had snapped instantly.

"It seems he couldn't bear it any longer," remarked one of the forensic experts who stood next to the gate.

"Who found him?" she asked.

"One of his neighbours. He noticed smoke and came over. There was a fire in the living room, but fortunately he managed to extinguish it before everything went up in flames here."

"His family?" Adel inquired.

"The children no longer live with him, and his wife is with relatives in Normandy," Sandrine said. "At least, that's what Dubois claimed. We need to notify them, and get Dubois here."

"Should he see him like this? After all, he was his best friend," Adel questioned.

"Renard Dubois is the only one who can tell us if anything unusual catches his eye in the garage or the house. Perhaps Poutin mentioned his suicidal intentions to him," Sandrine replied.

"Do you believe it's a suicide?"

"Hanging is the most common method of suicide, at least among men," she said without really answering his question, and walked outside. She was unsure how to view his death and wanted to wait for evidence from forensics. "Let's leave the garage to the forensic experts. Our new medical examiner should be able to give us more information soon."

As if Jean-Claude Mazet had been waiting for the cue, he arrived in his private car. Sandrine and Adel went outside to meet him.

"I'm sorry, but I was at my aunt's in Morlaix and came as quickly as I could," he apologised as soon as he got out of the car. "Is it really Luc?"

"Yes," Sandrine confirmed.

"Suicide? I wouldn't have expected that from him. What's your assessment?"

"Hard to say," she replied. "What strikes me is the chair lying on the side of the garage. I would have assumed that in the struggle of death, he would have swung back and forth. So, I would have expected to find him by the gate or in the rear area."

"We'll look into it," Jean-Claude Mazet promised. "He was one of us; we will be extra thorough."

"There was a fire in the living room too. That needs to be examined," Sandrine added.

"Did he want to guarantee it got him for sure?" Mazet scratched his cheek and looked at Sandrine sceptically.

"Or someone wanted to erase potential evidence," she shrugged. "Both are possible. Perhaps we'll know more tomorrow."

"If there's anything to find, we'll find it," Mazet assured her and walked past her to one of his colleagues. The man was always meticulous in his work. In the case of a colleague's death, whether he liked the person or not, he would re-examine every piece of evidence two or three times. She had no doubt about his commitment.

A car approached, the engine noise indicating it was well above the speed limit. It braked hard and came to a stop at the barricade. A man jumped out and ran towards them, leaving the car with an open door in the middle of the street.

"Here he comes," Adel said, blocking his path.

Renard Dubois arrived, panting heavily.

"Is he...?" He couldn't finish the sentence. Begging for her to contradict him, he stared at Sandrine.

"I'm very sorry," she said. "A neighbour found him."

"That's impossible. Luc would never do something like this. It's out of the question."

"We will find out what happened. Jean-Claude Mazet is in

the garage with his team, collecting evidence. We can rely on him."

"Sure," he said, fidgeting. "I want to see him."

"Do you really want to put yourself through this?" She knew it was necessary; he would notice small details that would escape them, but she also knew how distressing the sight would be for the brigadier. It was his closest, perhaps oldest friend, lying dead on a gurney in the garage. Nobody wanted to remember a friend like that.

"Want to? Definitely not. But Luc deserves it. Someone did this to him. Maybe I'll discover something that helps us catch the guy behind it."

"Come on," Sandrine said and led the way.

One of the forensic experts handed him shoe covers and gloves. She returned to Adel. Dubois was in good hands with Mazet. The two had been working together for years and respected each other.

"It's getting crowded," Adel said in a hushed tone, looking towards the patrol car that had stopped by the roadside.

"It was hardly avoidable," Sandrine replied.

Commandant Jogu and Major Baud stepped out of a patrol car and approached them.

"What happened here?" Baud asked directly, while Jogu at least nodded briefly in their direction.

"The neighbours found the body of Brigadier Poutin. He was hanging in the garage."

"Suicide?" Jogu asked.

"There is no evidence to the contrary at the moment. However, no suicide note was found."

"What does the medical examiner say?"

"He's on his way. Right now, the forensic experts are in the garage and the house."

"We'll take a look," Major Baud said.

"Not until the forensic examination is complete." Sandrine

stood in their way. The woman paused and stopped. Apparently, she wasn't used to being put in her place.

"We're investigating the case of Brigadier Poutin. You understand that, don't you?" Commandant Jogu sounded more conciliatory than his stern colleague.

"You're investigating his misconduct from a few months ago. I'm investigating his death. Two different cases loosely connected."

"Do I need to remind you of my rank, Capitaine Perrot?" Commandant Jogu asked softly but seriously.

"Do I need to remind you that you're not in charge of Saint-Malo?" Sandrine retorted and didn't budge an inch.

"There is an obvious conflict of interest in your case, Capitaine Perrot. The man who died here is accused of wanting to harm you personally. You cannot investigate his death," Jogu said. "Furthermore, he was part of your department."

"We'd better leave this decision to Commissaire Matisse and the two prosecutors," she replied. "Until then, this is my crime scene."

"Are you seriously trying to prevent us from entering the house?" Major Baud's voice sounded even more gruff than usual. She glanced at Commandant Jogu, signalling him to intervene.

"Absolutely not. But only after the head of forensics gives his approval. The fewer people enter the house, the easier it is for the forensics team to do their work."

"As you wish," Jogu reluctantly agreed. "We'll wait in the car until forensics is done." He turned and walked back to the patrol car they had arrived in. Major Baud hesitated, gave Sandrine an irritated look, and then followed her superior.

Adel moved closer to her.

"You do realise that Hermé will prevail, right? Tomorrow we'll be off the case, if there's even a case to begin with."

"I'm aware," she agreed.

"Then why the dispute over jurisdiction?"

"It wasn't a suicide. Someone killed him."

Adel raised his eyebrows in surprise. "What makes you think that?"

"I talked to Luc Poutin today. The man didn't feel the slightest hint of guilt or remorse. In his opinion, I had more than earned what he had done to me and Léon. On the contrary, he sounded defiant and felt untouchable. No one with that attitude takes their own life."

"Maybe he was lying."

"You know Poutin, he was a terrible actor. Whatever came to his mind, he said it out loud. The man had little impulse control in that regard. I'm convinced he was sincere with me. There must be someone with influence who assured him they would protect him from the investigation. At least Poutin believed that."

"Why is he dead then?" Adel asked.

"Because someone promised more than they could or would deliver, and that someone is covering their tracks. In any case, Luc Poutin won't be able to make any statements that would incriminate him."

"You suspect this de Saint-Clair?"

"Or someone working for him. I can't imagine he would personally kill a police officer. He's too clever for that. I'm sure he can provide a rock-solid alibi for tonight. But we won't be able to question him about it until we have more clues about what happened here."

Not knowing where the man was exactly and what his next moves were, would likely keep her up tonight.

Adel took a step closer and looked at her in disbelief. "You suspect one of the two investigators from Rennes is doing the dirty work for de Saint-Clair? Seriously?" Adel glanced at the patrol car. Major Baud was leaning against the fender, smoking. Her features were only vaguely visible under the streetlight, but the way she pulled on the cigarette showed her tension.

Commandant Jogu sat in the passenger seat, looking over at them.

"I'm not suspecting anyone at the moment, but I'm also not ruling out very many people. I can't yet gauge the two investigators from Rennes."

"You wanted to keep the crime scene uncontaminated. That's why you intervened when they tried to enter the house."

"If any evidence is found that points to either of them, it has to be clear that they were inside the house before they entered the crime scene. What they do in there after Mazet finishes his work is of no further concern."

Dubois emerged from the house and slumped onto the low garden wall. His upper body sagged forward, and he hung his head wearily. The sight of his dead friend was clearly hard to digest. Sandrine gave him the time he needed and silently sat down next to him.

After a while, Dubois raised his head and looked at her. "It wasn't a suicide," he said with a shaky voice.

"What leads you to that conclusion?" Sandrine asked. Though she herself was convinced of that too, she still wanted to hear his reasoning.

"Luc wasn't an emotional man, especially when it came to feelings, but he would never have taken his own life without thinking of his wife or children."

"The absence of a suicide note?" Adel inquired.

"Luc wasn't one for writing letters, and he despised modern stuff like emails or text messages." He shook his head. "I wouldn't have expected a letter from him."

"What then?" Sandrine had a sense of where he was heading.

"Once he had made up his mind, it was nearly impossible to talk him out of it. If he had been determined to commit suicide, he would have contacted me beforehand, asking me to take care of his family: helping with paperwork, checking in on them from time to time, keeping Anne company."

"I see," she said thoughtfully. It made sense, and it would have been in line with Poutin's character.

"Then there's something else," he continued. "One of the forensic technicians mentioned a bottle of Cognac."

"We saw that. The forensic pathologist will take a blood sample. It's not unusual for suicides to have a drink for courage."

"Luc detested Cognac. There was only a bottle in the house because Anne used it for cooking or making Mousse au Chocolat when she had guests. He exclusively drank Pastis or Lambig."

"Lambig?" she inquired.

"Fine Bretagne. It's an apple brandy, similar to Calvados in Normandy," Adel explained. It always surprised her how well-versed he was in alcohol. He wasn't particularly devout, but he only consumed high-quality spirits on special occasions and in moderation.

"He would never have reached for Cognac. If the doctor finds any of that stuff in his stomach, someone forced him to swallow it. Probably, he went along with it because he expected me to notice."

"Thank you for your help. I can imagine how difficult it must have been for you to see your friend like that." That's precisely why she hadn't stopped him from entering the crime scene. He was one of the few people she definitively ruled out as a suspect, and such details caught his attention.

"He would want me to find his killer," he said.

"Is there anything else we can do for you?" Sandrine asked. "If you need company later tonight, I can offer you a sofa at my place."

"Very kind, but I need some time alone."

"Consider taking the day off tomorrow," she suggested.

"That's out of the question. I want to catch the guy who did this."

"He won't get away," Adel promised.

"Either way, you'll be driven home. I don't want you behind the wheel of a car in this state," Sandrine decided. "Someone will bring your car to you later."

Brigadier Dubois straightened up, and though he initially wanted to protest, the determined look from Sandrine silenced him. Eventually, he nodded.

Adel escorted the brigadier to one of the patrol cars, while Jean-Claude Mazet emerged from the house and joined Sandrine.

"Did Brigadier Dubois mention his reservations to you?" Sandrine asked the forensic expert.

"He did. We're looking into it, but the decision on how the case is handled will have to be made by you."

"In this case, it's more likely to be the colleagues from Rennes. It's only a matter of time before they get the green light to take over the investigation."

"I understand," he said, looking briefly in the direction of the two investigators.

"What can you tell me?" Sandrine asked.

"He probably died about an hour ago. The exact time of death will be determined by the forensic pathologist. I'm guessing because at the same time, a fire broke out in the living room. Who else could have started it if not Luc? At that point, he must have still been alive. Fortunately, a neighbour passed by shortly after and noticed the smoke. There's a water supply and hose in the garden. The man quickly broke a window and turned on the water, otherwise the whole house could have easily burned down. Only the living room furniture is ruined. The man climbed in through the window to check on the family and found Luc in the garage."

"Arson?" Adel asked.

"Definitely. You can still smell traces of the accelerant. The lab analysis will determine what it was, but I'm sure it was gasoline."

"Was someone trying to make sure he wouldn't survive the night, or was someone trying to eliminate all traces that would cast doubt on it being a suicide?" Sandrine mused.

"Fortunately, that's your job. The death of Luc and the fire are so closely connected that based on the evidence I have right now, I can't determine the exact sequence of events."

"The forensic pathologist will find out if there are traces of gasoline fumes or smoke in his lungs," Sandrine said. "It's hard for me to believe that Luc would want to harm his family, either by committing suicide or setting fire to the house where his children grew up," Adel said.

"Dubois said the same," Sandrine replied.

"What he doesn't know about is this," Mazet said, holding out a transparent evidence bag containing a rope about the length of her forearm, and roughly as thick as her little finger.

"Where did that come from?" she asked.

"It was in his pocket, under the Cognac bottle."

"What could it mean?"

"I have no idea yet, but we'll thoroughly examine it."

Sandrine snapped her fingers. *So, this is where it's heading.* Mazet looked at her questioningly.

"What's it made of?" she asked.

"It looks like the kind of rope you can buy at any hardware store. Probably synthetic fibre. My kids have jump ropes that look similar. I use them on the sailboat."

"Could you compare the fibres to those found around the woman's neck at the beach?" Sandrine inquired.

"You don't seriously believe..." Mazet didn't even try to hide his surprise.

"It puzzled me that both silk and synthetic fibres were found on the victim. A strange mix."

"At first glance, yes, but it can be explained. She might have been wearing a silk scarf and later strangled with such a rope."

"That's possible, especially since we haven't found her clothes yet," she conceded, but her thoughts were going in a completely different direction. "Can we have a look inside the house?"

"Yes. We're just taking crime scene photos, then we're done here. An investigator from the fire department will come, but he won't be interested in shoe prints or fingerprints."

A hearse passed the barricade and stopped in front of the house. They would take the body and deliver it to Dr Mason. Sandrine hoped that the autopsy would provide clear evidence of whether it was a murder or suicide. Otherwise, de Chezac might consider Brigadier Poutin's death as an admission of guilt and not pursue it further. Especially if the analysis of the rope yielded the results she feared. It would be a quick investigative success in two cases, something the man highly valued. Blaming the murder of the woman on Brigadier Poutin would be a temptation that Prosecutor de Chezac would find hard to resist.

Sandrine waved Major Baud over and pointed to the house. The woman flicked her cigarette to the ground and stamped it out. Sandrine didn't wait for them and went with Adel to the open front door.

The house was compact, no more than three rooms and a kitchen. The windows were open, but the acrid smoke of the fire still hung heavily in the air. Ashes were scattered on the hallway dresser, and greasy stains covered the floor. Curtains, sofas, and a chair had gone up in flames before the neighbour could extinguish the fire. Sandrine walked around the puddles of water on the floor, her shoes crunching on glass shards. She sniffed the air.

"Gasoline," Mazet said from behind her. "It was poured over the furniture and set on fire. When you get closer, it's unmistakable. The lab analysis will undoubtedly confirm this."

"Not unusual," she said, looking around more closely. "Where's the container?"

"Good question." The forensic technician nodded. "There's a half-full reserve canister in the garage, probably for the lawnmower."

"Poutin wanted to set his house on fire but only took half the gasoline to start it. Why? Did he want to save money?" Adel wondered.

"I wonder more why he put it back," Mazet replied. "If he had succeeded, the canister would have burned up anyway. So why the effort? I've known Poutin for almost twenty years, and you could say many things about him, but compulsive neatness was definitely not one of his defining traits."

"No, you can't say that." What Sandrine had seen of the house so far was untidy but not dirty. Why did he put the canister back in the garage? It didn't make sense.

She walked over to Adel, who was looking at framed photos on a sideboard. Mostly family photos, but also several of Luc Poutin with Renard Dubois. Pictures of fishing trips or playing boules together.

"His wife looks nice," Adel remarked. He clearly hadn't expected a pleasant woman to be with Luc Poutin.

Sandrine picked up one of the pictures showing the brigadier, his wife, and their daughter. She recognised the area; the Cap Fréhel lighthouse was in the background. Both women were laughing, and even the brigadier wore a smile. She couldn't recall ever seeing him smile at work. *Schadenfreude*, yes, but a genuine smile? She shook her head and put it back. Did Dubois take this photo? Poutin wasn't the kind of person who would ask a stranger to take one. He despised owing anything to anyone, even for small favours. He had rubbed some people the wrong way because he rarely acceded to others' requests.

"It's late; let's go. Tomorrow will be a long day," she suggested.

"All right."

They left the house and bid each other farewell. Adel drove off and disappeared around the next bend. She yawned and reached for the helmet hanging over the BMW's side mirror as Commandant Jogu and Major Baud emerged from the garage. She wanted to avoid another discussion about who was in charge of this investigation, so she started the engine and drove off.

* * *

The next morning, Sandrine stood at the terrace door, looking out into the garden. Summer was taking a break today. Thick grey clouds piled up over the Bay of Mont-Saint-Michel. A cold wind howled around the corners of the cottage and rattled the pine branches that covered the steep slope to the sea. She had woken up early to secure the garden furniture and had managed to do so before the first rain started. Definitely not a good day for riding the motorcycle.

The hissing of the coffee machine stopped, and she took the full espresso cup, poured it into the frothed milk, and held the large coffee bowl in both hands before sitting down in one of the reading chairs by the window. The fire crackled in the fireplace stove and filled the room with pleasant warmth. She would have preferred to spend the rest of the morning here instead of struggling through the impending storm to the police station and dealing with the death of a man who had once been under her command. She had accumulated enough overtime hours in recent months, but she pushed the thought aside. She would definitely not leave Adel and especially not Brigadier Dubois, who had lost his best friend, alone today. However, she would still take the time for her coffee before venturing out into the rain.

At that moment, her phone rang, and a premonition told her

that she would have to leave the house earlier than planned. She picked up the phone, looked at the unknown number, and pressed the green button.

"Perrot."

"Surely you're in the kitchen, preparing yourself a balanced and hearty breakfast." The man didn't need to introduce himself; she recognised the voice instantly. It was Major Martin Alary, her former partner in the Paris Homicide Division. They had worked together for several years, and he knew her breakfast habits well enough to tease her about them.

"The coffee is ready, at least. I'll grab the rest on the way, as usual."

"You should get yourself a boyfriend who ensures you live a healthier lifestyle."

Sandrine paused for a moment. Either he knew about Léon, and this was his subtle way of inquiring without directly addressing it, or it was just a coincidence. Considering the nature of the policeman, the latter was unlikely.

"I'll think about it. But I'm sure that's not why you're calling. Have you found something?"

"I have."

She listened to him for a while before they said their goodbyes. As always, Major Alary had done an excellent job. *I need to repay him. There will probably be an opportunity sooner than I think.*

She sent a message to Adel, grabbed the key for the Citroën from the hook, and put on a light rain jacket. It would take a little longer to reach the police station than usual.

* * *

Sandrine parked on Quai Saint-Vincent in Saint-Malo and climbed the stairs at the Grand Porte, leading to the city wall. The wind blew harshly over the parapet of the fortress. She tightened her jacket and tucked her hands deep into her pockets. In front of her lay the Saint-Malo marina. The howling of the increasing wind rushing along the masts and ropes of the sailing yachts' rigging filled the air, and a sinister premonition crept over Sandrine. More deaths would follow if they couldn't stop the killer soon, she was convinced of that.

A luxurious-looking snow-white motor yacht with three decks was clearly too large for a berth at a pier. The Ariste VI was moored to the quay in front of it. The man had arrived with his own yacht. No wonder Inès hadn't found him in the city's hotels. Only the owner was registered in the harbour, not the guests. For tax reasons, he surely hadn't registered his boat under his own name. *Well done, Martin,* she praised her former colleague silently.

Lights were on in the rooms of the middle deck. De Saint-Clair was probably having a much more luxurious breakfast than Sandrine. She couldn't see him behind the tinted windows, but she knew the man was on board. Maybe he could see her. This time it was her turn to look down on him.

"Hello, Sandrine."

She flinched when someone spoke to her from behind. It was Suzanne Leriche, a psychologist she had come to know and appreciate in several investigations.

"I'm sorry if I startled you."

"It's not your fault, I was lost in thought," she replied. "You're up early."

"You know, I take a walk around the old town every day. Exercise is good for me, and I love the view. The weather is supposed to get so awful later in the day that I woke up early. I refuse to skip my walk just because of some rain."

Sandrine nodded. She had accompanied the woman on her walk before.

"Beginning or end?"

"I've just finished going around." Suzanne Leriche looked

towards the old town. "How about you? I could use some coffee. Would you like to join me?"

"Of course."

They walked along the harbour wall until they reached the city gate and descended the stairs into the old town. Directly opposite the Grand Porte was a small café with pleasant seating on the upper floor.

Sandrine held her tray with a blueberry muffin and freshly squeezed orange juice in her hands. She looked in amazement at Suzanne, who ordered a *Kouign amann* (a sugary Breton butter cake), several macarons, an almond croissant, and a large café au lait. Her metabolism must be working overtime to maintain her slender figure with such an opulent breakfast. Or perhaps it was due to her daily walk around the old town?

They found a seat upstairs at a small table in front of one of the windows facing the city gate. Just then, a deep rumble of thunder rolled over the view, and the sky opened up. Rain splattered against the windows, and the outlines of the city wall and the nearby Hôtel de Ville blurred behind the curtain of rainwater.

"Just in time," Suzanne Leriche said, poking her fork into the round cake. A good *Kouign amann* didn't require much—just butter, sugar, more butter, more sugar, and even more butter. At least, that's what a sign in Sandrine's favourite bakery claimed. She occasionally bought one and believed every word of it.

"Busy?" Suzanne asked with her mouth full.

"Unfortunately, yes."

"The body on the beach?"

Sandrine nodded.

"The news said it was an unidentified woman."

"She had too little on her to identify her, and there hasn't been a missing person report yet. If we don't make progress today, we'll release her photo."

"Have you arrested anyone?"

"No, not yet." It wouldn't happen anytime soon. The prosecutor would have to swallow his pride and consider de Saint-Clair a suspect, which he would never do. Admitting to a mistake wasn't in his repertoire.

"What do you think of narcissists?" Sandrine asked.

"I try to stay away from them, which isn't easy in my profession," the psychologist replied.

"I suspected a prominent man of murder in Paris. I haven't met a bigger narcissist since."

"Murder," Suzanne repeated, taking a thoughtful sip of her coffee.

"Multiple murders. Quite cold-blooded."

"Many psychologists differentiate between two types of narcissists," the psychologist explained. "One would be the grandiose narcissist. They see themselves as special, they're highly self-centred, and don't see their narcissism as a bad thing at all. They are considered boastful, self-satisfied, but also self-confident. They dismiss attacks on their superiority or contradictions as envy from completely inferior and irrelevant people. It doesn't bother them much because they never question their own superiority."

"That describes my suspect perfectly," Sandrine said thoughtfully. "The man thinks he's the crown jewel of creation. He probably gazes at his extensive family tree lovingly every day."

"However, grandiose narcissists tend to be less prone to violence."

"That wouldn't apply to my suspect."

"The other type is the vulnerable narcissist. These individuals tend to act bitter and defensive because they aren't quite as certain of their superiority as the grandiose narcissist. They tend to bully or intimidate others who they perceive as challenging their superiority, as far as they are capable."

"I unfortunately know one of that type too," Sandrine

replied bitterly. The description fitted de Chezac perfectly, to whom she would likely have to report today.

"While the grandiose narcissist can be incredibly frustrating to deal with, the vulnerable narcissist can also be dangerous. The mix of pent-up anger and hostility can explode. I would be more likely to suspect a murderer in the second category."

A group of tourists stormed up the stairs, chattering loudly. They shook water from their umbrellas and occupied a wide sofa on the opposite side of the room, which encircled the bakery like a balustrade.

Did she think de Chezac was capable of murder? Probably not. The man wouldn't engage in any physical confrontation unless he was absolutely desperate or in mortal fear.

"But narcissism is just one character trait of the dark triad," Suzanne continued.

"I've heard of that: narcissism, psychopathy, and Machiavellianism, right? Or am I misremembering?"

"That's correct. Some psychologists also include sadism."

"Weird name: the dark triad."

"It refers to a study that examined so-called dark personalities. Personally, I don't like the term. It refers to people with socially undesirable traits that aren't fully developed enough to be diagnosed as personality disorders."

"So, even a grandiose narcissist could be prone to violence?" Sandrine inquired.

"If they are a Machiavellian willing to use morally questionable methods to achieve their desirable goal or a psychopath lacking empathy, why not? A dash of sadism might also be helpful to shed inhibitions," Suzanne replied.

"People I encounter fairly frequently in my job." These character traits certainly applied to de Saint-Clair. He would go to great lengths to protect himself and his lifestyle, and empathy wasn't a trait often associated with him.

Sandrine's phone vibrated.

"Excuse me. Technically, I'm already working," she said.

"It's me, Arianne," the editor-in-chief of the local radio station announced.

"I'm sorry, but I don't have any news about the body on the beach yet."

"I might have something."

"What do you mean?"

"I showed the photo around the newsroom. One of our staff members recognised the woman from an interview. She forgot the name, but the woman works at an art gallery in Saint-Malo."

Sandrine noted down the address.

"Thank you very much. As soon as we can identify her, I'll get in touch with you."

"All right, we'll hold off on the news until it's been verified."

Sandrine ended the call and sent Adel a message to meet her here.

"Everything okay?" Suzanne asked, pushing the remaining crumbs of her pastry together with her fork.

"We have a lead we need to follow up on."

"That's a shame. I was hoping for a pleasant breakfast."

"I have to go to a shop in the old town. My colleague will pick me up, so I still have time for my muffin," she smiled and broke off a piece of the cake. The blueberry filling glistened in the light of the ceiling lamps, and Sandrine took a bite with pleasure.

* * *

Through the window on the upper floor, she saw Azarou, wearing a beige knee-length raincoat with the collar turned up, coming through the city gate. The rain had moved on and left wide puddles on the cobblestones that the brigadier carefully avoided in his new hand-stitched shoes.

"I have to go. Work is calling," Sandrine said, placing her plate on the plastic tray and looking for the waiter.

"Me too. The first client will be buzzing soon," Suzanne replied, grabbing her jacket and standing up.

"It was nice seeing you again."

"Just drop by on the weekend. I have no plans and would appreciate some company. You can tell me more about your narcissist."

"I'd be happy to." She was actually looking forward to having a nice chat with the psychologist. Suzanne was a pleasant woman who always had a well-informed view in response to her questions. They walked down the stairs together and said goodbye in front of the bakery.

"That was quick," she greeted her colleague.

"I was on my way to the police station when I got your message. So do we know who the dead woman is?" Adel asked.

"Not yet, but we know where to find out," Sandrine replied.

"I'm curious," Adel said.

Together, they walked up the Grand Rue. The rain and the early hour kept most tourists in their hotels, but delivery vans clogged the narrow alleys. In a side street, they found the gallery that Arianne Briand had mentioned. It was located on the ground floor of a four-storey building, sandwiched between a toy shop and a bookstore. Sandrine stood in front of the shop window and looked at the displays of oil paintings and some smaller watercolours, mostly featuring local views. The nearby islands were clearly visible, as were parts of the city wall. Sailboats passed in the background. Skilfully done, but not remarkable—only well-known motifs that defined the area around Saint-Malo.

"Better souvenirs for tourists who want to splurge a bit more, or something to decorate holiday homes to give them a maritime chic and a more authentic look. According to the price tags, nothing overly expensive," Adel commented.

"But it fits the profile," Sandrine muttered to herself more than to her colleague. The three victims of the Necktie Killer in Paris were art students or models. She wasn't surprised that this victim also had a connection to art.

"We're early. The shop doesn't open until ten," Adel said impatiently, glancing at his wristwatch.

Arianne Briand had mentioned that the owner lived in the same building. Sandrine checked the names on the doorbell and pressed one of the buttons. Apart from the gallery, there were only apartments in the building.

The door buzzer sounded, and Adel pushed the door open. A ground-floor apartment door was ajar, and a woman in her fifties stepped out. She was wearing elegant black linen trousers, fluffy pink slippers, and a loose, light-coloured T-shirt with some baguette crumbs stuck to it. They must have interrupted her breakfast. Probably a matching and elegant blouse, which she didn't want to spill coffee on, was ready on a hanger for her to wear to work.

"Madame Clarot?" Sandrine asked.

"Yes, I'm sorry, but the gallery doesn't open until later," she said.

"We're from the police," Sandrine said, showing her badge.

With one hand, Madame Clarot brushed the crumbs from her T-shirt and pushed a strand of hair away from her face. She seemed uncomfortable with the visit, likely being quite meticulous about her appearance most of the time.

"I'm having breakfast and was about to get ready for work," she apologised.

"Usually, we would announce our visit in advance, but unfortunately, we're a bit pressed for time at the moment. We hope you understand. Just a few questions, and then we won't bother you any longer," Adel said.

"I'm always happy to help the police," she claimed, but she didn't invite the two inside her apartment.

"Do you know this woman?" Sandrine held out a selected photo of the victim, where the wounds were concealed. "I was told she works here."

Madame Clarot took the photo and froze. She stared at it for a long moment, then raised her head and looked at Sandrine with wide, unbelieving eyes.

"That's Miriam Mignon," she stammered. "What..."

"She has passed away." Adel kept it vague.

"Not the woman found on the beach?" Madame Clarot sought eye contact with Sandrine. She had already heard about it, perhaps even read about the deceased in the newspaper during breakfast.

"Unfortunately, yes."

"But who would do such a thing? Miriam was always friendly and helpful. A truly likable person."

"She worked for you?" Sandrine asked.

"Yes, in the gallery. She was very popular with customers. We also sell some of her paintings."

"Paintings of Saint-Malo and its surroundings, like the ones in the storefront?"

"The watercolours are Miriam's work. She was very talented and versatile. She only painted occasionally; photography was her main focus."

"Did you notice anything unusual about her in the past few days? Was she nervous or anxious?"

"Quite the opposite. She spoke about a visitor who was very interested in her photographs and wanted to take some to an exhibit. An extraordinary opportunity for such a young girl. She had just turned twenty last month."

Madame Clarot went to the stairs and sat on one of the wooden steps. She clearly didn't think about dirtying her clean trousers. The girl's death had shaken her.

"Did she mention the visitor's name?"

"No... Not that I can recall. She acted somewhat mysteriously, actually."

"Is there anything you remember? Perhaps where the paintings were supposed to be exhibited?"

"Miriam was somewhat superstitious. She thought that if she talked too much about it, her wish wouldn't come true. But I also got the impression that the man wanted to remain anonymous. She hinted at it several times."

"Did that not strike you as strange? A stranger appears and promises to exhibit your young employee's paintings." *And asks her to keep quiet about him.*

"She was talented and hardworking."

"That talented?"

Madame Clarot shrugged. "I didn't want to be pessimistic. She was so excited. If only I had been." She looked up at Sandrine, tears filling her eyes. "Then maybe she would still..."

"We don't have any indication yet whether this stranger is even connected to her death,"

Sandrine interrupted the woman, who was surely not at fault for what had happened to her employee.

"Where did she meet this person? In the shop?"

"He probably saw her paintings here, but I didn't notice anyone. I'm not always in the gallery. I often visit my clients to deliver paintings or collect them for re-framing. I suspect, though, that Miriam invited the man to her studio. Most of her work is there."

"Do you have the address?" Adel took out his notepad and a pen.

"Of course." She dictated it to the brigadier, who nodded in acknowledgment. Apparently, he was familiar with the location.

"We'll need to take a look at the studio."

"I have a key that she left with me for emergencies. She wasn't a particularly practical person and had locked herself out of her apartment more than once." The memory brought a faint smile to Madame Clarot's face, but it quickly faded. She reached for the railing, pulled herself up, and disappeared into her apartment. Shortly afterward, she returned and handed Adel a key-chain.

"Thank you very much. We'll head there now," the brigadier said to the gallery owner. "If we need any further information, we'll get in touch with you."

"Please do. If there's any way I can help catch the guy who did this to her, I'd be pleased."

They said their goodbyes and headed for the door when the woman stopped them.

"You found Miriam at Tour Bidouane, didn't you?"

"That's correct. Is there any connection between her and that place?" Sandrine asked.

"It could be a coincidence, but I want to mention it at least. The interior of the tower has been converted and is used for rotating exhibitions."

"Mademoiselle Mignon exhibits there?"

"No, she isn't that well-known... wasn't. But she helped prepare the next exhibition in her spare time. She knew and admired the photographer."

"Do you know who this photographer is?"

"Of course. His name is Duval, and he's from the area."

Sandrine gave the brigadier a surprised look, which he acknowledged with a nod.

"Is it Monsieur Sébastian Duval from Saint-Lunaire?"

"You know him?" the gallery owner asked with a suspicious tone in her voice. "He has nothing to do with your investigation, does he?"

"Monsieur Duval? Not at all. I've seen some of his pictures. Very impressive."

Sébastian Duval was the boyfriend of a young woman who had been murdered in Saint-Malo some time ago. Sandrine was pleased that the man was preparing a new exhibition. Perhaps it helped him deal with his grief better.

"I wouldn't have expected that from him either." The gallery owner seemed visibly relieved.

"I didn't know that the tower was used for such purposes. Who has a key?"

"Definitely the city administration, and probably the artist who needs to make preparations."

"Could Mademoiselle Mignon have had a key?"

"I know she spent a lot of time in the tower, but as for whether she had her own key, I'm not sure." Madame Clarot shrugged.

"We'll find out," said Sandrine. "Thank you for your help."

"If you have any more questions, you know where to find me."

She stood up from the stairs and waited at the door until Sandrine and Adel had left.

"Do you recognise the address?" Sandrine asked as they walked onto the street.

"Yes. The street is in the direction of the Rance, near the Port des Sablons."

"There are a lot of boats in that harbour, right?"

"It's slightly larger than the marina at Quai Saint-Louis, but there are mostly smaller boats there."

"How far is it to get there? Two or so miles?"

"That sounds about right."

The Ariste VI would have caused a stir in the harbour if there was even a suitable berth, but de Saint-Clair could easily have made the trip with the dinghy without attracting attention.

"Let's go there right away," she decided.

* * *

Adel stopped in a narrow side street in front of a grey stone house.

"This is the address. It's just a few minutes' walk to the harbour."

Sandrine got out of the car. The unassuming house was slightly set back behind a waist-high hedge. Brown spots dotted the lawn, where a brightly striped lounge chair sat, and wind turbines rattled in the gusty wind. The plants in the pots drooped halfway, almost wilted. Sandrine doubted whether the recent rain had come soon enough to save them. It seemed like no one took responsibility for tending to this small garden.

The gate was unlocked, and they walked to the door. Adel glanced at the doorbells.

"The apartment is on the top floor."

"I'll go first," Sandrine decided and opened the front door. "Do you want to question the neighbours?"

"Sure."

She climbed the creaking stairs and entered the apartment. The door led directly into a small living room, which also served as storage for paintings that covered almost all the walls or were lined up in cheap frames. Musty air greeted her. No one had ventilated the place in the last few days. Sandrine put on disposable gloves and looked around. The watercolours resembled those she had seen in the gallery's storefront. But most of them were photographs, some in black and white. Pleasant motifs from Saint-Malo, mostly of the sea, but also some cityscapes. Nothing extraordinary, but good enough to be purchased occasionally as souvenirs. The room was messy but appeared to have been cleaned at least recently. The tiny kitchen barely had enough space for a folding table where no more than two people could sit. Miriam Mignon obviously hadn't been able to invite many visitors to her apartment. Sandrine doubted that the young artist would have asked anyone here she expected to exhibit her paintings. She couldn't imagine snob Ariste de Saint-

Clair here. He probably wouldn't have even sat on one of the sofas with the worn-out covers.

Sandrine entered an adjacent room that was slightly larger and had one more window. This was where Miriam Mignon had painted. In the centre of the room stood an easel. This time, it wasn't a watercolour but a charcoal drawing. She approached it and looked at the half-finished portrait of a man. In her mind, she completed it with the remaining features. It was Ariste de Saint-Clair, she had no doubt about it. The lips that refused to smile and the cold eyes made him unmistakable, at least for her. She doubted whether it would be sufficient for a court-acceptable identification. She quickly took a photo of the painting and the room. She looked at the remaining pictures standing upright against the wall, but there was no other portrait among them. Sandrine wondered if de Saint-Clair knew that his victim had drawn him. Probably not, otherwise it would have been destroyed long ago, not still here. The man usually took great care not to leave any traces. But here, he appeared to have been careless.

On the shelf was an expensive camera with multiple interchangeable lenses and a padded bag. Next to it was a waterproof case for memory cards. Sandrine opened it; about a dozen cards were in the designated slots. Some work for the forensic experts who would have to go through them.

The apartment door creaked open then Adel entered the living room.

"I'm over here," she called out, folded the memory card case, then locked it.

"No luck. The first-floor apartments are rented to vacationers who just moved in, and the owner, who lives on the ground floor, went to a family gathering in Languedoc last week."

"Our victim made a phantom drawing of the man she met. At least, I suspect it's him. He left such a strong impression on her that she drew his portrait." She pointed to the easel. Adel approached and looked at it for a moment.

"I'd call it half a drawing, at most. Unfortunately, it doesn't help us much. It could be anyone."

Sandrine nodded thoughtfully. Anyone who didn't know de Saint-Clair as well as she did would react the same way as the brigadier. It wouldn't serve as strong evidence in court. But the forensic experts should still take it as a possible court exhibit and examine it.

"I'll call Jean-Claude Mazet right away," Adel suggested. "The forensics team needs to examine the apartment. If the unknown art enthusiast visited her and viewed her paintings, his fingerprints are bound to be found."

"Should we wait for them?"

"We have the only key, what else can we do?"

Her phone vibrated. She picked up the call.

"We'll be at the police station in an hour or maybe two," she said after listening for a while. "No, it can't be done faster. We have a murder case, and that takes precedence."

She ended the call and put her phone in her pocket.

"What's going on?"

"They want to speak with me at the police station," Sandrine explained.

"Who exactly?"

"Matisse, Hermé with his team, and de Chezac. I'm a sought-after person today."

"Does that surprise you? They want to pull us off the Poutin case."

"That was inevitable." The deceased Brigadier Poutin had not only been a colleague but Sandrine had also been involved in the investigation against him. Of course, she and Adel wouldn't be allowed to investigate, she was aware of that, and yet she didn't like hearing it from her superior. No one had more interest in finding out what had happened to Poutin than she did. Well, maybe apart from Renard Dubois, his best, probably only friend.

Adel glanced at his wristwatch.

"We won't need two hours to get back to the station, even if we wait here for the forensic team."

"I want to take care of something beforehand, something I probably won't be allowed to do after the meeting."

"You mean, after they've taken the case away from you?" He smiled knowingly. He knew his partner well enough to know that she wouldn't completely stop investigating the Poutin case.

"I want to talk to the neighbour who found him, Monsieur Senlis. Maybe he noticed some small detail that could help us."

"You mean that something could help Commandant Jogu and Major Baud, right?" His smile deepened.

"We all want the same thing: to catch the culprit," Sandrine said.

"If there is a culprit. We still don't have any results from the forensic team or the medical examiner pointing to anything other than suicide."

"But we have Dubois' observations, and he agrees with me," she said. "Let's wait in the car for the forensics team."

Adel nodded in agreement, and both of them left the apartment.

After handing over the key to a member of the forensics team, they drove back to the old town. Adel took Porte Saint-Thomas and parked in the cobbled courtyard of the Hôtel de Ville. Fortunately, there was no wedding taking place today, so there were plenty of parking spaces available. He placed his police badge behind the windshield and got out. Monsieur Senlis worked at the Hôtel France et Chateaubriand, which was only a few steps away. The sun had broken through the clouds and was shining on the square, whose cobblestones still glistened with rain. Adel looked at the sky and left his raincoat in the car. It wouldn't be long until the next downpour started, but it should suffice for a brief conversation with the witness.

"There he is," Adel said, looking towards the café attached to the hotel, where a stocky man in a dark suit was serving drinks to one of the few occupied tables.

"Monsieur Senlis?" Sandrine addressed him and showed her police ID. "I am Capitaine Perrot and my colleague is Brigadier Chief de Police Azarou."

"You must be here about Luc. What else could it be?" His shoulders slumped tiredly, and he placed the empty tray on a table.

"Do you have time for a few questions?"

"Come with me." The man led them to a table in the back of the brasserie. "We'll be less disturbed here. I don't want to upset the guests with the terrible story."

"I understand. You found Monsieur Poutin?"

"That's right."

"How did it happen that you visited him so late?" Sandrine asked.

"We've been neighbours for as long as I can remember. His parents lived in that house."

"So, you knew him well?"

"As well as neighbours do. We sat in the garden together from time to time, grilled, and had a drink. But lately, he seemed troubled and avoided us. Especially since Anne went to her sister's. She didn't say why, I assumed it had something to do with their marriage, but I didn't ask. Maybe I should have."

"Don't blame yourself; there's little you could have done," Sandrine tried to reassure the man.

"He didn't seem like he was planning to do something to himself. Why else would he borrow my lawnmower?"

"When did he do that?"

"On Saturday morning. I also heard him mowing the lawn

and working in the garden." He looked at Sandrine curiously. "Do people do that when they want to commit suicide and set the house on fire? It seems strange to me. The lawn would be the last thing on my mind."

"Who can really look into another person's mind?" Adel said. "Maybe he just wanted to distract himself from the thoughts he was carrying around."

"That could be, but setting his house on fire? That seems absurd to me. It may not have been much, but Luc loved his place, just like Anne. I never would have thought he'd do something like that."

"What? Take his own life or set the house on fire?" Sandrine asked.

"Both, of course. And he would have definitely returned my lawnmower before doing anything like that." The man nodded emphatically with each word.

"Back to that evening. Why did you go to Monsieur Poutin's?"

"As I said, I heard he had finished mowing the lawn, and I wanted to retrieve the lawnmower and invite him for a drink."

"Apparently liked a good Cognac," Sandrine remarked, keeping a close eye on the man. She didn't want to miss his reaction.

"Oh, where did you hear that from? He couldn't stand that stuff." Monsieur Senlis shook his head. "But he always had excellent apple brandy at his place."

Dubois had made the same claim; they needed to examine the Cognac bottle more closely and determine its origin.

"Did you also lend him a canister of gasoline?"

"It's a new four-stroke lawnmower, it takes regular gasoline. After the last mowing, I filled it up, but as a precaution, I gave him the canister. It was still half full, so it would have definitely been enough."

"You rang the doorbell?"

"Yes. But he didn't answer. He used to sit in the garden in the evenings, so I went around the house, but he wasn't there. Then I noticed the fire in the living room. Fortunately, the hose was still connected. I grabbed one of Anne's garden gnomes, broke the window with it, and turned on the water. If I had come a bit later, the whole place would have gone up in flames."

"A lucky coincidence," Adel said.

"I have to confess about the garden gnome to Anne."

"Is that a big deal?" The brigadier gave him a puzzled look.

"She loved those ugly things, but there's a gang around here that claims to be liberating garden gnomes. They're just a bunch of nuts with nothing better to do, stealing other people's stuff. Anyway, they completely cleared out Anne's front yard. It really got to her. She hid the remaining gnomes behind the house." He turned his head to Adel, looking at him sternly. "The police should really do something about that."

"I'll see what can be done," he promised the man.

"You'll need to come to the police station in the next few days and give your statement."

"I will, but for now, I need to get back to my guests. Most of them are here on vacation, but they don't even have five minutes to wait for the server."

"Then we won't keep you any longer," Sandrine said, bidding farewell.

* * *

"They postponed the start of the meeting until you arrived at the police station," Inès informed Sandrine as she entered the office. "De Chezac seems quite tense; he called twice to ask where you were."

"Then the press conference probably didn't go well?" Sandrine guessed.

"I hope that's the only reason."

"In that case, I won't keep them waiting any longer." She turned to Adel. "It's enough if I come under fire; you better stay here."

"I can have your back."

"De Chezac will suspect which direction I'm investigating, and he won't like it. It's better if you stay out of it; otherwise, he might remove both of us from the case."

"He doesn't have many options left if he excludes us."

"That will be secondary for him. Plus, knowing him, he'll blame Matisse for the problem."

She took another cookie from the tin that Inès offered her. Apart from the muffin, she hadn't had anything to eat, and it seemed like she wouldn't be leaving the police station anytime soon.

"Inès, could you arrange for me to get the key to Tour Bidouane or find someone who can unlock it?"

"I'll call the city administration; it shouldn't be a problem. When do you want to go in?"

"As soon as I get out of here. If I'm not back at my desk in two hours, come in and get me out, no matter what excuse you use."

"Will do," Inès assured her with a broad grin.

On her way to the conference room, Sandrine encountered Jean-Claude Mazet and Commissaire Matisse. The team from Rennes had arrived before them, just like Antoine de Chezac.

"Where were you all morning?" de Chezac snapped at her as soon as she sat down.

"Doing my job, what else?" she replied.

"In the future, at least let us know where you are and when you intend to be in the office," he admonished her.

"I'll do that," she said casually, trying to appease the prosecutor.

"As I can see, everyone is here," Matisse began. "We all need to come to terms with the news of a colleague's death. Brigadier Poutin had been with the Saint-Malo police station for three decades. One of the most senior members of the force. Whatever allegations were made against him, he did not deserve this end."

Sandrine and Mazet nodded, while the others appeared indifferent. The investigators from Rennes had only encountered him once during an interrogation where he had refused to speak and behaved with hostility. De Chezac had worked with him directly just once, during the raid at Équinoxe, which had not gone particularly well. Sandrine wondered if he welcomed the policeman's death. The case would be closed, and no further questions would be raised about his involvement.

"I assume our team will be responsible for the investigation," Major Baud said. She skipped any sentimental phrases, as few would believe her sincerity.

"It's likely a suicide and it occurred in Saint-Malo," replied Matisse. "I see no compelling reason why it shouldn't be handled by my team."

"In normal circumstances, I would agree with you, but in this particular case, I insist on leading the investigation." Sébastian Hermé spoke in his calm manner that left no doubt about his demand. "We were investigating Brigadier Poutin, and now he's dead. It's impossible not to see the connection."

"Perhaps these investigations themselves triggered his suicide." De Chezac leaned back in his chair, his gaze fixed on his colleague from Rennes. Even though he hadn't explicitly stated it, everyone understood that he wanted to blame him for the brigadier's suicide.

"If you want to know if I see Brigadier Poutin's death in connection with the investigations against him, then the answer is definitely yes. Therefore, we will investigate it." The prosecutor from Rennes made it clear that he still saw the case within his jurisdiction. Sandrine suspected he might even escalate the matter to the Prefect. However, she also noticed that Hermé referred to the brigadier's death rather than his suicide. Did he also have doubts about that theory?

"If you insist on having the case, I won't oppose it."

Sandrine's head jerked towards de Chezac. Her surprise was evident. The fact that he was giving up the case without a fight astonished her.

"Then it's settled," Commandant Jogu said. "What do we know from the forensics team?"

Mazet placed the file on the table in front of him and opened it.

"Luc was found dead in his garage by his neighbour last night. The man cut the rope and tried to resuscitate him, but without success. Doctor Mason believes he was already dead at that point. There was a significant amount of alcohol in his stomach, but his blood alcohol level was unexpectedly low." Mazet looked up from the report and glanced at Sandrine. "He must have taken a substantial gulp from the bottle shortly before his death."

"He was probably trying to muster some courage, not uncommon," de Chezac chimed in, and Hermé nodded in agreement.

"We found his fingerprints on the bottle, but also those of a second person. So far, we haven't been able to identify the other set of prints."

"A family member?" Sandrine inquired.

"It's possible. We found a second partially full bottle in the kitchen. The family hasn't had any previous police involvement, and we don't have their fingerprints on record for comparison purposes. I spoke with Madame Poutin on the phone, and she will return later today. One of my officers will take her prints so we can eliminate her as a match."

"Please inform me when she arrives. I'd like to offer my

condolences and see how we can assist her in this situation," Commissaire Matisse requested.

"I will. She will appreciate it." Mazet knew that Matisse wouldn't stop at just offering condolences. The Commissaire had a reputation for pulling out all the stops to assist his colleagues in times of need.

"What did you find out about the bottle, aside from the unknown fingerprints?" Sandrine asked.

"Why do you think that the bottle could be important?" Major Baud didn't seem to appreciate Sandrine's interference in the investigation she had just been removed from.

"It's unusual." Mazet wasn't rattled by the interruption and flipped through his file. "It's a vintage Cognac, Albert de Montaubert, 1963."

Sébastian Hermé whistled softly. "Not bad. The man had refined taste, it was quite expensive." He turned to face de Chezac. "What would a bottle cost? 200 Euro?"

"Around 250 to 300 Euros, I'd estimate."

"We met Brigadier Poutin yesterday. It's not the brand I would have expected him to have," Hermé remarked.

"His last sip was worth splurging on." De Chezac raised his hands defensively when he noticed the irritated look Matisse shot his way. "Apparently."

"If the alcohol in the bottle is different from what was in the dead man's stomach, Monsieur Mazet would have already informed us, wouldn't you?" Commandant Jogu didn't want to waste more time discussing a bottle of Cognac. "What else do we have?"

"No traces of smoke were found in his lungs, but there were traces of gasoline."

"What do you think that means?" Hermé asked.

"He might have started the fire and left the living room before smoke developed," Mazet suggested.

"Sounds logical."

"We also found that gasoline was used as an accelerant, as we suspected at the crime scene."

"It had a strong smell," Commandant Jogu concurred with the forensic expert.

"Where did it come from?" Sandrine inquired. Major Baud once again shot her a look, making it clear that her involvement was no longer appreciated.

"There was a half-empty canister in the garage," Mazet said. "It was filled with gasoline for the lawnmower."

"I would advise looking into that more closely," Sandrine said, recalling the neighbour's statement vividly.

"We will definitely do that. This isn't our first investigation," Major Baud retorted in her direction.

"The crucial piece of evidence could be the rope we found in his pocket. It's made of the same material used to strangle the victim at Tour Bidouane," Major Baud explained.

"Have they found any traces of skin on the rope?" Sandrine asked.

"Yes, there are skin samples on it. They're currently with Dr Mason in the forensic lab. We should have the results by tomorrow."

"This changes the perspective on the investigation," de Chezac interjected. "He killed the woman, and his guilty conscience drove him to suicide."

"But what would be the motive?" Sébastian Hermé pondered. He had observed Brigadier Poutin during the interrogation, and it was likely that he found the idea of the man having any connection to the beautiful young woman as absurd as Sandrine did. She forced herself not to shake her head. Poutin did not fit the profile of a murderer. Who would believe the man to be a connoisseur of art with connections to galleries in Paris? It was ridiculous. But perhaps he was the second man who cleaned up the crime scene and erased the evidence. That could be possible. Any lawyer could now cast doubt on whether the murder weapon was an expensive silk tie or a piece of rope from a hardware store.

"We'll find out," Commandant Jogu said, likely wanting to avoid further speculation.

"No," Sandrine interjected. "The death at the beach is my case. If there are any links or insights that connect Poutin to the Saint-Malo murder, it's our responsibility."

"Didn't you listen to your boss? The investigation into Poutin's death has been assigned to us," Jogu objected, giving his colleague a hint not to interfere.

"Your task is to determine whether it was a suicide or not. That's all. If he was involved in a murder in Saint-Malo, that's our business," Sandrine asserted, casting a glance at Matisse, who nodded in agreement.

"The deceased at the beach is your investigation," Hermé conceded. "If there are any leads or findings that further connect Poutin to the murder, you will inform us."

"Exactly, just as you'll keep me updated on your findings in the Poutin case," Sandrine replied, seeking the gaze of the prosecutor. A faint smile curled the corners of his mouth.

"We will keep you informed about the events in his house," he assured her. However, she was excluded from the rest of the investigation against the brigadier.

"Please make yourself available for questioning later this afternoon," Major Baud swiftly stated and stood up. She obviously didn't want to engage in further discussion; Sandrine had already kept her waiting.

"I'll be at the crime scene after lunch, and then you can have my time," Sandrine agreed.

The woman hesitated, then packed up her documents and left the room with Commandant Jogu.

"Our collaboration will surely improve once we get to know each other better," Sébastian Hermé said with little conviction and followed his colleagues out of the room.

The door closed behind Hermé, and de Chezac let out a deep sigh. "What a dreadful woman. I'd rather work with you," he said in Sandrine's direction.

That might have been meant as a compliment. *I'd much rather work with Hermé than with you.*

"Poutin's death was not a suicide," she said. "But he definitely had a connection to the death of Miriam Mignon, the woman found on the beach."

"He knew we were closing in on him. The murder weapon was still in his pocket. No wonder he chose the noose rather than getting arrested by you. Poutin thought of you as a snooty Parisian who didn't belong here and enjoyed harassing him for no reason." While these might have been Poutin's words, de Chezac spoke them with such conviction they may as well have been his own.

"Did he tell you that?" asked Sandrine.

"Word for word," replied de Chezac.

"Then he must have had a bad day. You are quite popular among your colleagues and have nothing to blame yourself for." Matisse tried to diffuse the tension that had settled in the room. "Now, back to the investigation. Where do we stand?"

Sandrine brought them up to date.

"We've searched Mademoiselle Mignon's apartment, but found nothing suspicious at first glance. The camera and memory cards are in the lab and will be examined. We'll let you know if we find anything that looks interesting," Mazet reported.

"Please make copies of the last pictures taken by the victim," Sandrine requested.

"No problem, you'll have them on your desk in two hours."

"No rush." De Chezac waved it off. "We have the murder weapon and a basic confession through suicide. If the forensic expert can match the skin particles on the rope to the victim, the case is closed."

"There were two people at the crime scene at different

times. How can we be sure Poutin didn't arrive after the crime was already committed?"

"That's once again a far-fetched theory. Can you prove beyond a doubt that the murder and disposal of the victim were done by two different persons?"

"Not yet," Sandrine replied. "We still need to—"

"As long as you can't do that, I consider Poutin the perpetrator. It's obvious."

"I—" she began, but the prosecutor didn't let her finish.

"You're trying to complicate a straightforward case that's already been solved. Do you have a guilty conscience towards Brigadier Poutin?"

"There's absolutely no reason to accuse me of such a thing."

"Then we'll close the case. Poutin hanged himself to avoid arrest and punishment. Policemen don't have an easy time in prison, and he knew that very well."

"Is that your decision?" Matisse asked, surprised.

"As long as I don't have compelling evidence to the contrary, yes." In his role as a prosecutor judge, this decision rested in his hands. Even though Sandrine was convinced he was wrong, enough evidence supported his theory to make it defensible.

"Miriam Mignon was in her early twenties, blonde, blue-eyed, extremely pretty, with a petite figure. She was a photographer and painter who exhibited in a gallery in Saint-Malo. She was strangled and left naked. There were silk fibres around her neck. Does that sound familiar to you?" The sentences came quickly, and they hit de Chezac, who moved his chair slightly away from her.

"Of course. We both know about the murder series in Paris. The Necktie Killer, that's what the press called him, right?"

"The similarities are striking."

"Not every young and beautiful artist who meets a violent death is part of a series of crimes. We both know that the victims in Paris still had the tie around their necks. It was missing here.

Instead, we find fibres of a rope. She might have been wearing a silk scarf that evening. Also, the modus operandi is different. The body was thrown from the tower, and someone tried to make it disappear into the sea. Probably Brigadier Poutin was interrupted, or else we wouldn't have a body today. It would be floating somewhere in the English Channel."

"You are aware that de Saint-Clair is in Saint-Malo?"

De Chezac stared at her angrily. The tension between them seemed almost palpable.

"Of course. But you've targeted him before, even though he had solid alibis. It nearly cost you your job. If you do it again without evidence, this time no one will save you." The last part was directed towards Commissaire Matisse, who had brought Sandrine to Saint-Malo.

"I will provide the evidence, don't worry."

"Leave him alone," he snapped at her. "That's an official order. Do you understand?"

"Absolutely," she replied, as calmly as she could, though she was seething with anger inside. Her hands were firmly on the table, or else she might have clenched them into fists.

"Make sure she stays away from de Saint-Clair," he instructed Matisse, then stood up. "Close the Poutin case."

"Another official order?" she couldn't help but ask.

"Absolutely." He turned and left the room.

Matisse exhaled deeply. "Why do you provoke the man like that?"

"The real question is why does he get so angry every time I mention de Saint-Clair?"

"Is that the man you suspected in Paris?"

"Exactly. Now he's in Saint-Malo, and a young woman dies. To me, that's not a coincidence."

Matisse remained silent for a moment. Only the creaking of his chair, on which he swayed lightly, interrupted the quiet in the room.

"The investigation into the death of Brigadier Poutin is solely in the hands of Prosecutor Hermé. I think it's appropriate to inform him of your suspicions. It's then his call what to do with it, but he seems like a reasonable person to me."

"I think so too."

"Prepare the documents in the Miriam Mignon case so we can close it."

"Commissaire..." she began.

"No need to rush," he interrupted. "Perhaps something will come up over the next few days. As for this de Saint-Clair, I advise you to stay away from him, which doesn't mean we'll take our eyes off him. The safety of the residents of Saint-Malo comes first."

"I understand." Officially, they could close the case, but unofficially they would investigate and keep an eye on the suspect as long as he remained in the city. She hoped that time would be enough to link him to the crime.

Sandrine sat down at her desk, stretched her legs, and sighed deeply.

"That bad?" Adel opened the drawer, took out a chocolate bar, and pushed it towards her. "With chocolate, everything is only half as bad."

"Thank you." She broke off a piece and took a bite. She pushed the rest back to Adel. "Save it for the next meeting with de Chezac or Major Baud. I'll probably need some cheering up then."

"What happened?"

"As you suspected, Hermé and his team are taking over the investigation."

"The man seems competent; if there's something to find, he'll find it. Plus, he has Jean-Claude's help," Adel said.

"That's not the end of it. De Chezac wants to pin Miriam

Mignon's murder on Poutin. We're supposed to consider the case closed."

"He can't be serious. A woman like her wouldn't be walking the ramparts at night with someone like Poutin." He shook his head in disbelief.

"Matisse instructed me to prepare everything and close the file. However, without any hurry. So, we have until the end of the week to make progress."

"Then we need to get going. What's your next move?"

"Your chocolate was delicious, but my stomach is growling. I'm going to take a proper lunch break. The meeting was exhausting, and I definitely don't want to go for questioning by Major Baud on an empty stomach."

"Interrogation, not questioning," Adel corrected her.

"With her, every conversation feels like an interrogation."

Adel laughed. "That's true. She's not exactly a gentle person."

She glanced at her phone. She had missed several calls and a message from Léon.

"Sometimes you get lucky. Léon is in town and wants to have lunch with me." She typed a message to him and set the phone aside. "I'm taking a break now. After that, we'll figure out how to get into the tower."

"Inès ran into a friend in city hall. The last pictures will be hung this afternoon, and we'll be able to get in. The photographer will probably be present."

Someone else Sébastian Duval knew had died, and once again, she was the one delivering the news to him. *He probably won't be happy to see me again after this.*

"Then we'll meet at the tower entrance in an hour and a half." She said goodbye to her colleague.

* * *

Leon was waiting for her outside the Brasserie du Sillon. He had his raincoat's collar flipped up, and he crossed his arms in front of his chest against the strengthening wind.

"You're my saviour," she said with a smile and kissed him. "At least a bright spot on this miserable day."

"Thanks for the compliment. I assume you're hungry."

"Starving," she replied. She looked through the window of the brasserie, where there were hardly any free tables. "But unfortunately, I don't have much time for a leisurely meal. I'm afraid a baguette and a coffee on a bench will have to do today."

"We'll manage it. I've reserved a table, and I've already ordered for both of us. The server knows me and will be quick."

"But just one course, otherwise I'll really be late."

"That should be enough." He took her hand and led her into the restaurant to a table by the window overlooking the beach. She looked outside and watched the waves that ran far onto the beach. The wind was blowing frothy flakes of foam in all directions. Apart from a few joggers and walkers, the beach was deserted today. Only the kite surfers and sailors were enjoying the weather. A waiter brought a glass of wine and a bottle of water, placing them on the table.

"Was your day that bad?"

"Can't you tell?"

"If I'm the only bright spot, it says a lot."

She placed her hand on his and gave it a gentle squeeze. "You're always a bright spot, that's the nature of optimists like you. But what brings you to the city?"

"The prosecutor wanted to talk to me, and I didn't feel like going back home without seeing you."

"I didn't know that. How was it? Did you meet his team?" She was surprised that Hermé hadn't mentioned anything about it.

"No, he was alone."

"What did he want from you?" She wondered why he had

excluded Jogu and Baud from the questioning. She knew Hermé didn't do anything without a good reason.

"Nothing unexpected. He wanted to know what had happened that evening at Équinoxe." A playful glint appeared in his eyes, and the wrinkles around his eyes deepened. "Since I was with an exciting woman in Le Mont-Saint-Michel instead of my club, I couldn't tell him much about the events. I've never seen that brigadier in my life, just like your prosecutor, this de Chezac."

"That's not much of a loss," she said, taking a sip of her red wine and shifting slightly in her chair, which creaked softly. She seemed to have found an uncomfortable one. She glanced enviously at the comfortable benches along the wall, which were all occupied.

"Simone will have to appear in a few days and give her statement."

"Your manager?" She had seen the woman at the club occasionally but had never spoken to her. Mostly, Sandrine remembered her tattoos.

"Exactly. She was there, although she wasn't allowed into the office when that cop pulled the drugs out of the top hat."

"It's clear now that he planted them on you. You're out of the woods. I'm really sorry for all the trouble."

"It turned out all right. The police gave my club some good publicity, and I got to keep my license. Besides, your colleagues won't be showing up at my place anytime soon. Otherwise, I'll complain about police harassment, and they definitely want to avoid that. I assume this will all be over soon, especially now that this brigadier has taken his own life."

"You know about it?"

"Heard it on the radio. Is it your case?"

"If it ever was, it's officially in Hermé's hands now. I'm out of the game."

"You probably have your hands full with the woman from the beach."

She nodded silently. It would depend on whether she could uncover anything crucial before de Chezac put on the brakes for good.

"There's one more thing." He reached into his pocket and pulled out a photo, sliding it over to Sandrine. "Do you know this woman?"

"*Mon Dieu*," she exclaimed, looking at him in disbelief. It had taken her a moment to recognise the woman with the long curly hair, the tight dress leaving little to the imagination, and the high heels. It was Major Baud, holding a glass of champagne and clearly flirting with the bartender. "How did you get a photograph of her?"

"That's from the surveillance camera. I had a feeling you'd know her. The question is, is she a dealer or a colleague of yours?"

"Why do you think she could be an investigator?"

"She was at Équinoxe on Sunday night and was conspicuously asking the staff where she could get some pills. She didn't seem like a prostitute to me, so I thought either a dealer checking out the competition or an undercover cop trying to get information from me."

"That's the woman who was supposed to question you today, Major Baud, one of Hermé's associates."

"I see. So they still don't fully trust me, do they? Although that prosecutor seemed really nice."

"He is, but in his job, he has no choice but to double and triple-check everything."

"Then they should send someone who behaves less conspicuously. And, above all, someone who doesn't wear a dress that will remain vividly in the memory of any of my male staff."

The waitress brought two plates and a bowl of fries, placing them on the table.

"A Chateaubriand. Looks delicious."

"The dark pepper sauce they serve here is extremely tasty. Could have been made by me."

She took one of the thin and crispy fries, called alumettes, dipped it into the sauce that generously covered the beef tenderloin, and took a bite.

"Absolutely. Excellent choice. You know my taste."

Leon pointed towards the tidal islands, easily accessible by foot at this time. "We're sitting here in warmth and comfort, enjoying the view of Grand Bé. There lies the tomb of the writer François-René de Chateaubriand. A true Malouin. What else could I have ordered?"

"Is it named after him?" She tapped the tip of her knife on the filet.

"Yes. The name is derived from him, but it was actually his personal chef who invented it. Maybe they should have named it after him instead."

Sandrine set the cutlery aside, leaned forward, and kissed him gently. "Thank you very much. I really needed some good company right now."

*** * * ***

The bright red door to the interior of the tower was slightly ajar. Sandrine pushed it open and entered. A half dozen steps led down to a platform made of ancient wooden planks that seemed to float freely. A chest-high railing made of sturdy horizontal polished wood and vertical metal rods surrounded it to prevent a fall into the depths. Below the apex of the ceiling, there was a light strip with spotlights attached. A man stood on a stepladder, aiming one of them at a photograph hanging on the ancient stone wall but behind the railing. She immediately recognised Sébastian Duval. The man looked at her, and wrinkles appeared on his forehead.

"Capitaine Perrot. What brings you here?" He let go of the spotlight and descended the ladder.

"I was told you would be exhibiting here."

"That's correct." He stepped away from the last rung of the ladder and made a sweeping gesture towards the large-format photographs hanging on the walls. At most a dozen. "But you're certainly not here to get a sneak peek at my pictures before the exhibition opens, are you?"

"You're not mistaken." Sandrine approached the railing and looked at the photo of a shepherd holding a lamb in his arms. "Did this picture belong to the exhibition in Paris?" When she first met him, he had just come back from an exhibition at the Centre Pompidou. The man was a talented photographer and well-known beyond the borders of Brittany.

"The exhibition was only for a limited time. My gallery owner kept most of the pictures. I'm displaying the rest here for a few weeks. A unique place."

"No doubt."

"But my photographs haven't brought you here."

"No, it's about Miriam Mignon."

He turned away, went to a desk in the back of the tower, and sat down. Sandrine followed him.

"I've heard about it. The poor girl." He took her hand and squeezed it. Sandrine allowed it; it felt suitably familiar in that moment. "You have a profession that confronts you with the most terrible things our society commits. I don't envy you."

"I don't envy you either."

He tilted his head back and looked at the ceiling. His breathing sounded heavy.

"It still hurts. I don't think it will ever go away. That's why I work a lot, hoping it will distract me from the memory."

She vividly remembered Aimée Vilette, his girlfriend, whom they had found dead in her apartment in the old town. Like him, she would never forget the sight.

"She was killed here?" he asked without looking at her.

"On top of the tower." She wasn't entirely sure but didn't want to associate her death with his exhibition. That would only further burden the sensitive man.

"Did you know Mademoiselle Mignon?"

He let go of her hand, sat upright, and leaned on the tabletop with his arms.

"Vaguely. She knew my work and helped prepare the exhibition."

"She was also a photographer. Did she show you her pictures?"

"Yes. She had some with her."

"Someone promised the young woman an exhibition in Paris."

"Really?" His eyebrows raised a bit.

"What did you think of her pictures?"

"They were mainly motifs from the city or the surrounding area. Technically well done, but nothing really new. They didn't stand out from the crowd."

"Did she mention it to you?"

"No." He shook his head slightly. "I would remember that. I would have asked her to take her time and continue working on herself. She wasn't there yet. Technique is one thing, but she lacked a clear, recognisable signature to create an emotional impact. A failed first exhibition can easily ruin an artist's career."

"Did Miriam Mignon have a key to the exhibition?"

"I believe so. After all, she helped with the preparations. Wasn't it with her belongings?"

Sandrine approached the railing and looked down. "Pretty deep."

"There are three levels in the tower. Plenty of space for the pictures to have an impact."

"When does it open?"

"This weekend, but there's still a lot to do before then. We haven't even had a chance to put up a poster outside the tower."

"Then I won't disturb you further. I'll look around, and then I'll be gone."

"Go ahead. I'll be up here if you need me." The man got up and returned to the ladder, while Sandrine took the stairs to the lower floors. The middle level seemed to be ready for the upcoming exhibition, but the lower one had an open toolbox and several trash cans on the floor; otherwise, the space, more like a hall, was empty. Sandrine walked along the railing and looked at the pictures. Sébastian Duval captured impressions of almost extinct professions he found in Brittany. He captured the vitality of the people, the essence of what filled them. Some might call it the soul. That was what Miriam Mignon had lacked. She would never achieve it now.

Sandrine strolled back, glanced into the open toolbox, and lifted a piece of cardboard from the trash can when she suddenly froze in mid-motion. Black fabric peeked out from under the cardboard. She quickly put on her gloves. *So, it stayed here.* She pulled out a black dress. Judging by its size, it could fit a petite woman like Miriam Mignon. In the trash can, she found a handbag which she retrieved and opened. In a case, there was a credit card and Miriam Mignon's ID. Sandrine searched for a phone in vain. Her killer must have taken it. Perhaps she had taken a selfie with her murderer, and he couldn't leave it behind. If he had been smart, the phone would now be deep in the blue sea.

She called Inès.

"I'm at Tour Bidouane. Please send the forensics team. It's urgent."

"No problem, I'll do it right away."

"Where is Adel? He was supposed to meet me here."

"He's still in an interview with Commandant Jogu, so he's running a bit late."

"I'll wait here for the forensics team, then I'll take a taxi back."

She ended the call and climbed the stairs. Except for her and Sébastian Duval, no one was in the tower. It would suffice if she kept an eye on the door until the forensics team arrived.

* * *

Sandrine found Adel at his desk. He raised his hands apologetically.

"I'm sorry I wasn't able to get to the crime scene, but they were grilling me." The brigadier took a deep breath and rolled his eyes, which spoke volumes for the otherwise polite and reserved man. He couldn't stand Major Baud either.

"I still have that ahead of me, but first, some news," Sandrine said and informed him about the discovery of the victim's clothing. Before Adel could respond, Marie, a colleague from the forensics team, and Jamila entered the open-plan office.

"We've found something," Jamila blurted out immediately. The excitement was evident in her expression and her slightly flushed cheeks.

"Actually, Jamila found it," Marie noted, making Adel's sister beam. They took two chairs and sat down at the desk.

Jamila pulled a photo from a folder, showing the street facade opposite the crime scene. "There were no security cameras capturing that part of the wall, but then I found this." She tapped her index finger on a blurred spot at a window on the top floor of one of the nearby buildings.

"What is it supposed to be?" Adel pulled the picture towards him and examined it more closely.

"That's one of those small cameras people attach to bicycles or motorcycles. An action cam," she explained to her brother, as if it were obvious. "The owner attached it to the window with a suction cup. Naturally, I went there and questioned him."

Adel furrowed his brow and gave Marie a questioning look. He didn't like the idea of his sister leaving the police station on her own to interrogate a potential witness.

"I accompanied her, of course," Marie reassured him.

"The man had taken a time-lapse video of the beach. One picture every ten seconds, capturing an entire day of ebb and flow. The crime scene is quite visible on it." She pulled more pictures from the folder and spread them on the desk.

"We have the entire sequence of the crime," she said proudly, looking expectantly at her brother, who was focused on the images.

"Excellent work," Sandrine praised her. "Your discovery could solve the case."

"We have a single frame every ten seconds," explained Marie. "The quality of the footage is significantly better than regular security cameras, but due to the wide-angle view, we had to enlarge the frame significantly. The low-light conditions in the middle of the night weren't very helpful. It's not enough for identification. Also, we can only estimate the time of recording." Marie handed Sandrine a printout showing a man holding Miriam Mignon in his arms.

"She appears to be naked. At that point, she was already dead," Sandrine remarked, looking at Marie. "What's on the images before that? Shouldn't the crime be visible?"

"Before that, it's just the empty tower," Jamila replied.

"So, the crime really happened inside the tower, and he brought her body up afterward. I suspected as much, but now we know," Sandrine said.

"What were they doing there in the middle of the night?" Adel asked.

"Miriam Mignon was helping with the preparations for the exhibition and had a key. She might have wanted to impress the man from whom she hoped to get a career boost as a photographer and arranged a private tour. It turned out to be a fatal mistake," Sandrine explained.

"On the next picture, he places the body against the wall, right across from the entrance." Jamila handed a picture to Sandrine.

"This confirms my theory. The perpetrator wanted her to be found there in the morning," Sandrine added.

Adel gave her a questioning look, but she shook her head, indicating that her suspicion regarding de Saint-Clair should remain between them.

"Unfortunately, the man is not clearly identifiable. In the pictures, you either see his back or the shots are too blurry," Marie said. "He is white, somewhere between six feet to six feet two inches tall, strong enough to carry the woman up the narrow spiral staircase. The jacket he is wearing appears to be brown or a similar colour. I would guess black for the trousers."

"Could the jacket also be red?"

"It's possible," she answered vaguely. "With that lighting, it's hard to determine."

"But this is where it gets really interesting." Jamila handed Sandrine and Adel the next set of images.

"According to our calculations, about forty minutes passed."

"What happened during that time?" Sandrine asked.

"Nothing. Just the dead body on the tower," Jamila replied, somewhat surprised by the question.

"'Thank you." The perpetrator had staged the body and then left the tower, which definitely contradicted de Chezac's theory that the man had panicked after the murder and needed time to calm down and make a decision about what to do with the body.

Sandrine arranged several images in a row on the desk. Another man appeared on the tower, lifted the body, and rolled it over the wall into the abyss. Just as she had imagined. Something was vaguely visible in his hands, which could have been a rope.

"A second man cleaning up the crime scene and tampering with the evidence," she murmured thoughtfully.

"Definitely a second man," Marie agreed. "Unless the perpetrator changed clothes and shrunk about four inches."

"The rope that might have been used for strangulation was found in Poutin's pocket by the forensics team. Could the man in the pictures be Brigadier Poutin?" Sandrine asked, even though she had already ruled it out after a first look.

Marie pulled the picture towards her and studied it for a moment, while absentmindedly playing with one of her braids.

"The height might match, but in terms of physique, I'd say the man in the picture lacks several kilos to be Poutin, but it's hard to tell." She shook her head. "I'd be more inclined to say it's not the brigadier. But it's possible."

"How did the rope end up in his pocket?" Jamila asked.

"That's no longer our investigation," Sandrine replied. At least not officially. "Take the pictures to Prosecutor Hermé and his team. They are now responsible for the investigation into the death of Brigadier Poutin. For us, it would have been crucial to be able to rule out his involvement in the Mignon murder. But with the pictures we have..." She shrugged in resignation. The images probably wouldn't be enough to persuade de Chezac to continue pursuing the case.

"As you wish," Marie said slowly and deliberately, as if trying to understand what Sandrine was getting at. It wasn't typical for Sandrine to just give up on an investigation.

"But there's something else that definitely concerns your case."

"Go on," Adel prompted her.

"We went through the photos of Miriam Mignon that were on the memory cards." She sighed softly. "And that woman really took a lot of photos. But I noticed something. The memory card in the camera had been deleted and cleanly formatted. There was nothing left."

"What's strange about that?"

"Otherwise, she kept everything. There were tens of thousands of photos on the memory cards. Only this one was empty."

"Maybe it was new."

"Definitely not." She shook her head, and the wooden beads woven into her braids clicked softly against each other. "The other cards were high-quality with fast transfer rates; this one was standard from the electronics store."

"So someone wanted to make sure we didn't find anything on that card," Sandrine speculated.

"That's what I assume. But these printouts were in her desk drawer." Marie retrieved them from the folder and handed the images to Sandrine and Adel. "I have no idea if they have any significance for the case."

Sandrine turned the picture between her fingers. The victim had photographed de Saint-Clair's Ariste VI yacht. The man stood at the stern of the upper deck and was clearly visible. It was undoubtedly the port of Saint-Malo. In the background, she recognised the *Émeraude*, the Barnais' family's yacht. The woman on the *Émeraude*'s deck appeared to be Blanche, even though Sandrine had difficulty distinguishing her from her twin sister, Charlotte.

"That's Ariste de Saint-Clair." She pushed the photo towards Adel.

"Then he and Miriam Mignon knew each other," he said. "That should give the case a new twist."

Sandrine wasn't as optimistic as her assistant. Matisse expected hard evidence, and what she held in her hand was only a vague lead.

"It won't be enough," she finally said. "A photographer with thousands of pictures of Saint-Malo and its surroundings on her hard drive takes a snapshot of a luxury yacht in the harbour, coincidentally owned by de Saint-Clair. Any lawyer will tear that apart."

"True." He sounded frustrated.

Not as much as I am after chasing this man for almost a year and getting no closer. De Saint-Clair probably expects me to make another rash move, but not this time.

Inès waved at Sandrine and marched quickly through the open office space towards them.

"What's going on?" Adel asked. "You look like you have bad news."

"I can't assess it yet. But Capitaine Perrot is urgently needed." She sounded unusually formal in Jamila's presence, which made Sandrine smile.

"By Jogu or Baud, I assume. That can wait."

"No, Prosecutor de Chezac wants to see you. Urgently. At Commissaire Matisse's office."

"Everything that man does or wants is urgent." Her smile had disappeared. He rarely brought pleasant news. He probably wanted to wrap up the Mignon case quickly.

"He's not alone."

"Do you know who he brought with him?"

"The man at the reception said it's a group of three. I can't say more."

"Then I'd better get going. I don't want to keep our Prosecutor and his company waiting."

* * *

Sandrine knocked and entered. For a fraction of a second, her heart seemed to stop. She hesitated before continuing to the table. Sitting next to the prosecutor was Ariste de Saint-Clair. From the sly smile on his face, he hadn't missed her brief pause. He relished the impact his unexpected appearance had on her.

"This is the woman obsessed with trying to pin something on me," he said to his companion.

"Capitaine Perrot and I have already become acquainted," Lianne Roche replied.

Sandrine clenched her jaw tightly to avoid cursing out loud. Where had he picked up the damned lawyer? They had crossed paths in several cases, and Sandrine had seen the woman's dark side. If she had any other sides at all.

Sandrine pulled a chair closer and sat across from de Saint-Clair. Their eyes met, and she could sense the anger towards her beneath his sardonic facade.

"How nice of you to find the time to join us," de Chezac began, as if they had met for a friendly chat. "Since you have a suspicion against Monsieur de Saint-Clair, I took the liberty of inviting him for a conversation at the police station."

"Which I willingly accepted," he said towards the prosecutor. "As I seem to be under false suspicion once again, I asked Madame Roche to accompany me. She was highly recommended to me as a very competent lawyer."

In the first moment, only one person came to mind who knew how much Sandrine despised the lawyer, and a glance at the smirk on de Chezac's face confirmed her suspicion. He must have been the one who mentioned the woman to de Saint-Clair.

"Capitaine Perrot is quick to suspect law-abiding citizens," the woman remarked, trying vehemently to please him through her disparaging comments.

"If you need a Rottweiler in fancy clothes, you've found the right person in Madame Roche," Sandrine replied as calmly as she could manage, despite her tension.

"Capitaine Perrot!" the prosecutor interjected immediately, while Lianne Roche shot a venomous glance across the table, and de Saint-Clair chuckled softly. He knew that in this room, there were only two people of interest: him and Sandrine. The rest were mere extras in his performance.

"You haven't changed since we said goodbye in Paris," de

Saint-Clair said to her. "I like that." It wasn't a compliment; rather, an acknowledgment that she remained a formidable adversary.

"I can say the same about you," she replied.

"You flatter me."

"Not necessarily. You come to Saint-Malo, a young woman dies shortly thereafter, and you appear at the crime scene. It all sounds very familiar."

"Capitaine Perrot." Now the interjection came from Commissaire Matisse but Sandrine didn't respond to his interruption. She maintained her gaze with de Saint-Clair, like two boxers trying to assess their opponent and search for weaknesses.

"Monsieur de Saint-Clair was kind enough to come to us to dispel any suspicions," Antoine de Chezac said.

"That's correct." The man broke eye contact with her and turned to Commissaire Matisse. "Even though Madame Perrot may think I'm following her to Brittany, I'm only here to spend some time on my new boat, the Ariste VI. Business doesn't leave me much leisure time."

"What happened to the Ariste V?" Sandrine asked.

"You remember it, do you? Well, it's still docked at the Basin de l'Arsenal in Paris. I should've sold it, but I have some fond memories associated with it. Perhaps I'm too sentimental."

Sandrine scrutinised the man's face carefully. Sentimentality was certainly not one of his personality traits. What was he trying to convey? Maybe a reference to the last murder in Paris? The victim was found in the Canal Saint-Martin, which ended in the Basin de l'Arsenal. She had assumed the body was thrown into the canal from a dinghy of the Ariste V. *Is he mocking me, or is there more to it?*

"Enough chit-chat. Let's get to the point. We docked here last week, and I have never met this young woman. If I understood Monsieur de Chezac correctly, the woman was killed on Sunday night and found on the beach on Monday. Is that correct so far?"

Sandrine nodded in agreement.

"I was on the boat Sunday evening and didn't leave it. I had invited some guests for a casual reception. My crew can confirm that."

"Many people who depend on you. Not good witnesses." Just like in Paris.

"In these times, one should be glad to find any staff at all. There's no talk of dependency," Lianne Roche chimed in. She was trying to establish herself, but her sole purpose in being there was to provoke and tempt Sandrine into prematurely revealing her evidence.

"What interest would I have in this person?" de Saint-Clair asked.

"She fits the pattern we both know from Paris: young, blonde, blue-eyed. Add to that, she was an artist, and she was strangled. It should sound familiar to you."

"Of course. Since you suspected me, I've been following the investigations in the newspapers. You weren't particularly successful, as we both know." His smooth smile confirmed her suspicion that he was not only referring to failing to convict him but also to the file she had copied from him. He knew that she had struggled to open it, and failed.

She retrieved one of the photos Marie had given her from the file and slid it across the table to him. "If you didn't know her, why do we have a photo of you shot by the victim?"

"A nice snapshot." He showed the picture to his lawyer. "May I have a copy?"

"You can keep it. We have plenty more," Sandrine said.

"My client is a public figure and is frequently photographed by paparazzi. Additionally, a yacht of this size rarely docks in the marina. It doesn't seem far-fetched that a photographer would seize the opportunity for a picture," Lianne Roche defended.

Sandrine thought of the charcoal drawing she had found in the deceased's studio. However, she left it in the file. The resemblance to de Saint-Clair was too vague to pass as evidence. It would only highlight how thin their case against the man was. De Chezac had warned him, and he had gone on the offensive too early for her. She needed more time to investigate the case, but after this meeting, even Commissaire Matisse wouldn't have her back.

"I don't see how the police could maintain any serious allegations," Lianne Roche said. "We should end this charade. Do we want to waste more taxpayer money and endanger the good reputation of the Saint-Malo police?"

"Listen to my lawyer. It seems I have a permanent residence in your mind. Whenever a crime occurs, you seem to think of me first, for whatever reason," de Saint-Clair said, standing up. "Should you wish to speak to me again, contact me through Madame Roche." He shook hands with de Chezac and Matisse before leaving the room, ignoring Sandrine.

De Chezac waited until de Saint-Clair and his lawyer had left before turning to Commissaire Matisse. "I gave you a chance for questioning, but Capitaine Perrot had nothing but her gut feeling, no real trump card to play. Close the case. Brigadier Poutin had the murder weapon in his possession, and his suicide was practically a confession. For me, the investigation is closed."

Sandrine reached for the file to retrieve the photos of the two men on the tower, but she decided against it. The prosecutor had made his decision, and two blurry photos wouldn't be enough to change his mind.

"I expect the reports," he said and stood up.

"It was him," Sandrine muttered.

"You're getting lost in fantasies again. First in Paris, and now here. The man seems to be right; he practically lives in your head." He moved closer to her. "Suppose he were the Necktie Killer, which he's not. Why would he come here to murder a woman? Do you really believe he cares about you to that extent?"

"He made a mistake, and now he's here to clean up after himself," she said, addressing Commissaire Matisse, then turning to de Chezac. "There will be more deaths."

"Stop it," he said with resignation. "Or I'll have to have you evaluated for fitness for duty, and that's not in either of our interests." He nodded at Commissaire Matisse and left them alone.

"Do you really believe that?" her boss asked.

"I am convinced that de Saint-Clair is a murderer, and I fear the murders will continue."

"Do you believe he instigated Brigadier Poutin to plant drugs on your friend?"

"The attempt failed, and Poutin can't testify anymore."

"Who do you think the next victim could be?"

"I don't know; otherwise, I would issue a warning to them."

"You'd better take care of yourself. If your theory is correct, you could easily be the next victim." Matisse sounded concerned.

"That's possible, but rather unlikely. He would immediately become the prime suspect. Besides, he's more interested in destroying my reputation than suffocating me."

"Hopefully you're right. Should I assign a police officer to accompany you for safety?"

"No, that's unnecessary. I can take care of myself." She took the photos of the two men from the tower out of the file and handed them to her boss. "These are the two who were involved in the murder and its failed cover-up. Does either of them look like Poutin?"

He looked at the photos for a while before placing them on

the table. "It's hard to tell. It's dark, and the pictures aren't very clear. I can't rule out that it might have been him."

She closed the file and left his office. She sighed and let her shoulders slump. *That's enough for today.*

Sandrine decided it was quitting time. The questioning by Jogu and Baud could wait until tomorrow.

On the Run

The next morning, Sandrine sat in her garden in front of her cottage. The gloomy clouds of the previous day were just a memory, and a brilliantly blue sky stretched over the bay. She took a deep breath; the air was fresh and carried the scent of pine trees that covered the steep slope behind the hiking trail. A sailboat slowly cruised along the coast, and in the clear morning air, Mont-Saint-Michel on the horizon was clearly visible. A smile formed on her lips. Moments like this made her forget her frustration with de Chezac and the crimes she faced as a police officer. She was happy in Cancale and felt more at home here than she ever had in Paris. Yesterday, after the meeting with de Saint-Clair and his lawyer, she had briefly considered quitting her job, but her anger had quickly dissipated. Whether she liked it or not, she had to admit that the evidence against de Saint-Clair was too weak to lead to an indictment. Not yet. But one thing she would definitely not do was give up.

On the garden table, there was a bowl of freshly brewed coffee and a small pitcher of hot milk. In the kitchen, she had found a piece of yesterday's baguette, which she sliced, lightly toasted, and spread with coarse Pâté de Campagne. A dab of

Dijon mustard and the last pickles from the jar. A rather luxurious breakfast by her standards.

She heard the voice of Rosalie, her friend and the tenant of the main house, getting closer. Shortly after, she appeared around the corner of the former sheepfold.

"I guessed right; she's in the garden," she said to someone who seemed to be following her. Behind her, a petite woman in a vintage beige dress, about half a head shorter than Rosalie, appeared. Sandrine estimated her to be in her mid-fifties. She looked at Rosalie, as if she needed her permission to enter the garden. Only when Rosalie nodded did she cautiously step onto the neatly trimmed lawn.

Sandrine stood up and approached her. She had never seen the stranger before, but she believed she knew who she was.

"Madame Poutin? Anne Poutin?"

"Do you know me?" With wide eyes, the woman looked at her in astonishment. "We have never met."

Sandrine recalled the family photos on the sideboard in Poutin's living room. But it seemed inappropriate to inform the woman that she had explored the house without her consent, even though the circumstances had required it. There was no right to privacy when a violent death occurred.

"I'm very sorry for what happened to your husband. Please, have a seat." Sandrine pulled a garden chair up to the table. "Can I offer you something? Perhaps some coffee?"

"What happened to my Luc?" the woman asked in a toneless voice. Tears welled up in her eyes instantly. She seemed to have genuinely loved her husband. She sat down and looked around. "You have a lovely place here, and the garden looks so well-kept."

"I owe that to my friend, Rosalie. Unfortunately, I don't have a green thumb."

"Luc didn't either. Besides mowing the lawn, he wasn't much use in the garden." She pulled a tissue from her beige handbag and dabbed her tear-filled eyes. "Why did you say something happened to my Luc? Don't you believe it's a suicide?"

"Do you?"

"No," she replied instantly. "Luc would never take his own life. We've been married for over thirty years. He may have had his faults, but he would never leave me behind. He always took responsibility for his actions."

"I didn't know your husband well enough to assess that."

"That's why it's important for me to talk to you."

"I'm very sorry, but I'm not in charge of the investigation into your husband's death. You need to contact Prosecutor Hermé at the police station in Saint-Malo. He will answer your questions about the progress of the investigation." *And he will handle the woman with more sensitivity than de Chezac would.*

"I didn't want to leave him alone, but he insisted I go stay with my sister in Normandy for a while. If only I had stayed here…"

"You are not to blame for what happened. Please don't blame yourself."

"He must have had a premonition. He kept asking me to go to you if something happened to him. Only to you, to no one else. He was very insistent."

"To me? Honestly, I'm surprised by that. We didn't exactly have a harmonious relationship."

She studied Sandrine for a while, as if trying to figure out what she could say without offending

her.

"Luc couldn't stand you, I know that. Not a day went by at home without him cursing you."

"I'm sorry. I wasn't aware that I had mistreated him."

"My husband was certainly not an easy person. Once he got fixated on an idea, it was hard for him to let go. In any case, he thought you—forgive me—were an arrogant Parisian who had no idea about life in Brittany and didn't respect her colleagues."

"Then I see even less reason why he would have sent you to me." Sandrine was confused about what the woman wanted from her and mentally prepared herself for accusations that she was partly responsible for his death.

"Despite all his dislike, he thought you were a good investigator," she said, much to Sandrine's surprise. "He asked me to give this to you if something happened to him." Anne Poutin took a transparent bag from her handbag and placed it on the table in front of Sandrine. She could tell at first glance that it was an evidence bag containing a brown padded envelope. The woman's fingers nervously stroked the faux leather of her handbag. She clearly realised that her husband had gotten involved in criminal activities, and it seemed she deeply disapproved.

"Do you know what's inside the envelope?"

Madame Poutin nodded. Her fingers stopped running over the bag, and instead she clung to it, as if she needed some kind of support, no matter how useless it was.

"It's money," she said hesitantly, as if it was an admission of her own guilt. "But I didn't know about it until Luc gave it to me last week." She bit her lip and lowered her gaze. Sandrine waited until the woman was ready to continue.

"25,000 euros. That's what Luc claimed. I haven't touched the envelope. But I believe him."

"That's a lot of money." She knew what a brigadier earned. The man would have had to save for a long time to accumulate that sum. "Where did he get it?"

"He wouldn't tell me, but I suspect it's related to the events his colleagues are investigating him for."

Sandrine pulled the envelope towards herself. It felt heavier than expected. Besides money, there must be something else inside. She decided against opening it. It would be better for Jean-Claude or one of his forensic experts to handle it. She could easily destroy evidence by touching it.

"And he didn't mention who gave it to him?"

"No, not a word."

"You should talk to Prosecutor Hermé about this. He's in charge of the investigation. Unfortunately, my hands are tied."

"I will never go to the police station. His colleagues look at me with disdain. They all believe he was a criminal and that's why he hanged himself, but Luc wasn't." Anne Poutin turned her head and looked towards the bay, as if she couldn't bear to make eye contact with Sandrine any longer. She probably felt ashamed of what her husband had done.

Sandrine nodded sympathetically. Her husband had committed a crime, there was no doubt about that, but now de Chezac was trying to pin the murder of Miriam Mignon on him, and for all his faults, he didn't deserve that.

"I will hand over the envelope to Prosecutor Hermé. He will take care of it."

"Luc had placed his hope in you," she replied with a mixture of disappointment and determination in her frail voice.

"I'll do my best to see what I can do for your husband," she promised. "Are you here with a car? If not, I can give you a ride home."

"That won't be necessary. My sister brought me here, and she's waiting in the car."

"If you need anything, don't hesitate to call me."

"Thank you. Renard is helping us organise the funeral and get the house in order. I wouldn't know how to manage without him."

"That's a good thing." She hadn't expected anything less from Brigadier Dubois. "He can take as much time as he needs to support you."

"Thank you." She placed her hands on the chair's armrests, pushed herself up, and headed towards the main house. After a few steps, she turned back to Sandrine. "You're not at all like how Luc described you. I wish I had met you earlier."

Before Sandrine could respond, she turned and disappeared around the corner of the house.

* * *

Adel met her in the open-plan office.

"The people from Rennes are pretty upset that you stood them up yesterday. You better call Hermé right away and smooth things over. Commandant Jogu has already complained to Matisse about you."

"I wasn't in the mood to hear more nonsense after what de Saint-Clair and our prosecutor fed me."

"That bad?"

"Looks like it for now, but we'll see how it develops. Maybe I can get Hermé on our side."

"Good luck."

"First, I need to go to the forensics lab. Will you come with me?"

"Sure. Does it have something to do with our case?"

"Maybe. I can't say yet. It depends on what's inside this." She lifted the bag she held in her right hand. "Anne Poutin gave it to me this morning." *And it's surprisingly heavy for supposed cash.*

They found Jean-Claude Mazet at his desk, typing away with two fingers. Beside the keyboard, there was a half-full coffee cup and several torn sugar packets. It couldn't be his first coffee of the day.

"I hope you're bringing me something interesting. Writing reports is not exactly my favourite pastime."

"This might be a welcome change." Sandrine placed the bag on his desk.

"That's a bag we use, if I'm not mistaken. Where did the envelope come from?"

"It was given to me by a witness. It needs to be examined. Full analysis."

Mazet took the cup and finished his coffee, then put on a pair of gloves and opened the bag.

"Quite heavy." He weighed the envelope in his hand. "Feels like coins." With a letter opener, he cut it open at the top, looked inside, and carefully emptied its contents onto a tray. More than a dozen gold coins fell out.

Sandrine leaned over. "Krugerrands," she muttered as Mazet typed something into the computer and then photographed the coins.

"Each of these is worth almost 2,000 euros," the forensic expert said. "There are 13 of them, so around 25 to 26,000 euros. A nice sum. Where did it come from? A drug dealer?"

"Why do you think that?" Adel asked.

"Gold coins are freely tradable. Their origin is hard to trace, and you can easily turn them into cash. Ideal for illicit deals or as a fallback if everything collapses here."

Sandrine looked around. Except for Marie and Jamila, the office was empty.

"Anne Poutin brought it to me this morning."

"Anne? To you?" He scratched his head. "Well, that's something."

"Can we keep the source confidential until I've spoken with Hermé and Matisse? I don't want to further fuel the rumour mill about Poutin's death."

"Well, I have to enter a case number when I examine it. But I can wait until this afternoon. Any longer might be difficult."

"That's enough time. By then, I will have talked to Hermé. He'll have to decide whether the coins should be linked to his case or mine." What happens next will have to be worked out between the two prosecutors, Sandrine thought. *It's becoming increasingly difficult to sustain Poutin as Miriam Mignon's murderer and his death as a suicide.*

***

"Come in, Capitaine Perrot," Sébastian Hermé called out. He and Major Baud were sitting at an elongated table in a meeting room assigned to them by Commissaire Matisse for their investigations.

"You didn't show up for questioning yesterday," Major Baud stated accusingly.

"I had a tough day. Today, I'm at your disposal. How's your progress?" Sandrine inquired.

"Excellent," she replied. "Your boyfriend was questioned yesterday. He was much more cooperative than you. But you probably already know that."

"Léon is friendlier and more accommodating than I am," Sandrine commented as she took a step towards Major Baud. Her uniform looked as impeccably ironed and starched as always, her hair was neatly brushed back into a perfect bun. The woman seemed to abhor any variation, at least in her professional attire.

"I won't comment on that now," Major Baud replied, clearly expressing her opinion about Sandrine.

"You don't have to. It's evident," Sandrine said, pulling out the photo she had received from Léon from her back pocket, handing it to the policewoman. "The loose hair suits you. Personally, the dress would be a bit too daring for my taste, but you have the figure to carry it off."

"Where did you..."

Sandrine savoured the moment as the woman struggled to find words before finally sitting down beside Sébastian Hermé.

"If you're sending undercover officers into the club, they should behave and dress less conspicuously. Léon's employees mistook Major Baud for a drug dealer testing the market."

Sandrine kept the part about them mistaking her for a prostitute to herself, as the atmosphere between them was already tense enough. She decided not to further provoke the woman, which wasn't easy for her.

The prosecutor grinned broadly. "May I have a look?" he asked, reaching out towards his colleague, but Major Baud quickly tucked the picture into her trouser pocket.

"I was there privately to assess the club," she said. "Of course, I can't appear there in uniform."

"Unfortunately, I don't have a copy," Sandrine said, attempting to convey regret in her voice. "I suspect the drug haul at Équinoxe wasn't particularly significant."

"So, what brings you here?" Hermé interrupted.

"Prosecutor de Chezac has determined that Poutin was the murderer of Miriam Mignon. Therefore, I will have to halt the investigation per his instructions," Sandrine explained.

"A bold theory," she heard the investigator comment, and Sandrine turned around in surprise. She hadn't expected any support from Major Baud.

"I agree," Hermé also concurred. "Yesterday, the two forensic technicians were here. What a stroke of luck that you spotted the camera in the pictures. I probably would have missed it. I only knew Brigadier Poutin from one interrogation, but neither of the two men in the pictures bear a striking resemblance to him. The quality of the images is quite poor, and all we can deduce from them is that there are two different men, primarily due to their clothing. Based on these photos, I wouldn't dare connect Brigadier Poutin to the murder of Mademoiselle Mignon."

"The rope, which has skin traces of Miriam Mignon and was found with Poutin, is enough to link him to the murder," Sandrine argued. Her hope of gaining support from Hermé was growing. The man was rational and open to reasoned arguments.

"Major Baud already expressed some doubts about the

suicide theory yesterday. But please, go on," the prosecutor urged his investigator.

"These are just circumstantial pieces of evidence, but they contradict the suicide theory. Individually, I might not consider them significant, but together, they must be taken into account. There was no smoke in the man's lungs, which seems strange to me. The furnishings are not of high quality and consist mainly of plastic. There should have been a rapid development of smoke. If he didn't run away immediately, I would have expected smoke particles in his lungs. Then there's the matter of the gasoline canister. I spoke to the neighbour, and he's convinced that nothing is missing from it. So where did the accelerant come from? Not from inside the house. Another canister was never found.

"It's possible that the perpetrator brought gasoline and took it with him after noticing the canister in the garage. If it had belonged to Poutin, we would never have been able to determine if anything was missing or not."

Hermé nodded for her to continue.

"Then there's the issue of the Cognac bottle. The brand was too expensive for the man, and the unidentified fingerprints remain unexplained for now. In the kitchen, there's another bottle of Cognac from the supermarket, a rather cheap brand. Based on the layer of dust on it, no one in the household regularly drinks it. Anne Poutin uses it for the Mousse au Chocolat. Poutin only drank Lambig or Pastis," Sandrine explained.

"That's what Brigadier Dubois told us, and no one doubts it. So, where did the high-quality liquor come from, and who is the person who handled the bottle, besides Poutin? Probably the generous but anonymous donor. We need to find out who that is."

Sandrine looked at Major Baud. Perhaps she had been mistaken about the woman. It seemed she wasn't biased and was pursuing her investigation with determination and impartiality, like a steamroller. Her intuition told her that Major Baud wasn't involved with Poutin's accomplices. That left Commandant Jogu, whom she was still unsure about.

"Unfortunately, Madame Poutin has not contacted us yet. She is no longer in Normandy," Hermé said.

"She is back in Saint-Malo. She visited me this morning and gave me something from her husband." Sandrine placed her phone with the picture of the gold coins on the table.

"Krügerrand," Hermé murmured in astonishment. "How did she get her hands on those? They surely weren't hidden away in a piggy bank."

"Her husband gave them to her when he sent her to Normandy. According to her, he was afraid something might happen to him."

"And then she brings them to you of all people? Strange." Major Baud shook her head in disbelief. "The man couldn't stand you and got into trouble because of you."

"Not because of Capitaine Perrot, but because of a wrong decision he made himself," Hermé corrected the policewoman.

"He was sure that I would investigate the matter," Sandrine said.

"Which, in turn, would mean that he assumed other investigators wouldn't, but would sweep it under the rug." Hermé continued Sandrine's thoughts.

"At least, that's what he claimed to me, that nothing would happen to him in Saint-Malo, except for a slap on the wrist. Poutin was convinced he would be protected."

Hermé leaned back, interlocking his arms behind his neck. "There aren't many who would have such influence. Matisse, de Chezac, perhaps someone in politics."

"Or someone from our team," Major Baud added. "I think that's what Capitaine Perrot is getting at." Sandrine looked at her in shock. Today, the woman managed to constantly surprise her, and in a positive way.

"Don't pretend to be so amazed!" the policewoman snapped at Sandrine. "I had the same thought. Poutin sat here, exuding arrogance."

"It is certainly not me," Hermé said. "And I can vouch for my people. None of us protects Brigadier Poutin."

"The same is true for Matisse." Sandrine would vouch for him without a doubt.

"These are gold coins," Hermé noted. "Judas received only silver coins for his betrayal. Denigrating you is worth much more to someone."

"If we account for 2000 years of inflation, probably not," Sandrine replied, laughing.

"He probably received payment for planting drugs on Capitaine Perrot's partner. It underscores the doubts we had about the suicide," Major Baud remarked. "Someone might have silenced him as an undesirable witness."

She agreed with the woman.

"We need to speak with de Chezac," Hermé decided. "His secretary said he would be working from home today. I've tried calling him several times, but he's not picking up. Either he needs absolute quiet to work, or he's by the pool and doesn't want to be disturbed." By the way Hermé grimaced, he seemed to lean more towards the latter. He pointed his index finger at Sandrine. "The man lives near Cancale, just like you. It's best if we go together; it will be faster."

"I don't think that's a good idea. He's not exactly fond of me." Above all, she had no intention of getting involved in a dispute between the two men who outranked her in the hierarchy. It could mean her career taking a few more hits.

"Nonsense. We need to find a common approach in the investigations, and you're the only person involved in both cases." He retrieved the car keys from his desk. "Besides, you know the way."

She nodded. She had little choice. At least they wouldn't be interrupting de Chezac during brunch on de Saint-Clair's yacht.

* * *

Antoine de Chezac's house was perched on a hill above the wide sandy beach of Port Mer, a suburb of Cancale sloping gently to the sea.

"Not bad." Sandrine approached the hedge and admired her boss's home. It wasn't particularly large, but it had a panoramic glass front on the ground floor that offered a magnificent view of the beach and the sailing club. The man had only been in Saint-Malo for a few months and probably wouldn't stay long; he was too ambitious for that. Therefore, she assumed he hadn't bought the house but was renting it; if any house could be had in such a popular location at all.

"Come on," Hermé urged her. "We're police officers, not real estate agents. You can admire the house after we've spoken with him."

"Fine, I just didn't realise that prosecutors were paid well enough to afford such a gem in this location." She thought he deserved the pointed remark.

"We're not paid that well. But apparently, it's an advantage to come from a wealthy family."

The garden gate was unlocked, and Hermé marched straight to the front door. Sandrine followed him and watched as he pressed his finger to the doorbell. A sentimental melody sounded from inside. Another indication that de Chezac was renting. Otherwise, he wouldn't have tolerated such a thing.

"Come on," Hermé muttered impatiently, taking two steps back to look at the windows on the first floor. There was no movement.

"Wait here, maybe he's in the shower and needs some time to look presentable," Sandrine said. "I'll check behind the house;

perhaps he's in the garden." Which was unlikely. He was certainly not the type of person who enjoyed gardening, and it was too shady there for a pool or a nice terrace.

Even at the backside of the house, which looked far less impressive than the front, there was no sign of the man. Sandrine approached an unadorned door and pulled a pick lock set from her pocket. Something wasn't right. If de Chezac wanted to take a day off, he could have done so without bothering to come up with an excuse like working from home, especially not to someone who was subservient to him, like his secretary. He probably forgot her name regularly.

She pressed the doorknob, and it opened. The prosecutor seemed to have forgotten to lock it, which was something she found hard to believe. She put away the unused lock-pick and entered the house. The entrance led to a utility room. Next to the washing machine and dryer was a table with folded laundry, an ironing board, and cleaning supplies on a shelf. A suit, still bearing the dry cleaner's tag on the lapel, hung on a rod. The realm of his cleaning lady. She couldn't picture de Chezac using an ironing board.

She walked through the hallway into the living room and stopped abruptly. Several designer chairs made of chrome-plated steel and black plastic were arranged around an oval dining table, the sight of which made her back ache. Two more chairs were on the floor, next to a lamp and some cushions that had fallen off the beige sofa after someone had tipped it over. Books and magazines were scattered around. A fight had taken place here.

She quickly went to the door and opened it for Hermé.
"How did you...?"
"The back door was open."
"Really? That doesn't fit the man at all."
She stepped aside and let him pass.
"Take a look at the living room."

Hermé took a step inside and looked around. Sandrine remained silent behind him; she didn't want to disturb his concentration. Eventually, he turned to her.

"A definite fight has taken place here. There might be blood over there." He pointed to a smudged stain on the light sofa's cover.

"If it's blood, it's only a small amount. No one seems to have suffered a major injury. Which surprises me. The way it looks here, there was a serious brawl."

"Two people have died in Saint-Malo in the last few days, and neither of them lost blood. Who knows what happened here," he said, and concern was evident in his voice.

"Maybe one of the two got a hit on the nose or lip during the fight. It couldn't have been much more than that." Sandrine attended martial arts training several times a week and was familiar with the types of injuries one could sustain in a fistfight.

"Let's hope you're right, Sandrine." Hermé switched to the familiar form of address since they were alone. "But who could have attacked him?"

"Who knows, but it seems clear that someone is covering their tracks. First, Brigadier Poutin is murdered, and then Prosecutor de Chezac disappears."

"The two don't seem to have much in common."

"I am the link," she said. "Poutin tried to deceive Léon to harm me. When we ran into each other at the beach, he claimed to be protected from high up. Maybe he was referring to de Chezac, or maybe someone even higher, who knows? In any case, he acted on orders; he would never have confronted me without backup. It must be someone from the police force; Poutin would never have trusted a civilian."

For a while, she had been convinced that de Chezac had tried to get rid of her. The man had despised her for a long time. She remembered her conversation with Suzanne Leriche. The prosecutor was a narcissist, the kind she referred to as vulnerable narcissists. He had probably felt disrespected or even humiliated by her on many occasions. Someone like him reacted aggressively to such situations. She would have believed him capable of bribing Poutin to frame Léon with drugs, but murdering Brigadier Poutin? *Not to discredit me, but to save his own neck, I can believe that of him. If Poutin had spilled the beans, de Chezac would have gone down with him. But now I need to reconsider this theory. The man has become a victim himself. Who knows if he's still alive.*

"After his wife delivered the gold coins, it's hardly deniable that someone plotted against you. The question is, who is behind it?"

Sandrine remained silent. The list of suspects had greatly narrowed with de Chezac's disappearance, but she wouldn't be the first to utter the name de Saint-Clair. She possessed the file she had stolen from him, and she would bet everything on it containing information about the Necktie Killer. *But I can't open the damn thing.*

"Do you believe this Saint-Clair is the so-called Necktie Killer you were chasing in Paris?" he asked.

"I'm convinced of it."

"And now he has surfaced in Saint-Malo."

"And a few days later, a murder occurs that is identical to the ones in Paris, down to the last detail."

"There are some differences."

"Somebody made an effort to make the body disappear and contaminate the crime scene."

"But we don't know who that was."

"Someone who knew about the murder and wanted to cover it up. Committing a murder right under my nose was probably too risky for an accomplice. Maybe the same person who got rid of Poutin. One less witness."

"And now de Chezac?"

"Perhaps the prosecutor is also one of the accomplices and

was the one Poutin relied on. After all, he had already protected de Saint-Clair in Paris," she mused.

"He was the lead prosecutor in the case back then. Maybe he started to doubt de Saint-Clair's innocence, and someone got scared he might reopen the investigation here in Saint-Malo."

"Unlikely. He closed the case and declared Poutin the murderer."

"Based on the crime scene photos and the evidence Major Baud found, it's not that simple anymore. He'll have no choice but to reopen the case. I think it's possible someone wanted to prevent that or at least buy some time to disappear."

"Could be. But speculations won't get us any further." Sandrine took out her phone and called the police station. The forensic team needed to thoroughly examine the house. Afterwards, she took a chair from the kitchen and sat in the living room. Something about the room bothered her, but she couldn't quite put her finger on what it was.

* * *

An hour later, the black van from the forensics team pulled into the driveway of the house.

"You keep us quite busy." Jean-Claude Mazet greeted them at the front door.

"If it were up to me, you could sit in the lab and play on the computer all day. It's the criminals who keep you busy, not me."

Behind him, two of his team members appeared, along with Jamila, who had already put on the blue disposable coverall.

"She insisted on coming," the head of forensics explained, noticing Sandrine's gaze. "If I understood you correctly, there's neither a body nor pools of blood here. So, she can get a good impression of crime scene work." He turned to face Sandrine. "The tasks of forensics are at least as exciting as those of investigators, and highly demanding," he said towards the intern, as if conducting a job interview. She must have made a truly excellent impression.

"And Adel doesn't mind me being here," she said to Sandrine, likely trying to pre-empt the question.

"Then I'm reassured. I hope you asked him before getting into the van, and not just shortly before Cancale?" Sandrine asked.

"Of course, I did," Mazet assured her. "Although I don't think it's necessary, as Jamila works under my supervision. But I know that he's quite protective when it comes to his sister, so I gave him a call."

Sandrine nodded in agreement and led them to the living room.

"It looks like a mess. The prosecutor must have put up quite a fight. I wouldn't have expected that from the man," Mazet remarked, placing his equipment case on the floor.

"Can you tell me what that is and how old it is?" Hermé pointed to the dark stain.

"Probably," the forensics expert said. He took a bottle of luminol and a cotton swab, dabbing it onto the stain. "Looks relatively fresh. I'd guess it dripped onto the fabric only a few hours ago." He glanced at his watch. "Around breakfast time."

"Blood?" Hermé inquired.

Mazet held up the bottle. "This is a luminol solution," he said towards Jamila and sprayed some on to the cotton swab, which turned blue at the top. "When the solution comes into contact with iron, as found in hemoglobin in blood, it produces a bluish chemiluminescence, as you can see here." He handed the swab to the girl. "Take a close look at it and pack it carefully."

"Will do," she replied and went out, probably to fetch an evidence bag from the van.

"She's exceptionally clever and handles herself well. Make sure we keep her," Mazet said as he passed by. "Plus, she makes an excellent couscous with chicken."

The man's visible belly indicated his appreciation for a good meal. But she wouldn't argue with him; Jamila had left a positive impression, especially since she had discovered the camera by the window, which had been a significant breakthrough.

"We have evidence of a fight and blood. I've issued a missing person report for de Chezac," Hermé informed them. "He's unlikely to have stumbled and bumped his nose into the floor lamp."

"I need a signature, then I can prioritise the DNA lab tests. We should know by tomorrow at the latest if the blood belongs to de Chezac," Mazet said.

"You'll find it on your desk once you're back at the lab," assured the prosecutor.

"I have something here," one of the forensics experts said, entering the living room. He held a slim leather-bound appointment book in his hand, which he handed to Sandrine. The initials AdC were embossed on the cover, clearly belonging to de Chezac. It seemed that he only entered private appointments here. She quickly flipped to the current date.

"And?" Hermé prompted.

"There's nothing scheduled for this morning, but he was invited for dinner on de Saint-Clair's yacht yesterday evening."

"Then we'll scrutinise that man closely." He turned to Mazet. "Capitaine Perrot and I will head back to Saint-Malo and organise the search for the yacht. If you find any slightest hint about the man's whereabouts, call me immediately."

"Agreed."

* * *

They drove directly to the Saint-Malo marina, where Adel was already waiting for them with Commandant Jogu and two uniformed policemen.

"Do you have the search warrant?" Hermé asked his colleague.

"You just need to sign it." Jogu handed him an open folder with the document, which Hermé quickly signed.

At the railing, they were greeted by two men. The younger and more muscular of the two blocked their way.

"How can we assist you?"

"I'm Prosecutor Hermé," he introduced himself. "We have a search warrant. Where can we find Monsieur de Saint-Clair?"

"May I see it?" He reached out for the document.

"Who are you?" Hermé inquired.

"My name is Aubert, and I'm responsible for Monsieur de Saint-Clair's security and the yacht," he replied, pointing to the older man. "Monsieur Melan is the Capitaine."

"If you're the bodyguard, you should know where your boss is," Hermé said impatiently.

"Just a moment," he said and turned towards the entrance to the middle deck. In the doorway appeared Lianne Roche in a grey business outfit. "Our lawyer will review the document."

"She can do that while we start the search," Hermé said, taking a step towards the muscular man who didn't move from his spot.

"Move aside," Hermé warned him. A glance at Commandant Jogu, whose hand rested on the pistol grip, made him relent and he allowed the prosecutor to pass.

"That was very wise," Hermé remarked.

"Madame," he greeted Lianne Roche. "Where is your client? If his bodyguard doesn't know, perhaps his lawyer does. It should be within your purview, shouldn't it?"

The forced smile on the woman's face faded, and she shot an angry look at the prosecutor and Sandrine, conveying that she also had no idea of her client's whereabouts.

"He's away on business," the woman lied. Sandrine could assess Lianne Roche quite well. The lawyer hated having to admit she had no idea where her client was and, probably even more, knowing how unimportant she was to de Saint-Clair. Lianne Roche was smart enough to have figured out by now that she had only been hired to provoke Sandrine. In this game she was, at best, playing second fiddle, which she found difficult to bear.

"Then let's look around the boat and wait for his return," Hermé decided. He signalled to the police officers and Jogu to start the search.

Sandrine entered through the door onto the mid-deck of the yacht. In front of her stretched an expansive living area with nearly continuous windows. The tinted glass minimally obstructed the view outside but preserved the passengers' privacy. A table made of reddish shimmering wood, large enough to accommodate a dozen people, dominated the space. In the middle, there was a fruit basket adorned with flowers and an open bottle of champagne in a cooler. It appeared they had interrupted Lianne Roche's meal. A used plate and a half-full glass were still on the table. Sandrine paused at the door to take in the details of the room. Where would one hide something here? Nowhere. There would be too many people around. Unless it's something that looks inconspicuous and can be left out in the open. She snapped her fingers and crossed the room. At the back was the bar. She scanned the shelf of bottles, some worth the price of a mid-range car. *There it is.* She put on some gloves and took the oval bottle of Cognac from the shelf.

"Albert de Montaubert, 1963," she muttered. The same brand she had found at Poutin's. This couldn't be a coincidence.

Hermé joined her. "Do you believe the bottle at Poutin's came from here?"

"It's hard for me to imagine that de Saint-Clair invited our brigadier onto his yacht, but it's entirely possible that the bottle came from here. He might have given it to him."

"Hard to prove," Hermé mumbled.

"Unless the fingerprints on this bottle match the unidentified ones we found on the bottle at Poutin's."

"Do you think he was that foolish?"

"Everyone makes mistakes. Even someone like de Saint-Clair." That was her hope, even though her previous experiences with the man contradicted it. She considered him an inflated snob, but she had to admit he was highly intelligent and had not made any mistakes in Paris. After a year of intensive investigation, the police were essentially empty-handed.

Commandant Jogu came up the stairs from the lower deck, holding one of the evidence bags.

"I found this in the main cabin's desk. A key with a Saint-Malo city administration key-chain. It seems out of place here."

Sandrine moved closer to inspect the key, which seemed to fit a cylinder lock.

"Miriam Mignon had a key to Tour Bidouane. I found her clothing and personal items there, but the key was missing. We assumed the killer locked up after hiding the woman's things."

"And he takes the key with him," Jogu wondered. "I would have thrown it in the nearest trash can or into the sea. I have no idea what the man was thinking by keeping it. In any case, it was a terribly foolish idea. If we find Miriam Mignon's fingerprints on it, he won't be able to explain it away."

"Maybe he needs a memento of his victims. Many serial killers keep souvenirs that they look at to relive their deeds and revel in their power over their victims," said Sandrine.

"Regardless, let's secure the bottle and key as evidence and take them straight to the lab. Fingerprints will be taken, and then we'll know more. Commandant Jogu, arrange for the boat to be vacated by the staff and block access until the forensics team arrives. The forensics experts will have to work overtime today."

"Understood," the man agreed and left.

"This guy's days are numbered," Hermé said. "The net is closing in."

"I hope so."

Sandrine had been waiting for this moment. Excitement welled up inside her, making her legs tremble. It was crucial not to make any mistakes now. The man was intelligent, but he was at least as arrogant; otherwise, he would never have left the key here. The fact that the police would dare to search his boat clearly seemed beyond the man's imagination.

* * *

Hermé and Jogu had returned to the police station while she hoped to hear something from the forensics team that arrived about fifteen minutes ago. In these investigations, she had spent a lot of time waiting for Jean-Claude Mazet and his team. Now she hoped it had been worth it. While waiting, she made herself comfortable on one of the sun loungers at the stern of the yacht. If only someone would bring a colourful cocktail to her now, she could almost feel like she was on vacation.

Lianne Roche came up the short gangway and sat down across from her.

"I still have work to do and will leave now," she informed Sandrine.

"You're not arrested and can do as you please."

"Aren't you planning to question me?" The lawyer sounded irritated.

"Mr. de Saint-Clair hired you on what day?"

"Yesterday. When he found out you were after him. It's one of your preferences, making life difficult for people you don't like. In any case, I was highly recommended to him."

"Yes, I'm a real piece of work," Sandrine replied casually, wishing for a cocktail now that she could sip with boredom. Just to show the woman how little her attention was worth.

Lianne Roche looked at her in astonishment. She hadn't expected this response.

"What now?" she asked in a snippy tone.

"You have work to do, so go on your way, right? Have a nice day."

"That's it?"

"There's nothing you could tell me. You don't play a role in our investigations, so go. De Saint-Clair didn't hire you because he needed your legal counsel, but solely to provoke me. For that, he made an excellent choice. And now, I wish you a pleasant day."

The woman exhaled through her nose and practically jumped up. The lawyer excelled at letting insults and accusations roll off her, but being considered irrelevant was something she couldn't bear. She turned around and stormed off.

"Was that wise?" Adel asked, coming out of the cabin and having overheard the last sentences.

"What could she possibly tell me now that would help us in the search for de Chezac? She had nothing to do with Poutin's death; in fact, she was representing Léon at the time, against my advice. When the murders of Miriam Mignon and Poutin occurred, she didn't even know de Saint-Clair. She plays no role in our investigations, and I won't waste my time on that pompous woman."

Adel laughed. He had had an affair with Lianne Roche years ago, the end of which he didn't talk about. It must have been very bad. The woman, however, knew how to press the buttons that would drive him to distraction. So he probably enjoyed her departure very much.

"Could you please bring the bodyguard?" Sandrine asked Adel.

"Of course. He's waiting for us to leave."

Shortly afterward, he returned with the man, who sat down on the semicircular outdoor sofa and casually crossed his legs.

"Will you and your people be finished soon?"
"It depends on what else we find."
"My boss won't like what you're doing here. Mr. de Saint-Clair has excellent connections. This intrusion into his privacy will come back to haunt you."
"I'm tough. You wouldn't believe how often people threaten me with their connections. Eventually, you get used to it."
"De Saint-Clair isn't just some provincial bumpkin you deal with around here. You'd be surprised." His tone became more mocking, and he leaned against the waterproof cushion. Either he was convinced of his boss's invincibility or he was a good actor who didn't reveal his doubts. Sandrine hoped for the latter.
"When did you arrive here?"
"Last Friday, in the evening."
"And since then, you haven't left your boss's side?"
"Saint-Malo is not exactly a dangerous place. I'm mainly responsible for security on board here. The Ariste is a real gem, and Monsieur de Saint-Clair wants to protect his property from burglars and nosy paparazzi."
"So you're keeping kids from jumping onto the boat and taking a few snapshots?"
"It has happened," he replied. "But they might scratch the floor or spill some cola on the upholstery." He pointed to the living area. "There's quite a bit in there that would be worth stealing. The artworks alone are worth a tidy sum."
She nodded in agreement. De Saint-Clair owned some valuable items, for various reasons. Two of them were carefully concealed in her hands: a tie and a file she couldn't open. She chuckled briefly and bitterly.
"No need to be envious," commented the bodyguard, misinterpreting her laughter.
She pulled out a photo of Miriam Mignon from her jacket pocket and handed it to him.
"Do you know this woman?"

"She's really pretty," he said after taking a look at it. "I would probably remember her if I had met her."

"Perhaps here on the yacht, with your boss?"

"She's cute, but she doesn't have the class required to be invited here."

"And this one?" Sandrine handed him a photo of Prosecutor de Chezac.

"Of course. He has been on the boat several times. Monsieur de Chezac."

"For what occasion?"

"You'd better ask my boss. He wouldn't like it if I talked about his guests."

"I will, as soon as we locate him. But then he will be wearing handcuffs, and I'll have to decide whether you are an accomplice or a witness." Sandrine tapped the top of the picture. "Think carefully."

"What are you getting at?" The man's self-satisfied demeanour began to crack. He straightened up and leaned slightly forward.

"This is the Saint-Malo's Prosecutor. We suspect that your boss has abducted him from his house. Do you have any idea what's going on right now? No one takes a prosecutor without the police mobilising everything this state has to offer, no matter how influential that person may believe themselves to be. We will turn every stone, and it's up to you to decide whether you want to be an obstacle or a helpful witness. The choice is yours, but you will face the consequences."

It was not an empty threat. By now, even someone like de Saint-Clair should find it impossible to leave France. It was only a matter of time before they tracked him down. Hopefully, de Chezac would still be alive by then.

"Nonsense," he retorted. "De Saint-Clair wouldn't kidnap anyone. Why would he?"

"Then just take a look around with open eyes. I'm sitting in front of you, my team is searching every single room on the yacht, and there are enough police officers outside to drag you and the rest of the crew into a cell if I decide to. That should give you something to think about." She hoped that thinking wasn't one of the muscular man's weaknesses. But the fact that he was now almost perched on the front edge of the cushions showed how nervous and hopefully adequately intimidated he was to spill the truth.

"Your boss certainly won't send his hand-picked lawyer to get you out of a jam you've gotten yourself into, even if he demanded it of you. Right now, all he cares about is saving his own skin. And you should too."

"What do you want from me?" he said slowly and deliberately, as if the words were reluctantly coming out of his mouth. His situation seemed to be becoming clearer to him with every police officer who boarded the boat.

"Again. Do you know the woman in the photo?"

"No. Honestly. I've never seen her before," he replied almost urgently, trying to make her believe him.

"But Prosecutor de Chezac? When was he here?"

"I remember him well. A rather arrogant SOB who acted as if the yacht belonged to him. The cook and the stewardess had to jump to his every whim; he snapped his fingers frequently and took great pleasure in it."

"And de Saint-Clair?"

"He used to laugh at him when he was gone. I think he despised him."

"What makes you think that?"

"My boss asked me to keep a close eye on the man. He believed that this prosecutor couldn't keep his hands to himself."

"He harassed women? The stewardess?"

"Oh, not at all," the man waved it off. "That wouldn't have bothered de Saint-Clair."

"What are you getting at then?"

"What I mean is, things went missing after he had visited the boat, small but valuable items like a bronze figurine, a drawing, or a bottle of champagne. Just minor things."

"De Saint-Clair noticed this?" Sandrine asked in surprise.

"A bottle of that stuff costs a few hundred euros, but he didn't care about that. It was different when it came to his art collection; that is really important to him."

"Did you retrieve the bronze figurine?"

"The man went berserk and scolded us all, but in the end, he wrote off the figurine as a loss, which surprised me." He shook his head slightly. "It wasn't particularly pretty. Anyway, since then, he kept his lower deck cabin locked."

"If you were supposed to keep an eye on him, when was de Chezac on board?"

"He was here on Sunday for the party. It went on until the early morning hours. And then again yesterday. We had a small dinner party, and he was invited."

"And you were here the entire time?"

"That's part of my job."

"De Saint-Clair claimed to have been on the boat the whole day on Sunday, can you confirm that? Think carefully," she warned the man.

"As long as I was on board, I saw him."

"What do you mean, as long as you were on board? Did you leave the Ariste at any point?"

"I had to escort two ladies back home."

"I thought your job was to provide security here, not to play taxi driver?" she asked, slightly irritated.

"The two ladies were quite drunk, and my boss didn't want them to drive home alone in that condition. So, I had to take care of them and act as a babysitter. One of them even threw up in the taxi. The driver was furious and charged me fifty euros for cleaning."

"Where did you take them?"

"The beauties came from Rennes. The ride back had to be done with the window open. But at least it was pleasantly warm. Rare for this area. I much prefer the trips to the Côte d'Azur."

"Escort service?" Sandrine asked, and the man nodded. "Have you had to do this for him before?"

"Never. Usually, he doesn't care about the girls. It surprised me, but I'm not paid to ask questions, especially not to my boss."

"When did you leave?"

"Just after 11 o'clock."

"So, you have no idea if your boss was on board the Ariste between eleven and two o'clock?"

"I can't say."

"Who from the crew was on board?"

"The Capitaine was off duty. So, it was the chef and the stewardess, but they have the day off today and are out and about. We had hired a few temporary staff for that evening."

"I need a guest list," she requested.

"I can make a copy for you."

"De Chezac was here last night. Did anything unusual catch your attention?"

"Not that I can think of. It was just a small gathering, and the last guests left the yacht after midnight. Can I help you with anything else?"

"That's it for now. Come to the police station tomorrow and provide a statement."

"I will," he said without looking at her. His shoulders slumped, and he stared at the shiny wooden floor. He had definitely lost his job. Either his boss would go to prison, or he would kick him out as soon as he learned of his bodyguard's statement.

There was nothing more for her to do here so Sandrine

decided to go to the police station. Adel and Dubois could check the guest list. Maybe someone had noticed that de Saint-Clair had left his own party. To commit a murder.

The Manhunt

Sandrine stretched and let out a loud yawn. The thin blanket that had covered her had slipped to the floor. She sat up on the bunk and sighed softly. Her back ached as if she had slept on the concrete floor. *I'm not getting any younger; next time, I'm going home to sleep in my own bed.* Fortunately, no one had been locked up in the cell to sober up, and she had been able to sleep reasonably peacefully.

The search for de Chezac had kept her at the police station late into the night, but they had received no useful clues about the whereabouts of the prosecutor or de Saint-Clair. Police officers were waiting outside the yacht for the fugitive, but he was smart enough not to show himself. His crew knew nothing about his whereabouts, and he hadn't been seen in Saint-Malo. Patrol cars were on the lookout for de Chezac's car, which had not been in the garage or the driveway. De Saint-Clair couldn't show up at airports or ferry terminals anymore without getting arrested. If he wanted to leave the country, his only options were small private airfields or private boats.

"Damn it," Sandrine exclaimed and jumped up. She had completely overlooked something. She pushed open the door and ran down the corridor. One of the officers unlocked the door to the cell area where she had spent the night, and she raced up to her desk.

"A boat! How could we forget that?" she exclaimed to Adel, who was sitting at his desk, the phone receiver wedged between his cheek and shoulder as he jotted something down.

"A patrol car is stationed in front of the yacht. As soon as he shows up, he'll be arrested," Adel said, hanging up the phone. "You had a bad dream," he teased her. "You should be used to the drunk tank by now."

When investigations stretched into the night, Sandrine occasionally slept in a cell, while Adel always went home, even if he only had a few hours of freedom. He couldn't get used to the strong smell of cleaning agents, the noise, and the hard bunk.

"De Chezac lives just a few steps from the Port Mer Yacht Club. The man was obsessed with his reputation; I bet he owns a boat befitting a celebrity in this area. Can you find that out?"

"I'm on it," Adel replied.

Sandrine walked over to Inès, who was sitting in her office.

"Did you have a pleasant night?" the office manager greeted her.

"Not really. But it was too short to be truly bad," Sandrine replied.

"What can I do for you?" Inès had been in the office for an hour already and was more familiar with the progress of the investigation than Sandrine.

"Can I impose on you for an espresso?" Sandrine asked.

"Of course, no problem. I have a new blend I wanted to try anyway. A double shot?" She stood up and typed something on the coffee machine's display.

"How much caffeine can you fit in one cup?"

"Enough to keep you wide awake until tonight."

"That's exactly what I need. Nobody's going home until we find this guy."

The machine whirred to life, and the sound of the grinder

filled the room. Inès turned around and looked at Sandrine thoughtfully. "Did you ever think we'd go to such lengths to find that obnoxious de Chezac?"

Sandrine sat down in the visitor's chair, which swayed slightly under her weight, and stretched out her legs to loosen her stiff muscles. "At least he's one of us. That's enough to move heaven and earth," she replied, which was only partly true. In reality, de Chezac was secondary to her. What she wanted was to bring down de Saint-Clair, the man she believed to be the Necktie Killer. In Paris and even now in Saint-Malo, the arrogant man had done everything in his power to protect the person she considered the prime suspect. For this mistake, de Chezac might now pay with his life. Or he knew about his machinations and had to pay the price for it.

"Do you think he's already dead?" Inès asked, as if she had read Sandrine's thoughts, and placed a full cup in front of her.

"I don't know." She tore open the sugar packet and poured its contents onto the dark brown foam until a mountain formed, slowly absorbing the liquid and breaking through. Sandrine stirred and tried to put herself in de Saint-Clair's shoes. Why did the man suddenly turn against the prosecutor? Did de Chezac no longer want to protect him from the investigations, or was he one of the insiders de Saint-Clair wanted to get rid of, like Brigadier Poutin? The evidence against the man was mounting by the hour. If she were in his shoes, she would have quietly disappeared abroad, without making much fuss. He had the money and the connections to never have to face a French court. Something must have been known to the prosecutor that de Saint-Clair didn't want him to reveal, otherwise, he wouldn't have kidnapped him. The question was whether Prosecutor de Chezac had known the truth about de Saint-Clair in Paris or had stumbled upon some hint recently that had opened his eyes.

"I assume the prosecutor is still alive," she said to Inès. "De Saint-Clair holds a valuable hostage, if we find his hiding place."

At least until he crosses the borders of France and believes himself to be safe.

Adel stuck his head through the door and gave a thumbs-up.

"You were right. He has a sailboat that's moored in the Port des Sablons."

"That's the leisure harbour near Miriam Mignon's house, isn't it?"

"Exactly."

"Then let's go there." She drank the coffee in one gulp and got up. "Thank you, Inès. That saved my day."

"Always happy to help," said the woman who otherwise guarded her espresso machine like a Doberman guards its bones.

* * *

Two policemen were already waiting at the harbour. They had found the prosecutor's Audi parked in a lot. Sandrine opened the door and looked inside. At first glance, she couldn't see anything suspicious.

"No blood," Adel said, sounding relieved. It seemed that de Chezac wasn't injured, and the bloodstain in his living room had been small. There didn't appear to have been another struggle inside the car.

The harbour master was talking to one of the policemen while Sandrine opened the trunk and took a look inside. In one corner, there was an antique leather travel bag. She unzipped it and searched its contents. Under some clothes, a piece of fabric caught her eye, and it seemed familiar.

"Adel," she called to her colleague, then pulled out a silk tie, and held it up to him. "I think we may have found the murder weapon." On the back, she noticed the embroidered rose, just like on the other ties used in the Paris murders.

"How did this end up here?"

"We still don't know who the bag belongs to. Either de Saint-

Clair kept it as a memento of his murder, or de Chezac found it somewhere and took the tie. I doubt de Saint-Clair gave the prosecutor time to pack a bag, which means he must have taken the tie from de Chezac this morning and put it in the bag. I don't understand why he left it in the trunk if it was important enough to attack de Chezac over."

"If it belonged to de Chezac, he should have brought it to the police station immediately. Why didn't he? That was a significant mistake."

"Perhaps he wanted to give de Saint-Clair an opportunity to explain his involvement in the murder, or he wanted to solve the case on his own. He'll have to explain himself once we find him." Or he had doubts about reporting it at all. Admitting that his inaction in Paris had played a part in Miriam Mignon's death would have been difficult. It would have certainly damaged his career. Everyone in the Paris homicide division knew how much he had advocated for de Saint-Clair and obstructed Sandrine's work. He should never have been in charge of the investigation in Paris.

"When did the boat leave the harbour?" Sandrine asked the harbour master.

"Yesterday morning, around nine o'clock. At high tide."

"Have you spoken to the owner? Maybe he mentioned where he was heading."

"The Parisian who bought the *Justine*?" He shook his head. "The man hardly acknowledges anyone even on good days. Yesterday, he marched past me with another guy in tow. Shortly after, they set sail. I don't know where they were going, but you can locate them relatively easily."

"Was it this man?" She showed him a photo of de Saint-Clair.

"I wouldn't swear to it, but I think so."

"Thank you. You've been very helpful."

On their way back to the car, Adel called the police station.

Hermé would initiate the search for the *Justine* and request assistance from the maritime gendarmerie.

* * *

There wasn't much to do at the police station except wait for news of the prosecutor's sailboat. The tracking device was turned off, but Sandrine hadn't expected otherwise. De Saint-Clair's yacht was named Ariste VI. With Ariste I through V, the man had gained enough experience in handling boats to know how to make them vanish from radar. By now, he could have reached England and gone underground.

Adel's phone rang. Sandrine sat up and looked at him. The conversation was too quiet for her to hear anything, but the brigadier nodded several times.

"Do they have the boat?"

"No. It was Jean-Claude. They took fingerprints from the Cognac bottle on the boat. They match those of the bodyguard and de Saint-Clair."

"And?" she impatiently inquired.

"De Saint-Clair's prints match those found on the bottle at Luc Poutin's. The bottle undoubtedly came from the fugitive, at least from the yacht's bar."

"So, he had it in his hands. A clear connection between him and Poutin." It wasn't conclusive proof of his guilt, but a link between the two men was undeniable. What could two such different men have in common? *Nothing, except that they both wanted to get rid of me.*

"Those gold coins that Anne gave you probably came from him," Renard Dubois chimed in. She hadn't heard him approach.

"That's likely, but we can't prove it yet." She turned back to Adel. "Anything else?"

"There were traces of skin tissue on the tie. It will take some time for them to determine if it's from Miriam Mignon."

"Who else could it be from?" It wasn't a question to Adel; it was more of a realisation to herself. "Let's assume it's the murder weapon."

"Then de Saint-Clair killed her?"

"What's clear is that his alibi has fallen apart. We found photos of him on his boat in Miriam Mignon's possession, along with an unfinished portrait. Plus, the key to Tour Bidouane where the murder occurred, and we have the murder weapon. I hope we can find DNA traces from both on it, although I'm somewhat sceptical. In Paris, he was cautious enough to always wear gloves."

"And he also killed Luc?" Dubois took a seat in an available chair.

"The fingerprints on the bottle we found at Poutin's provide an indication of that," Adel reluctantly replied.

"But why?" His gaze shifted between Adel and Sandrine. He knew the answer but didn't want to hear it.

"De Saint-Clair paid him to harm Capitaine Perrot," Adel forced himself to answer. "The man didn't trust Poutin to keep quiet, so silenced him."

"Framing someone with drugs is one thing, but knowing a murderer and covering for him is another," Sandrine said. "Brigadier Poutin must have known who was behind the murder of Miriam Mignon. De Saint-Clair had crossed a line. Perhaps Poutin wanted more hush money or threatened to go to the police. We'll find out once we've caught the man."

"Luc wouldn't have covered up a murder." Dubois spoke unusually softly. He must have had doubts about his words. "Or do you think he was the one trying to conceal the murder and tampering with the crime scene?"

"To be honest, I don't know. The images are blurry. Personally, I don't believe it, but de Chezac seems to think so."

"But how is the prosecutor involved?" Dubois asked.

"He frequented de Saint-Clair's place regularly. Sometimes he would take small items, at least that's what the bodyguard claimed. Perhaps he stumbled upon the tie during one of his kleptomaniac excursions. Of course, he immediately realised what he had found. De Saint-Clair noticed the theft and figured out who had committed it, or de Chezac was foolish enough to mention his find. He must now face the consequences." This theory seemed the most plausible to Sandrine at the moment.

"They found the boat," Inès called out and stuck her head out of her office door.

"Where?" Sandrine jumped up and rushed to her.

"In the bay of Mont-Saint-Michel, not far from the abbey. It ran aground at low tide and is now in the mud. It won't move from there until the next high tide."

"How can we get there quickly?" Sandrine urged.

Major Baud entered the open-plan office at that moment and approached them. "As I heard, the news has already reached you. The helicopter and a small team from the tactical unit are ready in the courtyard. We can take off in ten minutes. Do you want to accompany me? After all, it's about your boss."

"Of course." The woman probably hadn't expected Sandrine to back down. She loaded a spare magazine and followed Major Baud to the courtyard. A blue and white police helicopter was waiting on the helipad. The engine was running, and the rotor blades were spinning. Two armed police officers from the tactical unit were strapped into the seats.

"What about Hermé?" Sandrine shouted to be heard over the noise of the engine.

"He's with Commandant Jogu at the maritime gendarmerie. We don't have time to wait for them. I've informed him, and he's coordinating the necessary activities based on what we find on board the boat."

Without waiting for a response, she turned away and climbed into the helicopter. Sandrine sat across from the police officers, nodding in greeting. The engine was now too loud for conversation without shouting. She closed the door and fastened her seat-belt as the helicopter lifted off from the helipad. Saint-Malo quickly shrank below them and disappeared from her view. It was about 25 miles as the crow flies to the tidal island of Mont-Saint-Michel. It took her nearly an hour by motorcycle from Saint-Malo. The helicopter should make it in a good fifteen minutes.

Below them, the bay came into view, and the pilot followed the coastline towards Normandy. To their left was Le Mont-Saint-Michel. The mountain with the abbey rose steeply from the mudflats, and she looked out the window to savour the sight. She wouldn't have the chance to do so again for several miles, as there was a strict no-fly zone in this area. The ebb tide hadn't reached its lowest point yet, but the mountain was already accessible on foot from the mainland. Only the tidal channels of the three rivers that flowed into the bay presented challenging obstacles.

"Ahead of us is the boat," the pilot said to them through the headphones. She couldn't see the *Justine* yet, but the helicopter was rapidly losing altitude. The two elite police officers checked their sub-machine guns. Their movements were precise and without any nervousness. It wasn't their first operation where a shootout was possible. De Saint-Clair must have felt like a cornered predator. One that could react aggressively and unpredictably. However, it wouldn't come down to the marksmanship of these two men, but rather her negotiation skills in getting de Chezac off the boat alive. She wondered whether de Saint-Clair would surrender to go to prison or choose to go down in a dramatic showdown. With a narcissist like him, she feared a theatrical gesture that could easily cost de Chezac his life.

The helicopter gently touched down on the wet and soft mudflat. One of the policemen opened the side sliding door, while the other pointed his sub-machine gun outside, as if expecting de Saint-Clair to engage in a firefight with them. *Better safe than sorry,* thought Sandrine, making sure not to get in their line of fire. The pilot had landed the helicopter parallel to the boat, which was in her line of sight. The approximately thirty-two-foot-long sailboat was slightly tilted with its keel in the mud. There was no sign of movement on board. Sandrine leaned her head out of the door, and there was no indication that the two men were on the boat. Had they escaped? There were no footprints in the mudflat suggesting that. However, the sailboat might have had a motorised dinghy with which they could easily reach the Normandy shore, at least when the water was still high enough in the bay. What had prompted de Saint-Clair to sail here? The man was an experienced sailor. He must have known that the ebb tide was starting, and he would run aground in the shallow waters of the bay.

Sandrine unbuckled her seat-belt and made sure she could easily reach her weapon. One of the policemen signalled her to wait in the helicopter. They would proceed to secure the boat first, and only then would she and Major Baud be allowed to investigate. That's how the regulations worked.

As soon as the two officers had disembarked and approached the boat, Sandrine, too impatient to wait, jumped out of the helicopter. Water and mud splashed under her shoes. She was glad she had chosen sturdy and waterproof footwear. Major Baud got out behind her, but she made sure not to soil her uniform trousers. They followed the two men, who soon reached the tilted side of the boat. No one was in sight. The first officer expertly climbed aboard and waited for his comrade. They signalled Sandrine to keep her distance, then the first officer disappeared into the cabin.

"It doesn't look like de Saint-Clair is still on board," Major Baud said. The woman had stepped up behind her and was attentively observing the boat, its sails lightly fluttering in the wind.

One of the policemen appeared in the cabin doorway.

"We have a dead body."

"*Merde*," Sandrine cursed and hurried to the boat. She grabbed the lower gunwale and pulled herself up. A table and some sun loungers had shifted on the slanted deck, and Sandrine pushed them aside. She couldn't stand de Chezac, but no one deserved this. No one.

"He's in the main cabin."

Sandrine balanced on the slanted deck towards the open door. The officer inside reached out a hand and pulled her in.

"Damn it," she exclaimed. The dead man sat in a pool of blood on the floor with his back against the kitchen cabinets. However, it wasn't Prosecutor de Chezac but de Saint-Clair. Next to him lay a pistol that must have slipped from his hand. Major Baud entered the cabin behind her and leaned against the door frame. Sandrine took a step forward and knelt on the floor. The man's head was slumped on his chest. His hair looked tousled, as if he had spent time outside in the wind. It matched the red outdoor jacket she had often seen him in. The zipper was open, and his shirt in the abdomen area was soaked in blood. She looked across the floor for a cartridge case but couldn't find one. Hopefully, the forensics team would have better luck.

He wasn't holding the pistol; he had used his hands for something else. His fingertips were red. De Saint-Clair had dipped them in his own blood and drawn a pointed diamond shape on the wooden floor. She had no idea what he meant by it, but it must have been important if he used his last strength for it.

A commotion at the front of the cabin startled her. The two policemen had gone ahead and were examining the two sleeping cabins.

"Someone's still here," one of them called out.

Sandrine reached for the table bolted to the floor and pulled herself up. Careful not to slip on the slanted floor with her muddy shoes, she made her way to the bow. Through the open door, she saw de Chezac handcuffed to a bed. His face looked badly beaten. De Saint-Clair must have delivered some powerful blows. None of the wounds were bleeding, but they were swollen and starting to darken.

"We'll get him right away," one of the policemen said and unlocked the handcuffs. Together, they helped de Chezac to his feet, led him outside, and placed him on one of the lounges at the stern.

"What happened?" Sandrine asked.

The man turned his head in her direction and looked at her. His left eye was almost completely swollen shut. He could probably barely see with it.

"Capitaine Perrot. I never thought I'd have to admit this, but I'm very glad to see you," he said. Speaking was clearly difficult for him, and she had to listen carefully to understand him. He reached for her hand and squeezed it tightly. She almost pulled it away but then let him be. De Chezac had been through a lot in the past few hours, and he could use some compassion.

"I'm sorry. You were right, and I was completely wrong the whole time," he said, breathing heavily. Admitting this must have been very hard for him. Sandrine raised the lounge chair higher and placed a pillow under his head.

"It's okay; we've caught him."

"Yes, we have," he replied.

"Why is that man dead, and you're alive?" Major Baud asked in her usual direct and unsympathetic manner.

"He came into the cabin to humiliate me. I resisted, and he struck me with the pistol grip."

"That wasn't very clever," she commented.

"Without aiming much, I kicked at him and managed to hit the pistol. A shot went off and hit de Saint-Clair. I think it was in the abdomen. But the guy was tough and struck me again. He forced me to put on the handcuffs and left me alone. I suppose he was looking for a first aid kit to tend to his wounds. I blacked out several times and can't remember everything. At some point, we ran aground, and the boat tilted to the side. Later, I heard you. At first, I thought it was de Saint-Clair and stayed quiet, and only when I could distinguish multiple voices did I hope for rescue. Where is he? I hope you've arrested him."

"I would have liked to, but unfortunately, it was too late for that. He bled to death. He had probably been dead for a few hours when we arrived," Sandrine explained.

"I can't say that I'm particularly sorry, considering it was my life on the line. If the shot hadn't gone off after my kick, I'd probably be floating dead in the water now."

"What prompted de Saint-Clair to kidnap you?" Sandrine asked.

"I was invited by him, and I was inspecting the yacht. He was bragging about his new toy. Curious as I am, I also went into the main cabin and looked inside the wardrobe. That's where I came across the tie. The same kind that was used in the Paris murders. I panicked, took one, and left, but the bodyguard took a peek into my bag and found it. He didn't buy my story that it was a spare tie in case mine got dirty; instead, he informed de Saint-Clair. The next morning, he showed up at my house with a gun and forced me to come with him. You know the rest of the story, or you wouldn't be here," de Chezac explained. Exhausted, he leaned back and closed his eyes.

"You should have handed over the piece of evidence at the police station," Major Baud scolded him.

"That was a mistake. I thought there was time until the next day; it was late when I left the yacht," de Chezac muttered. "But I almost paid for it with my life." After that, he fell silent. His breathing became slow and steady. Sandrine assumed he had fallen asleep.

Behind her, Major Baud was on the phone with her superior, providing a report.

"The pilot has already reported sighting of the *Justine*," she said, crouching down next to Sandrine. "The forensics team is on their way." She looked out over the flat mudflat that stretched before them. Only Mont-Saint-Michel and its little sister island, Tombelaine, broke the flat expanse. "I have no idea how they plan to get here. The ground is muddy, and the next tide will flood everything again in a few hours. There's no way to drive here, and the only available helicopter is here."

"Jean-Claude Mazet is resourceful. He'll come up with something. I would suggest going to Le Mont-Saint-Michel. There's a caterpillar vehicle from the fire department stationed there, perfect for use on the mudflats. If I recall correctly, it can transport more than a dozen people, should they bring the trailer."

"It's an hour from Saint-Malo to Le Mont-Saint-Michel, then they need to repack and make their way across the mudflat. So, it might be a while before we see the forensics team." She pointed at de Chezac, who still appeared to be asleep. "What should we do?"

Sandrine turned to one of the two police officers, whose weapon hung in a holster over the rail.

"Do you believe we're still in danger?"

"No." He shook his head. "The boat is empty. There's no one here anymore. It's hard to miss someone approaching the boat on foot. Besides, we've found the two individuals who were supposed to be on the boat, and neither of them poses a threat anymore."

"Then fly back," Sandrine decided. "The prosecutor urgently needs a doctor. He might have a concussion, which could turn serious. I'll stay here and watch over the boat until the forensics team arrives."

"Can you manage here by yourself?" Baud asked.

"What could happen to me?" she replied. "Getting robbed by random mudflat walkers? Or seagulls stealing my baguette?"

The policeman laughed. "You look like you can defend yourself, Capitaine Perrot."

"I can handle it. Get the man to a hospital."

"Alright," he agreed.

"I'll stay with you," Major Baud suggested.

"Why? The fewer people on board, the less evidence will be destroyed. Hermé will want to talk to you since you were here when we found him. While you start typing reports, I'll be here on the boat, enjoying the weather and the view. That's definitely the better choice."

"Perhaps he'd prefer to talk to you; after all, de Saint-Clair is your case." Sandrine detected a hint of jealousy. Did she assume her boss would rather work with her?

"He introduced you and Jogu as his most capable officers. Why would he turn to me? Probably de Saint-Clair committed Poutin's murder. That's your case, so finish it. Besides, our prosecutor is currently incapacitated. Hermé will also have to oversee the investigation into the Miriam Mignon case, for which he'll need you and Commander Jogu."

"Alright then. I'll fly back with de Chezac to Saint-Malo."

Slowly, the helicopter lifted off, turned towards the mainland, and left her in the mudflats. Sandrine watched it go, squinting as dirt and water droplets flew in her direction. Soon, the sound of the engine faded, and the helicopter became just a speck in the sky.

Sandrine set up one of the stretchers on the muddy ground and lay down on it. The sun beamed from a flawless blue sky, and the surface quickly dried. Some water to drink would be good, but she hesitated to go into the cabin. Valuable evidence could too easily be destroyed. She looked towards Le Mont-Saint-Michel, which was barely a half a mile from her. The buses were easy to spot as they travelled over the long bridge. Hordes of tourists poured out from the buses' bellies and would soon fill the alley leading from the main gate up to the abbey. During the summer, locals avoided the island for a good reason. She had enjoyed the quiet evening hours when the tourists left Le Mont-Saint-Michel, and the place returned to its tranquillity. She wondered how many photos had already been taken of the boat, which was clearly visible from the abbey's walls. None of them had the slightest idea that a murder had occurred here. And that was a good thing. Crime and tourism didn't go well together.

Less than an hour later, she noticed the red rescue vehicle approaching her. Jean-Claude Mazet had apparently had the same thought as she did. It briefly disappeared from her view to cross a deep channel and reappeared on the other side. It could easily cross water depths of up to three feet without the crew getting wet or the engine failing.

What stayed on her mind was the pointed diamond shape de Saint-Clair had drawn with his blood on the floor. He wanted to convey something with it, but she couldn't figure out what it might be. Maybe he didn't finish it. Who knows who the message was intended for. *He certainly wasn't thinking of me in his last moments.* De Chezac could say a prayer of thanks for his survival. Brigadier Poutin hadn't been so lucky.

She didn't doubt for a second that Ariste de Saint-Clair was the murderer of Miriam Mignon, just as she didn't doubt that he or someone on his behalf had bribed Luc Poutin to discredit Sandrine. He knew she would never give up pursuing him until she could pin the Paris murders on him. Trying to push her out of the police force had been his first attempt to get rid of her. When he failed, he killed his accomplice. But there had to be more than one person who knew about his crimes. She didn't believe Poutin was the one who tried to clean up after de Saint-Clair on Tour Bidouane. Who could it be? And had that person also helped with Poutin's murder? She had suspected the two police officers from Rennes. Major Baud was now ruled out, leaving only Commandant Jogu. She couldn't yet assess the man well. They had hardly spoken to each other. She rummaged in the side pocket of her trousers and pulled out the crumpled photo that Miriam Mignon had taken of de Saint-Clair. The man stood on the upper deck of his yacht, holding a glass of champagne in his hand. He appeared to be very content with his life, but now he sat dead in his own blood on the floor of the cabin of a small sailboat. In the background, the Ariste VI was anchored, along with the *Émeraude* belonging to the Barnais family. She still believed that the woman was Blanche. Sandrine smiled thoughtfully. She had liked her and her twin sister Charlotte, even though she had met them during a difficult time for the family.

The tracked vehicle stopped next to the boat, and the driver skilfully climbed out. Jean-Claude Mazet had a bit more trouble getting out of the narrow driver's cabin.

"Hello, Capitaine,' he called and waved to her. "We've come to relieve you."

"Thank goodness. I was afraid the tide would arrive before you. I have no experience with boats. Who knows where I would have ended up?"

The forensic technician approached her. "A beautiful boat," he said appreciatively. "We'll collect the evidence, and then I'm treating myself to a sailing trip. Olivier and I will take the *Justine* back to Saint-Malo."

"You can sail?"

The man shot her an irritated look. "I'm a native of Saint-Malo. Of course I can handle a boat."

"How soon we meet again," the driver interrupted. "Haven't I driven you to a dead body in the mud flats before?"

"Yes, indeed." She remembered the man who had not only safely guided her through the mud flats but had also acted as an enthusiastic tour guide.

"Five-cylinder diesel engine, 160 horsepower, and a top speed of 30 miles per hour, right?" she said, pointing to his rescue vehicle, from which water and mud were dripping.

"You have an excellent memory. It's actually 163 horsepower."

"This time, I got to fly in, but I'd be happy to ride back with you."

"Of course. Hop in. I'll pick up your colleagues later."

"Is that alright, Monsieur Mazet?"

"We have quite a bit to do here. There's no reason for you to keep us company." He glanced at the lounge chair. "Although you seem to have made yourself quite comfortable already."

"Then I'll see you at the station." She bid farewell to the forensics technician and climbed into the cramped driver's cab.

"Here we go." He shifted into first gear and stepped on the gas. A dark cloud of diesel shot out of the elevated exhaust as they moved. The driver curved around the *Justine*, then set his sights on Le Mont-Saint-Michel and accelerated. The chains dug into the mud, flinging dirt into the air behind them. The man clearly relished the ride.

"You don't often get to take this puppy out for a spin, do you?"

"Not often enough," he replied with a broad grin. "This is better than riding a rollercoaster."

Barely more than ten minutes later, they rolled onto the paved courtyard of the tidal island, and Sandrine got out.

"You've got quite a bit of cleaning up to do," she said, looking at the mud-splattered vehicle.

"Yeah. But not until I've picked up the rest of the team, otherwise it's not worth it. And what do you have planned for the rest of the day?"

She wasn't sure if he was asking about her work or inviting her for a coffee.

"When you find a body, it comes with a ton of paperwork. That'll keep me busy."

"You'd better make it a nice day for yourself. I know I would, especially if I'd arrived too late to save someone." He tapped the firefighter badge on the door of his vehicle with his palm.

"You're right, I will do that," she decided, bidding farewell to the man. Some food and a little chat sounded just right to her.

Sandrine entered Le Mont-Saint-Michel through the main gate. As expected, visitors crowded the narrow alley in front of the restaurants and souvenir shops. She bought a bottle of water and headed towards the abbey until she reached Auberge Saint-Michel and peered into the restaurant through the window.

"Can I help you?" someone spoke to her from behind. The voice sounded familiar, and she turned around.

"Blanche. What a coincidence. You're exactly who I was looking for."

"Me? I hope it's not an official visit." The woman smiled at Sandrine, although their last encounter had not been pleasant. "Unfortunately, I can't offer you a spot in the restaurant. We're fully booked, as usual during peak season. But I can invite you for a bite at my place."

"I don't want to impose, and I'm more or less on my way to the station." She pulled out the photo from her pocket. "You were in Saint-Malo over the weekend. I happened to come across this and thought it would be a nice opportunity to drop by."

"Oh. That's me indeed on the *Émeraude*. We're considering selling it. None of us use the boat. It just sits in the harbour, costing money. So, we're tidying it up in case a potential buyer comes for a viewing." She looked at Sandrine, a mischievous glint passing over her face. "Léon often talked about getting a boat. Perhaps he'd be interested in the *Émeraude*. She's not the youngest, but still in really good shape."

"I'll mention it to him, but I'm afraid it's way too big for him to handle alone."

"Oh, nonsense," Blanche brushed aside her objection. "And besides, he wouldn't be alone."

"You mean me? I can't handle a boat. Who knows, I might get seasick."

"Consider it," Blanche insisted.

"We will. Thank you for the offer."

"But the photo isn't from the weekend. I thought the police would be better informed."

Sandrine hesitated. "What do you mean?"

"I was at a historical association meeting in Nantes until Sunday. That's why I only got around to cleaning up the *Émeraude* on Monday."

"That's not possible," she muttered, feeling confused.

"Absolutely. I still have the hotel receipts and seminar materials, in case I ever need an alibi again," the woman joked.

"No, you don't need that. I must have gotten the days mixed up," Sandrine said, looking at her phone's display. "It's getting late; I need to head out."

"Whatever you prefer. Come by for a meal sometime. We'd be glad to have you."

"I'd love to. Let's see when Léon has time."

"Then we'll talk about the boat."

"Perhaps."

She hurried to get out of the crowd and climbed a staircase up to the city wall. Finding a quieter spot, she called Sébastian Hermé. It seemed they wouldn't be wrapping up the Miriam Mignon case today. Nor the Poutin case.

Sandrine took the bus to the barrier at the end of the bridge. She found a vacant spot on the terrace of a restaurant. There would still be time for a snack before Hermé arrived.

Paris

The yellow Renault Alpine pulled over at the roadside in front of the restaurant terrace, and Sébastian Hermé looked around. Sandrine finished the last of her second espresso, left money in the tray with the bill, and walked over to the car.

"You must have hurried quite a bit to be here so fast," she greeted the prosecutor.

"You sounded on the phone like it was a matter of life and death. What choice did I have but to hurry?" he replied.

"Must have been fun," she said, walking over to the passenger side and running her hand along the fender of the sports car; Sandrine opened the door and jumped into the seat. Judging by his grin, her statement hit the mark. The man enjoyed pushing his car to its limits every now and then.

"So, what's going on? I thought we had the case solved. De Saint-Clair got his just punishment, and de Chezac is currently being examined at the hospital in Saint-Malo. They removed him from duty just before you called. The champagne was about to pop. Now the bottle's back in the fridge."

"Did he add anything to his statement?"

"Major Baud questioned him during the flight. De Saint-Clair confessed to him, admitting to murdering the young woman, just like the brigadier. You were right in your assumption; he wanted to eliminate an inconvenient witness. Now no one can deny that."

"But why did he murder the woman? He only knew Miriam Mignon for a few days."

Hermé avoided her gaze. Instead of giving an answer, he turned the car and drove away from Le Mont-Saint-Michel.

"So, it was to send me a message after all," she said softly. "He wanted to show me how powerless I am against him. That someone like me could never convict someone like him. That's what he believed and wanted to make clear to me."

"You're not to blame for what happened in Saint-Malo. The only guilty one is now dead," Hermé said sympathetically.

"Maybe," she muttered, but the certainty wouldn't come. A few clues made her doubt his sole guilt.

"He drugged Poutin with sedatives and Cognac and hanged him. The results of the blood tests came back this afternoon, they were conclusive. The brigadier didn't commit suicide; he was murdered."

"You want to close the case?"

"I don't see any more unanswered questions," he replied, casting her a curious sidelong glance.

I do. And more than just one, in fact.

"You've done great work. Even de Chezac admitted it. He intends to apologise to you. The shock must have hit the man deep in his bones, or he wouldn't even consider such a thing."

"That's not going to happen," she said with conviction. She could do without the man's platitudes. Above all, she wasn't willing to forgive him, which he would probably expect as appropriate. She shook her head. *Never.* Too much had happened between them for her to forgive the man until the end of her days.

"Back to Saint-Malo?" Hermé asked, assuming the role of taxi driver for Sandrine.

"I have something else to take care of. It's a detour, but could you drop me off at the train station in Rennes?"

"In Rennes? What's there that has to do with our case?"

"Nothing. I need to go to Paris today. In Rennes, I'll catch the TGV. I should be back tomorrow sometime during the day."

"Does it have any connection to our case?"

"Yes."

"Is it important?"

Sandrine nodded.

"I haven't been to Paris in a long time," he said unexpectedly. "Gérard will be green with envy," he added softly, seeming to chuckle lightly. It was the first time he'd mentioned his partner by name in her presence. Hermé accelerated and pushed the gear to its limit before shifting. The trees along the roadside flew past them.

Sandrine picked up her phone and made some calls, then rested her head against the seat and closed her eyes. It would take about four hours to reach Paris by the early evening. Even Hermé's rapid driving style couldn't buy them much time, as they would inevitably get caught in the evening traffic.

* * *

Shortly after seven, they stopped in front of de Saint-Clair's apartment in Saint-Germain-des-Prés in the 6th arrondissement, on a quiet street between Rue du Four and the Seine. It was a popular residential area for wealthy Parisians. The man occupied the top two floors of the building, which must have cost him a pretty penny.

Major Alary was already waiting with several policemen and two forensic technicians outside the building. The grey-haired policeman with the closely cropped beard and angular face greeted Sébastian Hermé before taking Sandrine into his arms and hugging her tightly.

"My long-lost daughter has returned," he said, smiling. "I hope you haven't forgotten everything I taught you in the provinces."

"I'm back, you can refresh my memory." At least for one evening, she was back in her old life. However, she had to go into de Saint-Clair's apartment only, nothing else drew her to Paris. At this point, she felt at home in Brittany.

"Everything is prepared. We can officially enter and search the apartment," he said, holding a keyring between his thumb and forefinger and jingling it softly. "We even have a key from the building management."

"That makes it easier." She knew he was alluding to how she had gained access to de Saint-Clair's apartment before. Sandrine had never admitted it, but her former partner knew her and her skill with lock picks quite well. Moreover, he knew how desperately she had searched for a clue to incriminate the suspect. Like Don Quixote, she had charged against the windmills of the police apparatus, but in vain. She remembered it well. She had almost been caught by security in the apartment and had to disappear recklessly over the rooftops. It was hard to believe it had been less than a year since she had left Paris.

Major Alary unlocked the massive front door and marched towards the antique-looking elevator. Sandrine was too impatient and stormed up the stairs. Hermé followed her at a more leisurely pace. A door opened, and an older woman peered out.

"What's all this noise?"

"Police," Sandrine said, flashing her badge as she passed by the woman, who promptly disappeared back into her apartment. The door slammed shut, and a bolt slid into place.

She had reached the door when the elevator also stopped. The metal gate creaked open. Major Alary and two policemen stepped out.

"Not really worth it," the man said to Sandrine, who stepped aside so he could unlock the door and deactivate the alarm. But he was mistaken in his assessment. She hadn't wanted to be the first at the door; she couldn't stand being stuck motionless in an elevator moving at a snail's pace. She needed movement to ease her tension. Sandrine forced herself to let Alary go first. The major worked in the Paris Homicide Division. Here, he had the authority, even though Hermé and she held higher ranks.

At the door to the living room, she stopped. Nothing had changed. Evening light flooded the room through the windows, making the parquet floor gleam. There was a faint scent of floor wax and leather polish. The staff must have taken advantage of the master's absence for a thorough cleaning. A leather seating area dominated the room, which was otherwise sparsely furnished. Modern paintings adorned the walls, ranging from surrealism to cubism. She was convinced that the drawing in a simple frame between two windows was a genuine Picasso, and the bronze sculpture on the sideboard looked like a work by Rodin. She couldn't deny that de Saint-Clair had possessed excellent taste. At least when it came to art.

"You start here," Alary instructed the policemen.

"He wouldn't have been foolish enough to hide anything incriminating here, where he received his visitors. I'll go upstairs."

"Go ahead. We'll follow," Alary said.

"Could you help me?" she asked Hermé. "It'll be faster and we'll overlook less together." It was not so much his assistance she needed but his presence. After all, she had been suspected of breaking in here almost a year ago. The prosecutor was perfect as a witness who could confirm she hadn't brought anything to incriminate de Saint-Clair. It would be even better if he or Major Alary found the evidence.

Hermé followed her up the narrow wooden staircase with carved railings to the upper floor, where the man's desk was located. This was where she had found the USB stick. She didn't believe the man had changed his hiding place. They needed the original USB stick so that the documents on it could be admitted as evidence in court. But most importantly, they needed the password to crack the encryption. He must have left it somewhere in the apartment. Or he knew it by heart, thus the data, due to his death, was lost forever.

Sandrine pushed open the door to the dressing room with the flat of her hand, and it creaked open softly. A freestanding mirror with an intricately carved and gilded frame faced her. The first thing the man would have seen when he entered the room was his own reflection. He must have taken great pleasure in admiring himself. Along the short wall was a massive wardrobe made of dark cherry wood. She approached it. The doors were closed, and ornate keys were inserted in the locks.

"This wardrobe must be several hundred years old and yet looks brand new," Hermé commented, coming over and gently running his hand over the finely grained wood. "Magnificent."

"It'll probably be up for sale soon. As far as I know, he didn't have any children who will inherit this," Sandrine replied.

"Far beyond the salary of a prosecutor." Hermé turned a key and opened the door. He quickly rummaged through the stacked clothes until he found a drawer with ties. Sandrine had wondered if de Saint-Clair had been arrogant enough to keep them after she had discovered them and taken one. The answer lay right before them, and it didn't surprise Sandrine. He had indeed thought himself untouchable. *Then we have an excellent chance that the USB stick is still in the secret compartment of the desk.*

Hermé held up a tie. "This one looks remarkably similar to the one we found in the car."

"It's identical to the ones used to strangle young women. Three of them are in the evidence room at the Paris Police," Sandrine said, recalling where she had found them with the victims.

"Now, that's a lovely surprise," Martin Alary remarked,

standing in the doorway and examining the tie. He pulled out an evidence bag from his pocket and held it open for Hermé to place the tie inside.

"There are even more," the prosecutor remarked. "They could have been used for a dozen more victims."

"That won't be happening now," the major replied, casting a relieved glance at Sandrine. "Where should we continue searching?"

"As I passed by, I took a look into his study. If he kept mementos of his murders, we're most likely to find them there," Sandrine replied.

Major Alary stepped aside, allowing Sandrine to lead the way.

The study was about the same size as the living room but had a sloping roof, making it appear smaller. Sandrine walked to the dormer window and looked out. The sun was setting over the rooftops of the neighbouring buildings, turning the clouds into a pink blanket that draped over the city. Behind her, Hermé perused the bookshelves. Glass doors protected the leather-bound first editions. It reminded her of Fréderic Savier's library, the passionate bookworm from Bécherel. She didn't expect a similar treasure trove in Ariste de Saint-Clair's library. Savier's death was the first case she had investigated with Sébastian Hermé.

"Where would you hide something?" Alary asked.

It was a bait, and she swallowed it without hesitation. She had no time to waste.

"I assume the man wanted to keep the mementos of his deeds close to him, so he could look at them whenever he pleased. I would first search in the desk or one of the dressers," she emphasised the word 'desk', and Alary nodded in understanding.

"They often have secret compartments," he remarked, pushing the chair aside and lying down on the floor to examine the underside.

"I'll check the dresser," she said without much enthusiasm, pulling out the drawers but finding nothing except business documents. She trusted that Alary would find the secret compartment even without tips from her.

"Who would have thought that of the man?" Hermé waved a handful of nude photos of young girls that he had pulled from a drawer.

"We did," Sandrine heard Major Alary say as he ran his fingers over the wood, searching for hidden latches or indentations.

"The first victim was a nude model who accused the man of sexual harassment during a photoshoot. That's how we initially became aware of him," Sandrine explained.

"And?" Hermé prompted.

"She withdrew the complaint shortly afterward. Either he threatened her or pulled out his chequebook."

Something clicked under the desk, as if a spring had come loose.

"I've got it!" the major exclaimed. Carefully, he pulled out the panel at the back of the desk, shining his flashlight into the fist-sized opening. With two fingers, he reached in and pulled out a USB stick. Sandrine shook her head slightly. She would never have left it in this hiding spot, but would have sought out a new one, perhaps even destroyed it. But he couldn't bring himself to do so. Surely, it gave him immense pleasure to look at pictures of his victims and his deeds, because there would hardly be anything else on it. She shook her head; nothing was so valuable that it was worth spending the rest of her life in prison.

Major Alary secured the stick in a bag and crawled out from under the desk.

"I'm curious to see what we'll find on it," the major said. "It's best to check; someone from forensics will have a laptop."

"You go ahead; I'll keep searching here," she said to Hermé.

"Do you think there's anything else interesting to find here?" His doubts were evident, as was his curiosity to take a look at the file.

"We won't know until we've searched everything," she replied. She continued to open drawers and sift through their contents. What she was looking for was a hint to the password. She relied on de Saint-Clair's word; without the access key, they would never uncover the secrets he had stored on the stick, even with the help of the police technicians.

Soon, she closed the last drawer, unsuccessful in uncovering anything new. She went down to Hermé and Alary, and sat on the wide leather sofa.

"How's it going?" she asked the major, who was sitting with a forensics technician in front of the laptop, his resigned expression already answering the question.

"There's only one file on the stick, but it's password-protected," Alary said, looking at the technician, who shook his head.

"Only a fool would leave an unsecured file lying around the apartment," Sandrine replied, as if the information were new to her. "I'm sure there's specialised software in forensics for cracking a password."

"We'll do our best, but I can't guarantee anything." Neither the voice nor the expression of the man seemed particularly promising to her.

"What are you hoping to find in the file?" Martin asked, sitting beside her. "The man is dead, and you have all the evidence you need to close the case. He ultimately admitted his deeds to de Chezac, our charming favourite." Alary made no secret of the fact that he disliked the prosecutor as much as Sandrine did.

"Like in a bad crime novel. The villain confesses everything in the end and gets his just punishment," she said in a bitter tone. "There's something about it that doesn't sit right with me."

"I know what it is. The bastard shot himself, stealing from you the satisfaction of arresting him personally," Alary said.

She pondered his words. He wasn't entirely wrong. She had often imagined herself handcuffing Ariste de Saint-Clair, and each time, it had brought her profound joy. His death had indeed stolen that from her.

"You're probably right. It feels wrong that he's not behind bars where he belongs. Somehow, it feels like he's slipped through my fingers again. And this time, there's no chance for me to bring him to justice," Sandrine said.

"Strange thought," said Hermé. "I'm convinced the man would prefer to be alive and serving his time in prison than lying in a grave."

"I don't think so. The man was a tremendous... no, a grandiose narcissist. Losing to me would be worse than death for him." *Someone who names their yachts after themselves deserves the title of narcissist.* "Damn. How could I overlook this?" she exclaimed, jumping up.

"What's wrong?" Sébastian Hermé looked at her questioningly, while Martin Alary remained seated, accustomed to her sudden insights.

"The diamond he drew on the floor was really a message to me," she said, pacing along the window front.

"Why would he do that? During his last breaths, he certainly had better things to do than think about you," said the major.

"No, he didn't," she replied. She walked to the last window, turned around, and moved back to the wall.

"Are you perhaps a narcissist too?" Hermé tried to make a joke to lighten the tension.

"I have no idea, but for him, it was entirely natural to believe that he was the centre of the world. He saw me as he saw himself. In his world, I would naturally assume that the message was addressed to me."

"What message?"

"He wanted to get me to do something for him." She stopped abruptly and turned to the two men.

"I just don't know what yet."

"I still don't understand what message you're talking about," the prosecutor admitted.

"The guy named his yachts after himself. In numerical order. In Saint-Malo, we have the Ariste VI."

"Yes. We've already searched it. No luck."

"Let's suppose it wasn't meant to be an acute-angled diamond but rather an A for Ariste, upside down on a Roman five."

"That would look like an acute-angled diamond. Is it about his boat?" Hermé asked.

"The Ariste V is moored in the Bassin de l'Arsenal, at the end of the Canal Saint-Martin," Major Alary said.

"I know. De Saint-Clair mentioned it to me. Now I understand why," said Sandrine pensively.

"Why would he send you to his boat anchored in Paris? It doesn't make sense," Alary said, sceptically quirking his mouth.

"He knew that I... we were looking for the password for the stick. I assume it was a clue to where we could find it."

"How could he know that?" the prosecutor asked. "At that time, we had no knowledge of the USB stick at all."

"What else were we supposed to do, except gather evidence? He knows police procedures, especially mine. He could assume that we would discover his hiding place." *And the man knew that I knew the hiding place. There's something on the stick that I'm supposed to find.*

Martin Alary smiled. He had never doubted that it was Sandrine who had broken into de Saint-Clair's place. Now he had her confirmation. But he wouldn't betray her. Her secret was safe with him.

"We need to go to the Ariste V," she decided.

"Alright. After you called, I pre-emptively cancelled my appointment. And I was right; it's going to be a long day again," Alary said, getting up. "Let's wrap up the search here and head to the Bassin de l'Arsenal. Hopefully, we'll find something useful there."

* * *

Major Alary led them to a sleek white motor yacht, which, at 65 feet, was one of the larger boats in the Bassin but appeared modest compared to de Saint-Clair's newest vessel. The Ariste V had been used for cruising along the Seine banks of Paris, to be admired and flaunt one's wealth. Sandrine wondered if the boat had ever seen the open sea. Probably not.

"It hasn't been used in a while," Alary said, pulling aside the transparent cover that protected the open stern from rain, dust, and, most importantly, prying visitors. "A shame. It's a beautiful boat."

"He has a new and much prettier toy," Sandrine remarked, squeezing through the narrow passage between the hull and the cover. "It's in the marina of Saint-Malo."

A glass sliding door separated the lounge at the stern from the living area on the middle deck. Before them lay an elongated space with several seating areas, a bar with its cabinets closed, and a dining table for a dozen guests. Only a faint glimmer of the city lights seeped through the dark-tinted windows.

"Nice place," Hermé commented, walking over to the bar, seating himself on one of the stools and turning to face them. "I could hang out here. Unfortunately, the bar is closed. I'm afraid the kitchen is closed, too."

"Wouldn't surprise me if it's up for sale soon," Major Alary remarked.

"Outside my pay grade, like most of what the man owned," Hermé replied, standing up and heading towards the stairs leading to the cabins.

Sandrine glanced around the living area before following him. They were unlikely to find what they were looking for here.

An hour later, they sat around the table. The search had been fruitless, and Sandrine stretched her legs tiredly. She had been sure they would find a clue to the password. *It was a message to me, I'm sure of it. Maybe I just misunderstood it. But what else could he have meant?*

"We didn't find anything," Alary addressed Sandrine. "The password could be anywhere here. We don't even know what it looks like. Is it in a notebook or on another USB stick? Who knows? The boat is big enough that we could search for days."

"I know," she said wearily. Midnight was approaching, and the stress of the past few days was weighing heavily on her bones. "Let's call it a night." The words didn't come easily, but it was the most sensible option. She couldn't afford to waste another day on a futile search. In Saint-Malo, she could use her time more effectively.

"I can recommend a decent hotel at a discounted rate," the major offered. "You're no longer with the Paris police, so our holding cells are off-limits to you." He turned his head to Sébastian Hermé. "I assume you'd prefer a proper bed to a hard cot?"

"If we take turns driving, we can easily make it to Saint-Malo before breakfast," Sandrine said. Hermé raised his eyebrows slightly. She wondered which part was more surprising, staying up half the night or offering to drive his car. Probably the latter; he most likely holds his car sacred and wouldn't let anyone else behind the wheel.

"It's a long haul, and you're bound to be tired," Alary said.

"I feel okay," she replied. In truth, her inner restlessness would likely prevent her from sleeping. "How about you?" she asked the prosecutor.

"I'm in. I would have stayed for a good meal, but all the restaurants are already closed. We'll be lucky to get more than a coffee from the gas station," Hermé said. He certainly wouldn't bail on Sandrine and choose a night in Paris over this.

"It's a lot to ask, but would you have the apartment and the boat searched again tomorrow? Perhaps we overlooked something," Sandrine requested.

"It'll take quite a few man-hours," Alary said thoughtfully. "But our boss will approve them without complaint. Catching the Necktie Killer will be the talk of the town next week. There will surely be several press conferences."

"I can only imagine," Sandrine nodded. That would be the first thing the leadership of the Criminal Investigation Department would organise tomorrow. The press had often accused them of incompetence. Now it was their turn to bask in some glory.

"They'll probably invite de Chezac as well. After all, he took down a serial killer. Literally," Hermé remarked.

"You deserve recognition for all your work, Sandrine," Martin Alary said, stepping closer to her and putting his arm around her shoulders. "Without you, he'd still be out there killing. That desk jockey just got lucky not to get shot himself."

"Thank you. But it's true, he found the crucial evidence and confronted him. There's no denying that. I'm just glad the bastard is no longer a threat," she replied. She had found one of the ties as well, but it had nearly cost her her job at the police, while de Chezac was now being celebrated.

"It's good that you see it that way," the major said, sounding unconvinced. And he wasn't entirely wrong.

"Then we'd better hit the road," Sébastian Hermé said, bidding farewell to Alary and walking with Sandrine to his car. It was going to be a long drive and a short night.

* * *

It was after nine o'clock when Sandrine rode her motorcycle into the courtyard of the police station. She hadn't gotten much sleep. Sébastian Hermé had insisted on dropping her off at home before driving to his hotel in Saint-Malo. The journey had been silent, leaving Sandrine with plenty to think about. The return to Paris and the search of de Saint-Clair's apartment had stirred up many memories of the murders. She had been convinced of his guilt back then, and it should have felt good that he had been brought to justice, but a sense of satisfaction eluded her. Instead, she felt a tension gripping her tightly, intensifying with every mile they drove towards Saint-Malo.

"It must be the lack of sleep," she muttered as she entered the police station.

She hung her motorcycle jacket over her desk chair and placed her helmet on a file cabinet. For a while, she stared at the computer screen but didn't turn it on. She couldn't bring herself to start typing up the reports to close the case.

"It was quite a long night," Adel said, bringing her a coffee and sitting down beside her.

"You could say that," Sandrine replied.

"I heard you were in Paris. Was it worth it?"

"Not really. We didn't find anything concrete." She didn't mention the USB data stick; without the password, it was worthless. Maybe the specialists in Paris could do something. "I had higher expectations, but I guess I was wrong."

"With what we have, we can close the case," Adel said.

"There's a meeting scheduled in the conference room in half an hour. They're expecting you."

"No surprise there."

"Hardly. We've never managed to convict a serial killer from Paris."

"And now they'll negotiate who gets what credit and who gets to attend which press conferences?" she asked her assistant, who typically had better knowledge of the station's internal affairs than she did.

"I can imagine. Anyway, de Chezac is with Hermé at Commissaire Matisse's office. The guy looks pretty rough. He must have taken quite a beating."

"I suppose he did," she said, recalling the prosecutor's swollen eye, but also how often she herself had wished to punch him in the face. De Saint-Clair seemed to have fewer inhibitions than she did. The urge to grin welled up inside her, but she forced herself to ignore it; it would have been inappropriate.

"Are you coming along?"

"I wasn't invited," Adel replied. "It's a meeting for the higher-ups. I'm not included in that."

"Not yet."

"I'm a brigadier," he reminded her.

Sandrine picked up her coffee and took a sip. Over the rim of the paper cup, she observed Adel. He was one of the best cops she had ever worked with.

"You should change that."

"What do you mean?"

She gestured with her thumb towards the courtyard. On the other side lay the police school of the Police Nationale.

"You'd spend a few more years hitting the books. But your salary would continue, and you wouldn't have to move. It couldn't be more convenient. If I ever wanted to ask for your advice, it's just a few feet across the yard."

Adel leaned over the desk, resting his forearms, and scrutinised Sandrine intently, as if to make sure she was as serious as she sounded.

"We make a good team, and the work is enjoyable. It would be hard for me to give that up to spend my days in a school," he said thoughtfully.

"Think about your future. Who knows how long I'll still be here?"

"What do you plan to do?" he asked suspiciously.

"The same thing I always do, solve my cases." *If I mess up this time, I'll spend the rest of my life sorting files or writing parking tickets.*

"Don't do anything stupid," he cautioned her sternly, as if he had a premonition of what was going on in her mind. "You've gotten too close to this case."

"When have I ever done something foolish?"

Adel rolled his eyes, and Sandrine grinned cheerfully.

* * *

The two police officers from Rennes were already in the conference room. Commandant Jogu flipped through a file, briefly glancing up as Sandrine entered the room. Major Baud nodded to her, which seemed to serve as a greeting.

Sandrine chose a chair near the door. She had just sat down when Commissaire Matisse and the two prosecutors entered. De Chezac's eye was still swollen and turning dark blue. He would hate to appear in the newspapers with that black eye. A beautician would have her hands full trying to make him presentable enough for a press conference.

Matisse took a seat at the head of the elongated table and looked around the room. His nod indicated that everyone he had invited was present. "I am pleased that we have prosecutor Antoine de Chezac back with us. With this, we can consider the current case closed. We have identified a serial killer, something to be proud of."

"Indeed," the prosecutor agreed.

"Perhaps you could briefly describe the events leading to your abduction and the death of de Saint-Clair," Hermé asked him.

"I have already provided all the details to Commandant Jogu in my statement. In full," he replied.

"A brief overview would suffice for me. I will review the protocol in detail later. I'm sure this request will be made of you frequently in the coming days. As far as I know, you have been invited to a press conference in Paris. Surely you will also have to answer to reporters in Saint-Malo beforehand."

"That's correct," he said, turning to Sandrine. "I intend to ask Capitaine Perrot to accompany me. She was the one who suspected Ariste de Saint-Clair from the beginning of the investigation. I did not give enough credence to her theory, and for that, I must sincerely apologise."

Her eyebrows shot up in surprise. Sharing the spotlight was clearly difficult for the man. To apologise to her on top of that almost took her breath away. What prompted this change? Had the near-certain death at the hands of de Saint-Clair triggered it?

"That's part of my job. No need to apologise," she deflected.

"Yes, it is necessary," the prosecutor insisted stubbornly. "I was very unfair to you. I should have been a better superior. In the process, I almost lost one of the best policewomen I've ever known."

"I agree," said Commissaire Matisse, "but now back to the case."

"Due to the events in Paris and the evidence from Saint-Malo, such as the photos Mademoiselle Mignon took of de Saint-Clair, the portrait in the studio, and the unusual bottle of Cognac at

Brigadier Poutin's house, the suspect was already under investigation. During a dinner on his yacht, I looked around and came across the tie. Unfortunately, de Saint-Clair's bodyguard suspected me of stealing it. I tried to talk my way out of it, but apparently without success, as he informed his boss," de Chezac explained.

Matisse opened the file. "The fingerprints on the Cognac bottle have been compared to those of the suspect, and they match. De Saint-Clair touched the bottle found at Poutin's, probably brought it along, and forced Brigadier Poutin to drink from it. We can definitely link him to Brigadier Poutin's death."

"He admitted it to me," de Chezac interjected. "He probably didn't expect me to be in a position to tell anyone."

"Hair traces from Miriam Mignon were found on the tie, matching those used in Paris," Matisse continued. "There is no doubt that it is the murder weapon. De Saint-Clair's guilt in the death of the young woman is beyond doubt."

"What happened on the boat?" Hermé asked.

"After he abducted me from my house and dragged me onto the boat, he locked me in the cabin. I suspect he needed me alive as a hostage until he could disappear. Financial resources for a longer escape were no problem for him. His company has branches worldwide. He threatened me several times with the gun or took out his anger on me." He pointed with a finger at his eye, through which he could barely see. "He hit me again, and I kicked desperately in his direction. By chance, I caught his hand with the gun. A shot went off and hit him in the stomach. He let go of me, forced me to put on handcuffs at gunpoint, and staggered out of the cabin. I heard him stumbling up the stairs, then there was silence on board. I assumed he was tending to his wound. I couldn't see how bad it was, as he was wearing a red jacket. We drifted at sea for several hours before running aground and getting stuck in the mudflats. Eventually, I was rescued." He turned to Sandrine. "I have never been so glad to see you as I was that day. Thank you very much; you probably saved my life." Tears glistened in his eyes. Then he looked at Major Baud. "The same goes for you, of course."

"That's part of our job," said the woman, visibly uncomfortable with de Chezac's attention and emotional speech.

"We have compelling evidence of his involvement in both deaths and an oral confession to prosecutor de Chezac. I suggest closing both cases with this." Matisse took over the meeting again. "But of course, it's up to the two prosecutors." He looked expectantly at the two men.

"I agree," de Chezac concurred.

"What's your take on this?" Hermé asked Commandant Jogu.

"I have no objections."

"Then I also agree. I have no doubt that de Saint-Clair knew Capitaine Perrot would continue to investigate him. He enlisted the help of Brigadier Poutin to tarnish her reputation, perhaps even to persuade her to leave the police force. When the plan failed, he got rid of his accomplice. That makes sense to me. Do you see it differently, Capitaine Perrot?"

"I have no doubt about his guilt in Miriam Mignon's death. I consider the case resolved."

"And what about Brigadier Poutin?" Hermé inquired.

"Brigadier Poutin did the dirty work for de Saint-Clair and was paid for it. That seems clear-cut, but I am convinced that there is another accomplice, one who was likely involved in the murder of Brigadier Poutin," Sandrine asserted.

"Someone else?" Commandant Jogu asked, surprised. "I see no need for a third person to be involved. After de Saint-Clair murdered the woman, the brigadier cleaned up the crime scene behind him. De Saint-Clair must have been furious that one of his lackeys dared to disrupt his staging. That probably made it even easier for him to decide to get rid of the accomplice."

"There is no evidence that it was Poutin who tried to dispose of the body," Sandrine countered.

"But there's no evidence against it either." The usually composed Jogu seemed unconvinced by her conjectures.

"Poutin was utterly insignificant to someone like de Saint-Clair. He was just a pawn in the game. Why would de Saint-Clair have to inform him that he had killed a woman? At most, he would have created a potential blackmailer, or someone who wanted nothing to do with a murder and would have snitched to the police," Sandrine reasoned.

"He paid well, as we have seen. As such, moral scruples often fall by the wayside," Jogu countered, appearing increasingly irritable.

"You experienced Poutin during the interrogation; the man did not feel threatened. He claimed to me that he was being protected by someone with influence," Sandrine explained.

"Who could that be more than de Saint-Clair?" Matisse inquired.

"Influence over the investigation from the police or a prosecutor? I highly doubt it," Sandrine pondered. "I am convinced he was referring to someone within the police force. Poutin was an old-fashioned man; he would never have trusted a civilian, but a policeman, yes."

"Is there anyone you suspect?" Matisse asked hesitantly, likely realising he might not like the answer.

"I have no evidence, but it is striking that the brigadier became increasingly confident after the team from Rennes arrived here." Sandrine dropped the bombshell, and the reactions were immediate. Matisse rolled his eyes and sighed deeply, likely regretting inviting her to the meeting. Hermé stared at her in astonishment, while Jogu jumped up.

"'This is outrageous. Are you suggesting we are corrupt?"

Only Major Baud looked at her unmoved, as if the accusation didn't particularly surprise her.

"As Capitaine Perrot already stated, there is no evidence to support your view. We've all had some long and exhausting days; let's conclude the meeting at this point." Commissaire Matisse attempted to defuse the tension before it could escalate into an open dispute. "We will follow the recommendations of the competent prosecutors and close the cases."

The team from Rennes got up and left the conference room. Commandant Jogu shot her an annoyed glance, and Sébastian Hermé briefly leaned towards her.

"What were you thinking?" he asked.

"It had to be done."

Without a reply, he followed his colleagues.

"You possess a self-destructive trait that evidently compels you to offend others." De Chezac closed the file lying in front of him on the table and stood up. "Send me your reports so we can close the case. If you insist on these accusations and cannot prove them, it will be very unpleasant for you." Then he left her with Commissaire Matisse.

"You didn't do yourself any favours just now, but I'm sure you're aware of that," Matisse remarked.

"I have no doubt about it."

"Was it really necessary to accuse the team from Rennes?" he asked.

"Yes, otherwise I would have refrained," Sandrine replied. "Contrary to de Chezac's assumption, it brings me no joy to accuse colleagues of a crime."

"I'm curious how you plan to extricate yourself from the mess you willingly got yourself into."

"I'm doing my best."

"And I hope you succeed, even if it means we still have a corrupt policeman on the force. Take the rest of the day off and reconsider your accusation."

Then Matisse rose, leaving her alone in the conference

room. As uncomfortable as the last few minutes had been, she felt relieved that her boss didn't consider her crazy, as de Chezac evidently did, but instead gave her the chance to prove her theory. Which wouldn't be easy.

* * *

She found Jean-Claude Mazet at his workplace in the forensics department.

"May I?" She placed her hand on the armrest of the chair opposite him.

"But of course. Please, have a seat. You've been keeping us quite busy lately. The paperwork is going to drag on for a few more weeks, and the evidence is piling up in the lab."

"That's why I'm here. What's new?"

The man gestured towards a row of file folders. "Where should I begin?"

"From the beginning. With my crime scene."

"There are no new developments there. The man left no traces; he knew exactly what he was doing. But that shouldn't surprise me, considering he's rumoured to be quite skilled."

"It was his fourth murder, as far as we know, following the same pattern. The evidence has always been extremely thin. After a year of investigation, the Parisian police still had nothing."

"Fortunately, things look much better here. Especially at Poutin's house. The bottle with the fingerprints was an unforgivable mistake. Perhaps Luc's death wasn't planned, and in the commotion, he overlooked the bottle."

"That could have been the case; at least, that's the official opinion of the prosecutor." She herself struggled to imagine de Saint-Clair in Poutin's house. The man would never have set foot inside if he hadn't intended to kill the brigadier. Why would he suddenly panic? He had seen enough corpses already.

"Are there any clues suggesting a third person at the crime scene? Someone who assisted de Saint-Clair in carrying out the act?"

"I can't disprove the assumption, but there's also nothing to support it. At any rate, we haven't found any clues. Should I send someone over again?"

"No. Your team works meticulously; if there had been any hint, it would have been noticed during the initial search. Besides, his wife has started tidying up the house again. She probably destroyed any potential evidence already."

"Then we have de Chezac's house." Mazet lifted a file. "Again, nothing. Nothing unusual outside the living room. The statement seems to be accurate; de Chezac willingly opened the door for him. There was a struggle in the living room." He paused and placed the file back on the table. "I ran into Prosecutor de Chezac this morning; he looks awful. But given the signs of struggle in his living room, I would have expected to find him in a hospital."

"He was lucky to be alive at all."

"More than just luck. I don't understand why there was a struggle in the first place. This guy threatened him with a weapon. Who starts a fight then?" Mazet said.

"Someone with a lot of fear and little sense," Sandrine replied.

"Anyway, we examined the travel bag found in the car's trunk in the lab."

"What did you find?"

"Except for the tie, everything was unremarkable. The skin traces indeed belong to Miriam Mignon. The results came in this morning. She was strangled with it."

"Twice?" Sandrine asked. "First with the tie, then with the rope found at Poutin's?"

"Both had the victim's DNA on them. The marks on the neck were caused by the tie, according to the forensic examination. The narrower and rougher rope was drawn over her skin post-mortem, probably to leave traces and manipulate the evidence."

"And on the boat?"

"That was a change from our usual crime scenes. We had plenty of time to search the boat while waiting for the tide and then sailing into the harbour. Now it's back in the Port des Sablons. The weapon found next to the victim was definitely the murder weapon. A Glock 17, the same as those used by the police. The shot was fired at close range, probably no more than a hand's breadth from the body. The gunshot residue on the clothing is clear. Only one cartridge was missing, and we found the casing in the cabin. That's also where de Chezac claims the shot was fired."

"Where did you find blood traces?"

"Only in the kitchen. He died where he was found."

"No drops between the cabin and the kitchen? The man must have bled quite a lot."

"That puzzled me too, and I had it checked twice, but there was no blood. Perhaps the fabric of his clothing absorbed it until he reached the kitchen. There, his strength left him, and he collapsed to the floor, where he died."

"Unusual, but possible. Thank you."

"Do you have any idea what the diamond he drew on the floor might mean?" Mazet asked. "I couldn't come up with an explanation."

"My guess was that it was an A and a Roman numeral five. A clue to Ariste V, hence my detour to Paris. But it was a dead end, leading to nothing," Sandrine explained.

"I'm sorry to hear that. But the case seems pretty clear as it is. The guy is responsible for the girl's death."

"I agree with you."

"We'll figure out the few remaining puzzle pieces, even if it means putting in some overtime."

Jamila waved to her from the opposite side of the lab, where she was sitting with Marie in front of a screen. Sandrine waved back.

"I'm glad she's enjoying her time with us."

"Jamila? Stay away from her!" the head of forensics replied in an unusually resolute tone. Sandrine turned to the man, surprised, as he grinned broadly at her.

"Adel was here last week and described to us a picture of a sheltered girl with little life experience and a dislike for blood and violence. I fell for it hook, line, and sinker. Do they really live in the same house?" he asked, shaking his head slightly.

"I don't understand what you mean."

"I greatly respect Adel. Honestly. But if that's his understanding of people, I wonder how he solves any cases at all. The girl is clever and has a quick mind. Moreover, she doesn't have the nature of a delicate flower; she's more like a bulldog."

"Bulldog," Sandrine repeated, looking over at the slender girl.

"When she's latched onto a problem, she won't let go until she's solved it. How long do you think Jamila sat here, staring at pictures, until she noticed the camera outside the window? She's among the first to arrive in the morning and the last to leave in the evening," Mazet remarked.

"Plus, she makes an excellent couscous," Sandrine muttered. *Or she gets it from her parents' kitchen, who ran a renowned Moroccan restaurant.*

"That's another point," Mazet agreed.

"Adel will be pleased when I pass on the praise. But why should we stay away from her?"

He turned to look at Jamila, then leaned in closer to Sandrine, speaking in a lower voice.

"She's practically born for this job here. But she also has ideas in her head that it might be more exciting to chase criminals and shoot guns around. Probably watches too much TV and wants to be a female James Bond. What nonsense. Most cases are solved right here in the lab."

"Jamila Bond. Sounds good, too," Sandrine teased the forensic technician.

"Like I said, she's made for this job here," he replied, sounding as if he could already see the day he would hand over his lab to her.

"Adel will be pleased; he doesn't want her working in our department. He's overprotective and won't admit it, but secretly he thinks I'm a bad influence on his sister."

"Where he's right, he's right," Mazet agreed.

"In that case, I'll make my exit before you further insult me," she said facetiously.

"Where are you headed?"

"I'm off for a quick chat with Dr Mason, then I'll head home. I've accumulated enough overtime to take the afternoon off." *Besides, after insinuating corruption in the police force, I'm not particularly welcome here at the station right now.*

* * *

"Glad to see you visiting me," Alexandre Mason greeted her. He wore a lab coat that was no longer quite white and had been patched in a few places. He didn't seem particularly vain, but the deceased would forgive him. He opened the compartment in the morgue and pulled out the gurney with Ariste de Saint-Clair's body.

"Do you really want to see him?" He held the cloth covering the man in his hand, waiting for her confirmation.

"I have a few questions about his death, and you're the expert."

"Indeed." With a flourish, he pulled the shroud down to the man's hips. The Y-shaped incision was neatly stitched, and the wound in the abdomen was clean. There was nothing more than a finger-width bullet hole to be seen.

"Tell me," Sandrine prompted the medic.

"The case is clear. This dead man on my table is one of the healthiest specimens of a human I've seen in a long time. Balanced diet, exercise, and a healthy lifestyle can work wonders."

"Killing people isn't exactly what I consider an exemplary lifestyle."

"I didn't mean it like that." The doctor's cheeks flushed.

"I know. But let's not forget who's lying here in front of us. He hardly deserves any special sympathy. Nevertheless, I want to find out exactly how he died. There are some things I still can't explain."

"That's pretty straightforward." He extended a telescopic pointer and indicated the gunshot wound. "The bullet entered fairly straight-on and nicked the abdominal aorta. The man bled out."

"How long would that have taken? Rough estimate?"

"Quickly. A few minutes."

"The wound would have bled instantly and heavily. Am I understanding that correctly?"

"Absolutely."

"How long could the shirt have contained the bleeding?"

"A thick coat might have contained some of the bleeding, but certainly not a thin summer shirt like he was wearing. His jacket was water-repellent, so it didn't absorb any blood. Why do you ask?"

"He managed to drag himself from the cabin below deck up to the kitchen without leaving a blood trail."

"I find that hard to believe."

"Would it have been possible?"

"There was no exit wound; most likely, the initial blood mainly flowed into the abdominal cavity. It's possible but rather unlikely. The bullet came directly from the front," the man positioned the telescopic pointer vertically on the wound, "and entered here."

"Directly from the front?"

"Yes."

"Interesting," she murmured. Slowly, the puzzle pieces fell into place, and the picture became clearer. An ugly picture, showing what had led to Ariste de Saint-Clair's death.

* * *

Sandrine parked the BMW on its kickstand and removed her helmet, hanging it on the right-side mirror before dismounting. To her surprise, Jamila was standing at the rear of the Ariste VI.

"Monsieur Mazet sent me to unlock it," she said, holding up the keys to the boat.

Sandrine had called him, asking for another look inside the boat. She still feared she might have overlooked something that de Saint-Clair had wanted to tell her.

"How did you get here so quickly?" Sandrine asked.

"A patrol car brought me. My parents used to be afraid of their kids ever having to ride in a police car, but now it's part of my job. Cool," she beamed at Sandrine. The internship at the police seemed to be a lot of fun for her.

"Jean-Claude Mazet says you're doing well. Adel will be pleased."

"Not so sure," she mumbled as she unlocked the boat.

"Sure he will."

"I think he'd rather see me working at my parents' restaurant or my sister's until I marry a nice man, have kids, and stay at home. He's not exactly a fan of equality."

Sandrine laughed at the thought, although she wasn't entirely wrong about it.

"It's quite nice here," Jamila said, standing behind the door and looking around the luxurious mid-deck. "My art teacher would go crazy seeing these paintings. It's like a museum."

"De Saint-Clair had a fondness for art," said Sandrine.

"And also the cash to afford it," Jamila added, stepping in front of one of the paintings and examining it for a moment. "In any case, he had good taste."

"Be glad you never met him. You would have appealed to him, which doesn't mean anything good."

"I have kind of an intuition for quirky people," Jamila said. "This one would definitely have been too rich for my taste. What are we looking for?"

"I'm not exactly sure. He left me a message: Ariste V. Written in his blood."

"The guy liked you," Jamila said abruptly.

"What?" Sandrine had never entertained that idea before.

"Well, his last thought was of you. He was probably secretly infatuated with you."

"That's more than far-fetched. He tried to ruin my career. I suspect he would have preferred to strangle me, like his other victims."

Jamila shook her head.

"You're not a victim; the man knew that if he wasn't completely blind. He was probably trying to lure you to the dark side. Maybe as his morbid companion."

"You watch too much TV." *She certainly has an imagination.* "Let's focus on looking around to see if we find anything related to Ariste V."

They started on the mid-deck and slowly worked their way forward to the cabins below deck, so far without discovering any clues.

"If it were important to me, I would keep it close to me," Jamila remarked.

"That's why we're going to check out the main cabin, where de Chezac claims to have found the tie."

"Claims?"

"He found the tie there," she corrected herself and pulled at the door of the cabin, but it was locked.

"Did your boss give you a key for the door?"

"There's no key for that." She stepped closer and pulled aside a curtain. Behind it was a keypad. Quickly, she entered the combination, which was written on a note she pulled from her pocket, and the door lock opened.

During the initial search of the yacht, the door had been left open, and Sandrine had missed the keypad. De Saint-Clair likely installed it after some art objects went missing. And it kept snoops like de Chezac out.

A double bed occupied much of the room. Cabinets of reddish-brown wood lined the walls, and a mirrored sliding door led to the bathroom. A seating area with leather sofas completed the furnishings. Pictures hung on the walls, but only photographs with maritime motifs.

"Here's something." Jamila waved her over. A row of framed photographs of his boats hung on the wall, from the Ariste I to VI. "He couldn't buy many more, or he'd run out of space on the wall," she commented.

"I think this boat would have sufficed for a while. This here is the Ariste V." She tapped on the picture of the boat she had been on yesterday. It wasn't docked at its usual berth but had been taken from the banks of the Seine. She recognised de Saint-Clair, standing at the helm on the upper deck. In the background stood the Eiffel Tower. She knew the spot where the picture had been taken. Her fingertip traced over the glass of the frame, following her searching gaze until it landed on a darker shadow, difficult to distinguish against the grey of the Seine. *That's what he wanted to tell me.* She took the picture off the wall and approached one of the windows. Upon closer inspection, the spot consisted of many different grey and white squares within a square outline.

"Do you know what this is?" she asked the girl.

"Looks like a QR code that leads to a website link."

"Exactly. And probably to the final pieces of evidence in our case." She pulled out her phone from her pocket and scanned the QR code. Instantly, a link popped up, which she tapped. A combination of numbers and letters appeared on the screen: the password she had been searching for so long. Quickly, she secured the code with a screenshot before it disappeared.

"Is this what we've been looking for?"

"I'm convinced it is. You're a real lucky charm."

"That's why you should take me along on your investigations more often." She instantly seized the opportunity.

"As soon as Adel agrees, you're welcome to join us."

"Awesome," she replied, almost bouncing with excitement. Her mind was probably already working on the problem of how to best to convince her brother.

"Don't get too excited. Most of our cases aren't as thrilling as this one. Luckily, people in Saint-Malo are pretty peaceful."

"If it's up to Adel, it'll definitely be something boring. Graffiti on a wall or a stolen bike," she said with subdued enthusiasm.

"Now you need to go back to Monsieur Mazet and give him the picture. It's an important piece of evidence."

"You can count on me. I'll deliver it safely."

Sandrine called the station to send a patrol. She couldn't take Jamila and the picture on the motorcycle.

Shortly after, a patrol car arrived, and the girl bid farewell. She had wrapped the picture in a towel and held it securely in her hands.

Sandrine remained seated at the table on the mid-deck. Even though she hadn't yet glanced at the file, she already had a sense of what she would find on it. The tension that had gripped her throughout the day fell away like a stone, and exhaustion took its place. She leaned back in the seat and closed her eyes for a moment. Tonight, she would be able to close the case.

* * *

Sandrine parked the motorcycle in the narrow alley below the Tour Bidouane and climbed the stairs up to the rampart. It was just after midnight. She had sent him a message, asking to meet him here to hand over the evidence of who the corrupt policeman was who had helped de Saint-Clair. She had doubted whether he would comply with the request to meet her at this location and so late at night, but in the moonlight, she recognised the silhouette of a figure on the tower.

"Good," she murmured. His curiosity got the best of him.

In her left hand, she held the motorcycle helmet, and with her right, she checked if she could draw the pistol that hung in a holster on her belt, half concealed by her jacket. With every step closer to the tower, her tension rose. She loosened her shoulders as she walked. *You have all the evidence you need,* she repeated in her mind like a mantra. If she had miscalculated, her time at the police would be over. Sandrine forced herself to ascend the narrow spiral staircase slowly, although she was eager to face the man.

She stepped out of the dark stairwell onto the platform of the tower. The man had his back to her, and she approached him.

"I'm used to many things from you, but what's the meaning of summoning me here in the middle of the night?"

"The case of Miriam Mignon started here, so I find it fitting to end it here as well. Besides, you came, that's what matters."

Antoine de Chezac turned around and scrutinised her intently. "Out with it! What new evidence do you have? And who is the corrupt policeman?"

Sandrine took a step back. "Right at this spot is where de Saint-Clair dropped off the victim."

"I know that; I read the reports," he retorted irritably.

"At that time, she was still wearing the silk tie with the embroidered rose around her neck. But you know that."

"I found the tie on the man's yacht; it was definitely the murder weapon. Everyone knows that. If you don't have any new information, I'll leave now." He took a step towards the stairs, but hesitated too much for Sandrine to believe him.

"I have one too. There are plenty of them." She pulled out the tie she had stolen from de Saint-Clair in Paris from her jacket pocket. It dangled from her hand like a noose.

"Where did you get that from?"

"De Saint-Clair came to Saint-Malo to send me a message."

"And what was that supposed to be?" He didn't hide his cynicism. "Why would he be interested in a small and insignificant policewoman like yourself?" The gratitude he had shown her earlier in the morning had completely disappeared by now. Perhaps it was because there were no witnesses to whom he had to perform his act.

"He wanted to show me that he can murder people anywhere. No one, especially not a small and insignificant policewoman, could touch him."

"A ludicrous idea. You massively overestimate your importance in these investigations."

"He must have been angry that you ruined his staging." Sandrine walked to the wall and placed a hand on the railing. "You rolled her over the wall here, didn't you?"

"Me? You're crazy." He took a step back and stared at her. In the moonlight, his skin looked pale, as if the blood had drained from his cheeks. His hands clenched into fists, which he pressed tightly against his legs. He had known Sandrine long enough to know that she could defend herself. He wouldn't attack her physically. Sandrine imagined his thoughts anxiously swirling around what she might have found out. After all, she had accused him of complicity.

"How did it happen? He murdered Miriam Mignon and

told you about it. Did he call you to boast about it, or did he casually whisper it in your ear at the party on the boat? He must have loved humiliating you."

De Chezac opened his mouth to retort, but no words came out, only an overwhelming anger distorting his expression.

"Anyway, you came here to make the body disappear." Sandrine moved around him in a semicircle, like a matador circling an aggressive bull. "I'm sure you ran to the crime scene as fast as you could. At any moment, a loving couple could have found a quiet spot and stumbled upon the body. You had to prevent that at all costs. The resemblance to the Paris murders was too striking. Even for you, protecting him from the police again would have been difficult."

"Why would I want to protect him?"

"Because you did it in Paris already, but with the murder in Saint-Malo, he went too far. You decided to put an end to it: to finally rid yourself of the man who loved to humiliate you. Inevitably, all the accomplices, like Brigadier Poutin, had to go too."

De Chezac abruptly turned away and went to the railing. He silently gazed over the silvery sea to the lights of Dinard on the other side of the Rance. The fingers clutching the railing betrayed his tension.

"You can't prove any of that. Those are just figments of your imagination. De Saint-Clair was right, he's inside your head, driving you crazy." The words came out choppy and harsh; the man seemed on the verge of panic, and Sandrine couldn't gauge what he would do next. She forced herself not to reach for her weapon. She wasn't in danger yet.

"De Saint-Clair was always cleverer than you," she said.

The prosecutor emitted a gruff sound. A vulnerable narcissist, that's how Suzanne Leriche had described him. He lashed out when he felt attacked. So Sandrine pressed on. She had to unsettle him.

"The man committed three murders in Paris without leaving a trace. We couldn't prove anything against him. He came remarkably close to perfect murders."

"He wasn't as clever as you think." The response came spontaneously, without much thought. He probably regretted his outburst already.

"Because you helped him erase his traces and keep the investigators at bay."

"Something else you can't prove. I think I'd rather leave now. See you tomorrow at your boss's office." Despite his threat, he didn't move. It was an empty threat; he would never leave without knowing what she knew.

"He was brilliant at leaving no traces, and here in Saint-Malo, he made one rookie mistake after another. I wondered why. What had happened to the man?"

"He got cocky after getting away with the murders in Paris. Arrogance is a pitfall where criminals trap themselves, thinking they're smarter than everyone else."

"Or the evidence was planted on him," she said.

"More fantasies."

"There was the connection to Miriam Mignon that made me think. Like a rabbit out of a hat, suddenly the photos appeared in her apartment."

"She was a photographer. What surprises you about that? Of course she would have taken pictures of the admirer of her art," he snapped at her. "Even someone like you should understand that."

"I'm just surprised by people who come back from the dead to photograph their murderer. If that happened more often, my job would be much easier."

"What do you mean?" The panic in his voice intensified. He obviously felt that he had made an irreparable mistake.

"In the background of the Ariste lies the *Émeraude*. A nice sailboat owned by the Barnais family. You met them in Le

Mont-Saint-Michel when you were there with me to investigate the death of their mother. The woman in the picture is Blanche Barnais, and she assured me that she had only boarded the boat on Monday. So who took the photos? Certainly not Miriam Mignon, who was murdered on Sunday night."

"You must be mistaken."

"Unfortunately, you had to delete the memory cards. Forensics would have found out if anything had been altered on the date of the recording. The woman kept tens of thousands of pictures, but these, to which she should have had an emotional attachment, were missing from the memory card, which made me suspicious."

"But the unfinished portrait of de Saint-Clair in her studio. Do you think I could draw a picture so quickly?"

"Of course not. But you wanted to make sure that we uncovered the connection between the two and stole it from the yacht. De Saint-Clair complained to his bodyguard about small art objects disappearing. That's why he also had the lock installed on his cabin. Do you know that he suspected you? That's why his bodyguard kept an eye on you."

"Nonsense."

"Mademoiselle Mignon painted watercolours, why would she suddenly radically change her style and technique? That's unlikely. Moreover, the forensic team found no charcoal pencils, erasers, or textured paper used for charcoal drawings in her studio, only the equipment she used for her watercolours. But even more surprising is that I didn't mention the painting during the interrogation with de Saint-Clair at all. How did you know about it?"

"It was in one of the reports."

"I haven't written a report about it yet. Therefore, you can only know because you stole it aboard the yacht and deposited it in the victim's studio yourself. I bet de Saint-Clair commissioned the portrait in Paris and left before it was finished. Major Alary has a photo of the drawing and is visiting the potential artists. It's only a matter of time before he comes across it. At the same time, you took the Cognac with de Saint-Clair's fingerprints from the bar."

"That proves nothing." His voice had lost its strength. De Chezac must have known that he was caught in a trap from which he could hardly escape.

"The portrait and the photos led you to Miriam Mignon's studio, and you put the Cognac bottle in the pocket of the dead Poutin. You are too wealthy to understand the living conditions of a simple brigadier. A two-hundred-euro bottle would catch the attention of the forensics. Besides, you didn't know the man well enough. Poutin only drank pastis and Breton apple schnapps. He detested Cognac. The rope in the dead man's pocket was just excessive; you bombarded us with clues and evidence against de Saint-Clair. Even Major Baud quickly realised that the suicide was staged. However, she still suspected de Saint-Clair was behind it, while you were the one who put the noose around Poutin's neck and got rid of a witness."

"It was de Saint-Clair. He admitted it to me."

"Another lie. The man would never leave a bottle with his prints behind," said Sandrine. "Besides, he would have put the tie in the man's pocket, not the rope. But that was impossible for him since he left the tie at the crime scene. The one who must have had it was the one who cleaned up after him. Also you. De Saint-Clair probably didn't even know about the existence of this rope."

"And then? Why did de Saint-Clair attack me, abduct me from my house, and try to kill me? If I hadn't been extremely lucky, my body would be floating somewhere in the English Channel right now."

"Your living room looked like a battlefield. That made me

think. It was grossly exaggerated. Plus, there was a tiny bloodstain. If I've ever seen a fake crime scene, it was this one."

De Chezac was about to retort, but Sandrine waved him off and the man fell silent, bewildered.

"The next mistake was the tie in the trunk. If de Saint-Clair had been on the run, he would have had to assume that we would find the car. The man would have taken the piece of evidence and thrown it overboard as soon as the boat left the harbour. It went completely differently. I assume you either lured him on board or forced him at gunpoint."

"And who beat me up and tied me to the bed?"

"You did that yourself, after you shot de Saint-Clair."

"More of your nonsense," he countered, but not nearly as vehemently as a few minutes ago. His fingers brushed over his neck, as if he could feel the noose tightening around it, slowly but relentlessly.

"The bullet hit him straight on from the front. The man was right-handed. If you had knocked his hand aside, the bullet would have entered at an angle, but not at a right angle. Wrists aren't that flexible. Furthermore, we found no blood traces from the cabin to the kitchen, something our forensic pathologist deems extremely unlikely. There's only one possibility: you shot de Saint-Clair in the kitchen, as blood was only found there. Then you went to the cabin, hit yourself in the face several times or smashed your head against the wall, and handcuffed yourself to the bed. Of course, Matisse and Hermé did everything humanly possible to find you. All you had to do was wait for us."

"This is all circumstantial evidence, not proof. You have nothing concrete in your hands."

"Now here's the astonishing part. De Saint-Clair didn't want to go down without taking his revenge on you."

"What?" he stammered.

"You know his USB data stick? Major Alary found it in de Saint-Clair's apartment. Surely we'll find on it the reason why he could blackmail you."

"The Paris police assured me this morning that it would be un-crackable. So you're bluffing."

"With his blood, he left me another message that led me to the password's hiding place."

She pulled out her phone with her right hand and loaded the screenshot of the password. De Chezac leaned forward and stared at it. Anger flashed in his eyes and a thin thread of saliva slid down from the corner of his mouth.

"You cursed bitch," he shouted, stepping back. Faster than Sandrine would have expected, he drew a weapon from his jacket pocket and pointed it at her. "My life would have been so much better if I had never met you. Why do you stick your damn nose into things that don't concern you?"

"It runs in the family, I suppose." With the phone in her hand, she had no chance to draw her service weapon in time.

"He feared that you might find some way to pin the murders on him, so he wanted me to get you out of the police force."

"That almost worked in Paris."

"But only almost. Because of you, I had to move to this godforsaken province and deal with an idiot like Poutin, who had a simple job but completely botched it."

"De Saint-Clair wasn't particularly pleased with you, was he? What did he have against you?"

"That's not relevant anymore. I had a streak of bad luck at the casino, and he helped me out of it. When he called me saying a prostitute had died in his apartment, I believed it was an accident during sex. He seemed to enjoy strangling his partners, and it got out of control. What was I supposed to do? De Saint-Clair could have financially ruined me, so I helped him make the body disappear."

"And he recorded everything in his apartment. Just like he recorded me when I broke into his place."

The prosecutor only nodded. He must have realised he was finished.

"Put the gun down, it will only end worse for you," she urged him.

"It's over anyway. And you certainly won't be arresting me. Definitely not you," he repeated, injecting his entire contempt for Sandrine into his hoarse voice. "Of course, I've made arrangements in case I need to disappear quickly. It looks like that day has come."

Sandrine noticed the sparkle in his eyes and hurled the helmet in his direction. The gun went off. A blow struck her chest, knocking the air out of her lungs. Arms outstretched, she flew backwards and crashed hard onto her back. Gasping for air, she struggled to breathe. The pain brought tears to her eyes, and the surroundings blurred as a beam of light cut through the darkness. Two figures appeared at the stairs, shining the flashlight beam on de Chezac, who spun around and fired a shot at them, the bullet ricocheting off the wall. The newcomers threw themselves to the ground, and the light went out.

Sandrine reached for her holster and managed to draw the pistol. Half-blind, she raised the weapon, pointing it in the direction of the man who was turning to face the strangers, and squeezed the trigger. He screamed and staggered backwards. Suddenly, he disappeared into the darkness. Exhausted, she lost her strength, and the gun slipped from her hand.

"Sandrine." Someone knelt beside her. It was Adel. Behind him, Major Baud appeared, still holding her weapon. "Where did he hit you?"

"You took your time," she said, still struggling to breathe and speaking in short, choppy sentences. Adel pulled down the zipper of her motorcycle jacket to tend to the gunshot wound.

He let out a sigh of relief. The bullet was lodged in the bullet-proof vest she had worn as a precaution.

"*Allah!* How could you meet with the man alone?" Even as he scolded her, she could hear the worry he had for her.

"At least she was smart enough to wear a vest and send us a message," Major Baud said, looking down at her. The concern Adel showed for Sandrine was completely absent from her. She reached out a hand to help her up. "Get up, or do you want to lie here for the rest of the night and bask in your glory?"

"Aren't you just a ray of sunshine?" Sandrine replied, taking the hand. "Single, I assume," she attempted a joke.

"Happily married, three kids," the woman countered, pulling her to her feet.

Sandrine held onto Adel's arm until she felt steady on her feet again. Her chest ached as if a horse had kicked her.

"Where's de Chezac? Did I hit him?"

"You did," Major Baud said. "Pure luck by the looks of it. You should spend more time at the shooting range."

Adel shot her an annoyed glance.

"It's true," the woman defended herself.

"You probably got him in the shoulder. The impact knocked him back, and he fell over the railing."

Every breath hurt, but she forced herself to walk to the wall. Gripping the railing with both hands, she looked down, but in the darkness, she could only make out the ground vaguely. Several men circled the tower, their flashlight beams cutting through the night.

"We didn't come alone, of course," Adel said.

"Here he is," someone who sounded like Dubois called out, shining his flashlight beam on de Chezac, who lay on the rocks in front of the tower.

"That was too damned close," Adel said. "Your solo missions will get you killed someday."

"By then, you should have completed your training and be

ready to take over my job, or do you want Jamila to surpass you and snag my position? She'd be your boss then."

"Jamila?" he exclaimed incredulously but with a hint of concern in his voice.

Sandrine's laughter turned into a groan. Her ribs would remind her of the bullet for several days.

Émeraude

Sandrine lay on a bench at the stern of the boat, watching Léon at the helm. The cool wind caressed her skin and tousled her hair. Her T-shirt fell to her hips, concealing the bruises that adorned her ribs. Breathing was no longer difficult, but it would still be a while before she could return to any kind of athletic activities including her beloved martial arts. However, not as long as it would take for de Chezac to recover. Besides the clean bullet wound on his shoulder, he had broken his pelvis and both arms in the fall from the tower. Once they released him from the hospital, he would be transferred to pretrial detention. Until then, she had a heap of paperwork to tackle, but she delegated that to Adel for the time being. Commissaire Matisse had forbidden her from showing up at the station until she was fully recovered; she would enjoy the time off.

"How do you like the boat?" Léon called out to her. He gripped the helm with both hands, beaming like a little boy at Christmas. Owning his own boat had been a long-standing dream of his.

"I'm just lying around here being lazy. How can I help?" she replied.

"That's exactly your job—to lie around until you're fully healed."

She listened to the waves splashing against the bow of the *Émeraude*, spraying off to the side.

"What a coincidence that Blanche called me and loaned me the boat for the weekend," he said.

"That was very generous of her," replied Sandrine.

"Did you know that the Barnais family wants to sell it?" He looked at her curiously, gauging her reaction.

"What a surprise," she lied. Blanche was a savvy businesswoman. She knew Léon well enough to anticipate his interest in the boat.

"Where are we headed anyway, or is that still a surprise?"

Léon pointed to a spot on the horizon that looked like any other.

"We're heading to the Channel Islands and staying there for a few days. I reserved a table at a first-rate restaurant for tonight."

She leaned back and enjoyed the rocking of the boat. There would be plenty of time until they reached the islands to find out whether she would get seasick or not. From the sparkle in Léon's eyes, it was obvious that this wouldn't be their only trip on the *Émeraude*.

Sounds good to me, she thought, closing her eyes.

Thanks

I am delighted that you joined Sandrine Perrot and Adel Azarou in their investigation in Brittany. Feedback from my readers is very important to me. Critique, praise and ideas are always welcome, and I am happy to answer any questions.

My email address is: Author@Christophe-Villain.com

Newsletter: To not miss any new publications you can sign up to the newsletter and get the free novella: Death in Paris - The prequel to the Brittany Mystery Series.

Free Novella

Subscribe to the newsletter and receive a free eBook: Death in Paris.

Sandrine Perrot's back story, her last case in Paris.

Sandrine held the warm coffee cup in her hands and looked out through the café window. The gusty wind drove dark clouds across the sky and swirled leaves along the boulevard. Pedestrians zipped up their jackets and scrambled to keep dry before the impending rain. She wasn't particularly excited about the prospect of having to take her motorbike on the road. Sandrine forgot to shop most of the time and hated to cook. Café Central was her salvation so she wouldn't turn up at work with her stomach growling.

"Would you like anything else to drink?" asked the waitress, who regularly saw Sandrine during her morning shift. She bet the young girl was a student who worked here to earn a few euros. Judging by her distinct accent, she was probably from Provence.

"Thank you but I have to get on the road pretty soon."

"Not a nice day." The young woman took a peek outside and picked up the used plate on

which the remains of scrambled eggs and baguette crumbs lay.

"That's why I hold on to my coffee cup for a while and enjoy the warmth in the café before I have to go to work." A bad feeling swept over her that she couldn't pin down to any specific event, but it nagged at her, as if the day could only get worse. The case she was investigating was stuck in her head and she couldn't shake it, which she usually could.

"No hurry," said the waitress, looking around the half-empty café. "It doesn't get crowded again until lunchtime, so until then I don't have much to do."

Sandrine's cell phone, which was lying on the table in front of her, vibrated and she glanced at the display.

"I'm afraid I have to take this call."

The waitress took the hint and took the dirty dishes into the kitchen. "Hello, Martin, what's up?"

She listened to her colleague in silence for a while.

"On the Richard Lenoir Boulevard? I'll be there in fifteen minutes."

Sandrine ended the call and cursed under her breath. Her gut feeling had proved to be right; the day lived up to its promise. She put money on the table, pulled on the waterproof motorcycle jacket and picked up the helmet that was lying on a chair. She quickly drank the rest of the coffee. The waitress gave her a friendly wave as she left.

Her motorcycle was parked on the wide sidewalk between two trees. She wiped the wet seat with her sleeve before climbing on and pulling on her gloves. She took a deep breath and started the engine. Shortly thereafter, she merged into traffic.

Half a dozen patrol cars and an ambulance were parked by the Saint-Martin Canal. The paramedics were hunkered down in the car and puffs of smoke rose through their slightly ajar windows. They were more comfortable than their police colleagues, who had to go out to cordon off the area. The first onlookers were already gathering on one of the narrow bridges that spanned the watercourse. Sandrine drove through a gap in the metal fence separating the canal from the boulevard and parked the motorcycle on the wide pedestrian promenade. Bollards – stocky

vertical posts – were set at regular intervals, but today no boats were moored here and the lock gate was closed.

"Good morning, Sandrine," a grey-haired man with angular features greeted her. His badge identified him as Major de Police. "Kind of shitty weather to be out on a motorcycle."

"Hello, Martin. It's still a lot quicker than driving a car. Not to mention parking." She stuffed her gloves and scarf into her helmet and stuffed it into one of the panniers. "Is it our guy?"

"The Necktie Killer? Looks like it."

"Is that what they call him now?" She shook her head in disgust. "Far too friendly sounding. He's a sadistic murderer and should be considered and referred to as such."

"I didn't invent it. We owe that to the journalists who needed punchy headlines." He held up his hands defensively.

"I'm sorry. I was thinking of the victims."

"That's all right. Whenever things like that don't get to you anymore, it's time to change careers."

"In there?" she asked, looking toward the entrance to the

Saint-Martin Canal, which ran underground for the next few miles. Even on sunny days, this gloomy place seemed ominous to her. "Who from our team is here?"

"Brossault, the medical examiner with the forensic guys and some cops cordoning off the area. The big boys are on their way, it was probably too early in the morning for them."

Sandrine laughed softly. The chief of homicide and the juge d'instruction, the prosecutor in charge of the investigation, would not be long in coming. They were forced to demonstrate that

the police were doing everything they could to take the perpetrator off the street since the series of murders was dominating the front pages of the newspapers. However, they hadn't even come an inch closer to him since they'd found the first victim in the summer. It was now February and two more dead women had joined the list of victims.

"Let's go then," she said, walking towards the scene of the crime.

The rain started, pattering on the dark water of the canal. Major Martin Alary pulled up the collar of his raincoat and walked faster across the slippery pavement. A uniformed cop stepped aside and waved them through the barricade.

"Was it closed?" Sandrine asked, looking at the lock where the water was damming up. The Saint-Martin Canal was just under two-and-a-half-miles long, and connected the Bassin de la Villette in the north with the Seine in the south. It had a total of five locks – enclosures with gates at each end where the water level could be raised or lowered.

"Most people only use the exposed area: a few tourist boats, but mostly paddle boats and small motorboats used for family outings in the Bassin de la Villette. Hardly more than a dozen boats a day traverse the entire length of the canal."

"The less water traffic, the more noticeable things are. Let's hope someone noticed something."

They entered the tunnel through an open metal door guarded by another police officer. Martin Alary wiped raindrops from his shoulders and adjusted his gun holster. A brick path, on which two people could comfortably walk side by side, ran along the length of the canal. The dim light of the rainy day reached only a few feet deep into the tunnel, and the antique-looking lamps that hung at regular intervals on the wall allowed one to see the way, but were useless for forensic work. The forensics team had already set up blazingly bright spotlights so they wouldn't miss a thing.

A thin man with a pointed beard and a bald head walked towards them.

"Ah. Capitaine Perrot and Major Alary. Already here?" Marcel Carron, the forensics manager, patted Sandrine's companion on the shoulder and gave him a wink before turning to face her. He refrained from giving her a chummy pat on the back.

"How far along are you with securing the crime scene?"

"Almost done. However, there was hardly anything to secure."

"What can you tell me?"

"An employee of the city building department discovered the body during a routine examination. She was floating in the water. He informed us immediately and left the site. Very prudent."

"Is this also the scene of the crime?" the major asked.

"There's no evidence thus far," Carron replied. "We've searched the path for evidence of a struggle, but to no avail. The corpse is unclothed, but we couldn't find clothes anywhere."

"Not surprising."

"I concur."

"Any idea how the body got here?" Alary asked.

"There aren't many options left. There is no current in the canal sufficient enough to move a human body. She would have been spotted within one of the locks."

"Then she was put here," said Sandrine.

"The question is how." The forensic scientist pointed to the metal door at the entrance to the tunnel. "Entry is forbidden and the door is normally locked. However, there's no problem climbing over the door but dragging a corpse of an adult person up and over would be almost impossible without risking being discovered."

"Then there's only one option left," Sandrine said, stepping up to the railing that was too dirty to touch. "The perpetrator threw her off a boat at this point."

"An ideal location," the major agreed. "Nobody would notice since people seldom come in here."

"I'm assuming there's no security camera in the tunnel." Despite saying this, Sandrine looked around.

"Maybe the doctor can tell us more." She wasn't particularly hopeful. So far, the killer had left no usable evidence.

"Good luck."

Sandrine pulled a pair of disposable gloves and shoe covers out of her jacket pocket and put them on. Even though the forensic scientist assumed there wouldn't be anything of interest here, she played it safe.

A few feet away, she found Doctor Brossault standing next to the victim, a blue blanket spread over it.

"Bonjour," she greeted the older man in a dark suit, bow tie and handkerchief in his breast pocket. He turned to face her and used his forefinger to push his rimless glasses up the bridge of his nose. "An ideal place to dump a body, isn't it?"

"Absolutely." He nodded enthusiastically. "The murderer has a soft spot for historical places. You have to give him that."

"The canal dates back from the early 19th century, from what I remember from my history class." "1825 if you want to be exact, but who cares about that anyway?"

Sandrine suppressed a grin. The medical examiner was the

type of person who always wanted to be as precise as possible and didn't withhold his knowledge.

"The canal, anyway. The structure built over the canal did not take place until much later: in 1860. At first, it was designed by Haussmann to improve traffic in the city."

"At first?" Sandrine asked. The man loved sharing his knowledge of history and enlightening those around him. It made him happy, so she let him have his fun.

"Naturally. Napoleon III was not exactly a popular head of state. Resistance to his rule simmered particularly in the revolutionary neighbourhoods such as Faubourg-Montmartre and Ménilmontant. So the plan to build over the canal came in handy. A wide swath through the city along which to send cavalry to maintain law and order."

"Interesting," said Major Alary, who Sandrine heard come up behind her. "But it didn't do him any good in the end."

"Fortunately," the doctor agreed.

Sandrine knelt down next to the body and looked inquisitively at the medical examiner. Only when he nodded did she lift the blanket under which the victim lay. A young woman's bloodless face stared at her with lifeless blue eyes. Blonde hair clung damply to pale skin. She wore a silk tie around her neck, where strangulation marks could be seen.

"She was strangled," Sandrine murmured, more to herself than to Doctor Brossault. "Just like the previous two victims," he confirmed.

"What can you tell me?"

"I'd put the woman in her mid-twenties, blonde and attractive like the other victims. She was strangled with the necktie. There are cuts on her wrists. Without wanting to commit myself, I would conclude that plastic restraints were used. The police use those things, too."

"Any other signs that she fought back?"

"I can't imagine that she didn't, but she had no chance of

surviving. Not with her hands tied. Of course we are also looking for narcotics."

"Maybe the tie will get us further."

"A silk tie. Quite expensive and downright exclusive. Forensics will confirm that, although I can't imagine Monsieur Carron being an expert on the subject."

She looked up at him probingly.

"Have you ever seen the man properly dressed before?" His brow furrowed as if surprised at her lack of awareness.

"What's so special about these ties?"

"The quality of the silk is impeccable. In terms of design, I would guess mid-century. In addition, our killer is able to tie a perfect Windsor knot, something that is becoming increasingly rare these days. People either forgo a tie completely or fasten it sloppily. I would narrow the circle of perpetrators down to people with style and money."

He finished the sentence and straightened his bow tie.

Sandrine put the blanket back over the woman's face. She would see her again in the medical examiner's office. She'd seen enough for now.

To subscribe to the newsletter, please use the QR code.

Other Books

Emerald Coast Murder

Sandrine Perrot's investigation takes her from the picturesque fishing towns to the rural hinterland of Brittany's Emerald Coast.

Police Lieutenant Sandrine Perrot is on leave from her post in Paris and has settled in Cancale, the oyster capital of Brittany. She is temporarily assigned to the Saint-Malo police station for this case. The body of an unidentified woman is discovered on the Brittany coast path along the bay of Mont-Saint-Michel.

With her new assistant, Adel Azarou, she takes on the investigation, which leads them to a cold case from Paris, but also deep into the tragic history of a venerable hotelier family.

Saint-Malo Murder

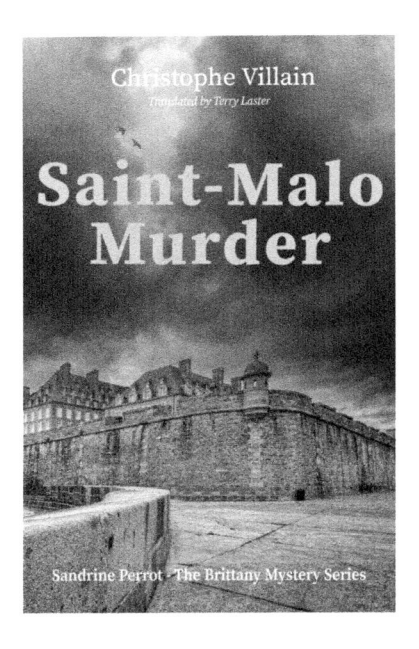

Death of an influencer

The tranquillity of the picturesque old town of Saint-Malo is shattered by a gruesome murder. The dead woman is a well-known influencer and radio presenter who has made many enemies in the region with her controversial opinions and themes. The killer has not only professionally staged the body and crime scene, but also meticulously recorded the crime.

Will she find the perpetrator in the dead woman's private surroundings, or will she have to dig deep into the victim's past?

Deadly Tides at Mont-Saint-Michel

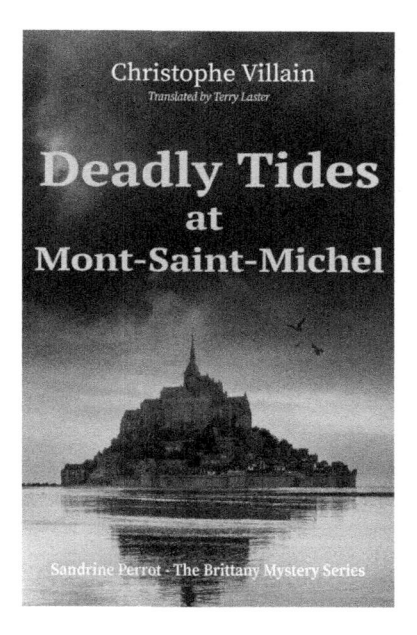

A dead woman loved by all.

Instead of spending a pleasant day with Léon on the coast and at Le Mont-Saint-Michel, Sandrine Perrot is called to a fatal accident in the Saint-Malo marina. The driver's death touches her personally, as she had just met the woman. In the course of the forensic investigation, she discovers that there is more to the alleged accident than she first suspected.

Her investigation leads her into the world of a well-known family in Le Mont-Saint-Michel, a family marked by antiquated traditions but also by conflicts between siblings.

Another person soon disappears without a trace. Was he trying to evade interrogation, or was an unwelcome witness being silenced?

Booklover's Death

A dead book collector

A new case takes Sandrine Perrot to Bécherel, the Cité du Livre of Brittany. A place where life revolves around books. The president of a well-known book club has been found murdered in his private library. Did contempt and rivalry among the book lovers lead to murder or does she have to look elsewhere for the motive?

While Sandrine investigates in the city of books, the prosecutor de Chezac builds a case against her. From the sidelines, she has to watch as the situation in Saint-Malo escalates.

Printed in Great Britain
by Amazon